Praise for the Sharpe & Donovan novels

"Neggers fashions a colorful landscape shaded with just enough darkness to create the brooding atmosphere in which her heroes best thrive…. Reels you straight in and doesn't let go."
—*Providence Journal* on *Impostor's Lure*

"Carla Neggers has long excelled at forging neo-gothic, brooding tales rich in setting and atmosphere. With *Thief's Mark*, though, she ups the ante in fashioning a crime thriller of rare depth and complexity."
—*Providence Journal*

"Everything is out of control, and nothing is as it seems, making for the intense, edge-of-your-seat whirlwind that bestselling Neggers does so well in her Sharpe & Donovan series. In this particularly wild cat-and-mouse installment, Neggers has her characters zipping from Maine to Ireland, where families form an alliance to take down a deadly killer."
—*Booklist* on *Liar's Key*

"The unforgettable characters make Neggers' story extraordinarily memorable."
—*RT Book Reviews*, **Top Pick**, on *Keeper's Reach*

"Neggers delivers another spellbinding, chilling, complex page-turner… Her characters will awe readers and the 'ah-ha' moment is priceless. Brava!"
—*RT Book Reviews*, **Top Pick**, on *Harbor Island*

"Well-plotted, intriguing and set mostly in the lushly described Irish countryside, the novel is smart and satisfying."
—*Kirkus Reviews* on *Declan's Cross*

"*Heron's Cove* gives romantic suspense fans what they want…complex mystery with a bit of romance."
—*RT Book Reviews*, **Top Pick**

"*Saint's Gate* is the best book yet from a writer at the absolute top of her craft."
—*Providence Journal*

CARLA NEGGERS

RIVAL'S BREAK

mira

mira™

ISBN-13: 978-0-7783-6091-9

Rival's Break

Copyright © 2019 by Carla Neggers

This edition published by arrangement with Harlequin Books S.A.

For questions and comments about the quality of this book, please contact us at CustomerService@Harlequin.com.

Mira
22 Adelaide St. West, 40th Floor
Toronto, Ontario M5H 4E3, Canada
www.Harlequin.com

Printed in U.S.A.

To my grandparents, gone before I was born,
well loved, never forgotten

RIVAL'S
BREAK

1

Emma Sharpe opened all the windows in the small Maine coastal house she shared with her husband of almost four months, ending with the stubborn one above the kitchen sink. A crisp, salt-tinged breeze blew in on her, and she shut her eyes, taking it in, relishing it after her slog of a drive up from Boston. She'd left her FBI office early, hoping to beat the worst of the foliage traffic. Maybe she had. Maybe it was even worse now, at rush hour.

The weather forecast called for a sunny, cool weekend, perfect for leaf-peeping, hiking, kayaking—or a family wedding.

I'll be there for the wedding, Emma. Promise.

That was three weeks ago. Long weeks, Emma thought. Hard weeks. The details of Colin's whereabouts were on a need-to-know basis, and in her role as an art crimes analyst, Emma didn't need to know.

But tomorrow, after many ups and downs, her brother-in-law Andy, a lobsterman and third-born of the four Donovan brothers, and his marine biologist love, Julianne Maroney, were finally getting married in their small hometown of Rock Point, Maine.

A fresh, gusty breeze caught the calendar Emma had bought in Ireland and hung on the wall by the refrigerator, one of her touches in the Craftsman-style house. Colin hadn't objected. They'd met a year ago… fallen in love fast…married in June…a whirlwind of a love affair, every second etched in her memory. But the last weeks of summer and first weeks of autumn had been a blur of grief, work and long walks in the Irish hills with her grandfather, mourning his only son, her father…gone too soon…and Colin, the hardheaded, hard-driving man she loved, away on his latest FBI undercover mission…

Emma noticed the calendar was still set to August. She pulled it off its prosaic nail and flipped past September to October. The blank weeks reminded her of the passage of time since she and Colin had last been here, in the house he'd bought before they'd met. She'd added a few touches of her own here and there. In time, she'd add more.

She hung the calendar back on its nail and admired the photo of Moll's Gap on the southwest Irish coast. She and Colin had stopped there in June on their honeymoon. Holding hands, taking in the stunning views of the mountains and lakes, it was as if time stood still and nothing bad could ever happen to them.

Faintly unsettled, she took off her lightweight leather jacket and hung it on the back of a chair at the table. She was in black slacks and a white blouse, but would change into something more casual for tonight's rehearsal dinner, a casual affair at Hurley's, a favorite Rock Point watering hole on the harbor. Would Colin get back in time?

Emma yanked open the refrigerator. Three bottles of a local craft beer sat on the top shelf. Colin wouldn't mind not coming home to actual food in the fridge, but beer? A staple for any Donovan. She wondered how many times in the past weeks he'd thought about the beer waiting for him when he finally made his way back home.

Then she spotted a glass jar of local, whole-milk yogurt tucked on a shelf in the door. Had she left it on her last visit?

She shook her head. "No."

As she shut the refrigerator door, she felt the flutter in her stomach she always felt when she knew Colin was near.

And he was, she thought. He was here.

Footsteps sounded on the back stairs. She saw him through the screen door as he pulled it open and came into the kitchen. Her heart skipped a couple of beats. The tousled dark hair, the blue-gray eyes, the small scar on his upper cheek. The broad shoulders. The slight, knowing smile. He wore jeans and a dark blue sweatshirt. His Maine clothes, his undercover clothes—it didn't matter.

He shut the door behind him. "Hey, there. Did you see I got you your favorite yogurt?"

"I did see that."

"I got your favorite granola, too. It's in the cupboard."

"You're the best, Colin Donovan." Emma smiled as he slipped his arms around her. She'd pulled back her hair, fair and straight, but a few strands came loose as she took in the feel of him, his warmth, his strength. "When did you get back?"

"After lunch. I went for a walk."

Of course. "Felt good?"

"Not as good as this." He drew her closer, opening his palms on her hips. "How are you, Emma?"

"Happy you're here, safe and sound." She eased her arms around his waist, settling them where sweatshirt and jeans met on his back. "How did you get here?"

"Mike picked me up at the airport in Portland. I didn't want to fly into Boston and risk not getting here in time."

Mike was the eldest brother, a Maine wilderness guide and an occasional security contractor. "You didn't want to miss tonight's rehearsal dinner," Emma said.

"And you. I didn't want to miss tonight with you."

Heat spread through her, a contrast to the cool late-afternoon breezes blowing through the small house. "Now here we are."

"Yes." Colin's eyes held hers. "Together again."

"And you are safe and sound, yes?"

"I am." He pulled her closer. "Our lives won't always be like this, Emma."

"Thinking about doing puffin tours again?"

"Cap'n Colin. I have three brothers in Maine. We'd make puffin and whale tours and such work."

He was at least half-serious. Emma was familiar with this reentry mood, understood the appeal of a quieter life here in his hometown. "No doubt in my mind. Whatever you decide is next for you is fine with me. Right now, the work you do, the absences…" She leaned into him, solid, warm, here. "That's fine, too."

"I love you, Emma," he said, as his mouth lowered to hers.

He lifted her and carried her into the front room and on to the entry. He was a strong, fit man, and although Emma could see the fatigue in his face, he continued up the stairs without a pause.

Their thing, from their earliest days together.

He carried her up the stairs without breaking stride, ducked into their bedroom at the back of the house and laid her on the bed. She sank into the soft quilt. He wasn't the least bit winded, but she could hardly get a decent breath. Nothing to do with exertion, everything to do with having him here again, with her.

"I'm sorry I had to leave when I did," Colin said. "Your dad... Emma..."

"I needed that time on my own. You knew that."

"Because I know you." He kissed her softly. "It's good to be home."

"I'm glad you're here," she managed to whisper, before speaking became impossible, and unnecessary.

Julianne and Andy chose to have their wedding at the old sea captain's house the Donovans had converted into an inn out on the harbor, and Emma couldn't imagine a more perfect day for the hometown pair. The bright, clear autumn weather continued through last night's rehearsal dinner and the wedding, held outside on the inn's expansive lawn, with colorful leaves reflected in the quiet water and coordinating with Julianne's golden-brown hair and warm white dress. The Donovans and Maroneys had simple tastes and a modest budget, but they knew how to have a good time.

Even gloomy Franny Maroney, Julianne's widowed grandmother, couldn't find much to complain about.

"Beautiful wedding," she said next to Emma at the cake table. Her white hair in tight, neat curls, she wore a flowing burgundy dress and sturdy shoes. At seventy-five, she was a bundle of energy. She sighed, eyeing the rows of cake slices on small plates. "No Donovans in tuxes, though. Andy nixed them. I think Julianne was in on it, though."

Emma smiled. "Disappointed, are you?"

"I'm not the only one. We had powder blue tuxes at my wedding. It was at the church. It seems like yesterday."

"Weddings bring back memories. Have you had cake yet?"

"I tried all three kinds."

"That's my plan, too."

Unable to decide on just one cake, Andy and Julianne had opted for three. Coconut, apple spice and chocolate. There were autumn-decorated cookies, too, but Emma had to draw the line at overindulging somewhere. She wore a deep coral knit dress, comfortable and forgiving even with how much food she'd been consuming, both last night—fish chowder, rolls, pie, whiskey—and today with the generous buffet and, now, cake and cookies.

Franny wandered off, and Emma helped herself to a small slice of the apple spice cake. Maybe she'd stop there, after all, or maybe she wouldn't. Colin was at the outdoor bar, looking sexy in his dark suit as he engaged in what appeared to be an intense conversation with his youngest brother, Kevin, a state marine patrol officer.

In another moment, Colin nodded and started across the yard to her. "Kevin's heading out to check on possible food poisoning at a yacht party. I'd like to tag along. Okay with you?"

"Of course. He looks as if he'd appreciate the company."

"He's miserable. He's feeling sorry for himself because he came to the wedding alone."

Emma grabbed a fork for her cake. "He's the only unattached brother."

"He's also the youngest. I told him he could have brought his dog. No one would have minded."

"And he was unamused?"

"Very."

"Was he as rough on you when you were unattached?"

"Rougher."

Emma was getting used to the banter between the brothers. She'd rarely seen it go too far, but she imagined sometimes it did, not that anything would ever break the bond between them. The Donovans were a tight-knit lot. In their own way, so were the Sharpes, but now it was just herself, her grandfather, her brother and her mother.

"Kevin's trying not to inflict himself on the rest of us," Colin added cheerfully. "Drunken partiers puking off the sundeck of a fancy yacht will give him perspective."

"Lovely," Emma said. "Wear gloves and a mask. And a gown. Maybe goggles, too."

"Kevin's got gear in his truck, but I'm letting the medical types deal with any bodily fluids. Fun talk at a wedding, isn't it?"

"You're a good brother. I'll save you and Kevin cookies."

Colin kissed her on the cheek. "Save us a good Irish whiskey instead."

He crossed the lawn to join Kevin, already at his

truck on the narrow outer harbor road. Colin had started in law enforcement with the state marine patrol. He'd know the drill, not that either of them needed to respond. But she loved seeing how relaxed Colin was, so soon after a weeks-long deep-cover mission.

As she ate her cake with its not-too-sweet cream cheese frosting, she noticed Finian Bracken, the Irish priest and friend who'd officiated the wedding, peel away from several guests and walk toward her. In his late thirties, blue-eyed and handsome with his angular features and dark hair, he'd also officiated at her and Colin's wedding in June.

"Emma," Finian said, kissing her cheek. "It's good to see you."

"It was a beautiful wedding, Finian."

Across the yard, Andy, with his strong Donovan frame and ocean-gray eyes, swept his bride into his arms and started up the front steps into the sprawling early nineteenth-century house, presumably to get ready to leave on their Irish honeymoon. Julianne laughed, the autumn sun catching the golden highlights in her hair. They'd known each other forever and had settled some epic battles between them before discovering how much in love they were, and how enduring that love was.

"They'll be at the cottage in time for lunch tomorrow," Finian said, obviously pleased.

Emma knew he was referring to the traditional Irish stone cottage he owned in the Kerry hills, with stunning views of Kenmare Bay. He seldom, if ever, stayed there given the bittersweet memories it held of his wife and two young daughters, who'd died in a sailing accident eight years ago, a tragedy that had ultimately led him to Rock Point.

He looked preoccupied as Emma set her cake plate on a stack of other empty plates. "I'm finished here," he said. "Why don't we drive to the rectory together? I could use your opinion on something."

She eyed him. He obviously didn't want to provide details. "Sure. Let me grab a few cookies."

She placed a dozen cookies in one of the boxes set out for that purpose and followed Finian to his BMW, the one obvious symbol of his past as a successful whiskey man, owner with his twin brother, Declan, of Bracken Distillers back home in Ireland. It was just a few minutes' drive to the residential streets above the harbor, and he said little before parking at the homely vinyl-sided Greek Revival house that served as the rectory for St. Patrick's, Rock Point's struggling, and only, Roman Catholic church. The small, granite-faced church was next door to the rectory, a short walk from the house Emma shared with Colin.

As she got out of the car, she saw what had prompted Finian's troubled mood, and his invitation to join him.

More specifically, who.

Henrietta Balfour stood in the middle of the rectory's front walk, twirling a red leaf by the stem, her reddish curls pulled back loosely with a large clip. She wore a long flowered skirt, a denim jacket and ankle boots, looking more like the garden designer Finian would know her as than the MI5 officer she was.

Behind Henrietta, Oliver York looked on from the front steps. Tawny-haired and green-eyed, he was a mythologist, a gentleman farmer, a former art thief and, lately, an MI5 asset.

They were all friends, after a fashion.

Henrietta greeted Emma with her infectious smile.

"What a stunning day for my first visit to Maine. I love the sea air this time of year. We left a dreary rain in London." She shifted her attention to Finian as he started up the walk. "Do you rake the leaves once they've fallen or just leave them on the ground through winter?"

"We rake," Finian said. "I should say, volunteers from the church rake."

"I love raking." She tossed her leaf into the grass. "It's relaxing, unless one gets blisters, which is utterly tedious."

Emma pinned her gaze on her priest friend. "What's going on, Finian?"

"Henrietta and Oliver are here for a visit. Oliver texted me as Julianne and Andy were cutting the cake."

"We didn't want to distract you and Colin from the wedding," Henrietta said. "We hopped on a plane and here we are. Sometimes one needs to do things at the spur of the moment."

Oliver got to his feet, his graceful movements suggesting his expertise in martial arts. He and Henrietta were in their late thirties, and they'd known each other forever but only recently had become a couple. He gestured to the bags at his feet. "We accepted Father Bracken's gracious invitation to stay here at the rectory." He settled his cheeky gaze on Emma with the slightest smile. "Separate bedrooms."

Henrietta nodded to the box Emma had tucked in one arm. "I hope that's wedding cake."

"Cookies," Emma said.

"Cookies, then. Brilliant. Shall we put the kettle on?"

Oliver picked up his and Henrietta's bags by the steps. "Where's your charming husband, Emma?"

Colin had warmed up to Oliver in the past year, but

it was a stretch to call them friends. "He's checking on food poisoning aboard a yacht in Heron's Cove."

Just the slightest flicker in Oliver's eyes, but it was enough to arouse Emma's suspicion. Henrietta, on the other hand, didn't give anything away.

2

"What about that ER nurse you were seeing before I left town?" Colin asked as he and Kevin approached the sleek, expensive yacht, moored among a half-dozen much smaller pleasure boats at a private marina on the tidal river in Heron's Cove. A knot of first responders were gathered on the pier. "Is she still in the picture?"

Kevin shrugged. "Sort of."

"Why didn't you invite her to the wedding?"

"Andy's wedding? With all three big brothers there?"

Colin could see Kevin's point. "So you'd have invited her if it hadn't been a family wedding?"

"Doubt it."

"Okay. I give up."

"Good. The wedding was nice. Glad those two figured out they're meant for each other. For a while I thought Julianne might throw Andy overboard and leave him to drown."

"More likely she'd have done him in on land. She wouldn't have left you to find his body."

"Ha. True."

Nothing like gallows humor while checking on a drunken yacht party.

The upscale marina was next to the main offices of Sharpe Fine Art Recovery, founded sixty years ago by Wendell Sharpe, Emma's Irish-born grandfather. Colin glanced back at the gray-shingled Victorian, newly renovated to the rigorous standards of Lucas Sharpe, Emma's older brother, who ran the family business. The offices were closed for the weekend, and Lucas was in Ireland with his semiretired grandfather, working and keeping each other company in the aftermath of Tim Sharpe's death. Wendell had moved to Dublin and opened up offices there after the death of his wife sixteen years ago.

Colin reminded himself he had no reason to suspect the yacht and its ill-fated party had anything to do with the Sharpes. He shifted his gaze to the narrow channel that marked the boundary between the tidal river and the Atlantic, sparkling in the distance. The channel was just wide enough and deep enough for the yacht in question.

"You're not going to tell me where you've been the past month?" Kevin asked.

"Nowhere I had to sidestep barf."

The smallest of smiles from his brother. "Life is good, then."

They slowed their pace as they came to an ambulance crew. Two khaki-clad middle-aged men staggered off the yacht onto the pier but shook off help from the

EMTs. Guests, not passengers, they explained. They were here just for the party and would make their way home after they got some air. They didn't get ten yards before one of them collapsed to his knees and barfed into the river. The EMTs ran to him.

Kevin grimaced. "Yeah, I know. We could be having cake and whiskey right now."

"I don't mind missing the cake." Colin got out of the way of an EMT pushing an empty stretcher. "Any idea whose yacht?"

"Money guy and his wife. They chartered it out of Boston. Own crew."

That didn't tell Colin much. He and Kevin boarded the yacht but didn't have to sidestep vomit until they reached the sundeck, where the party had taken place. Except for a few splatters and pools of vomit, the sundeck was appealing with its cushioned seating, bar and Jacuzzi. It looked as if people had been having a good time and then started getting sick with a sudden onset of symptoms.

A young woman in a navy polo shirt and tan khakis was loading plates, glasses, flatware and napkins onto a tray. "Not everyone made it to a head, as you can see. Whatever it was took people by surprise." She set the tray on the bar. She was small, even waiflike, with short blondish hair, pale blue eyes, freckles and an unexpectedly brisk manner. She spoke with an English accent. "My name's Georgina Masterson. I'm the chef. I'm not sick, but I didn't eat any of the food."

Kevin introduced himself, then Colin. "Is everyone on board accounted for?"

"Richie is doing a head count. Richie Hillier, the captain. I don't know the exact number who were on board. Six passengers and four crew, but how many guests came just for the party? I couldn't say. Another ten people, maybe. It was a last-minute thing. Heron's Cove wasn't one of our planned stops. It was added last night."

"Why's that?" Colin asked.

She shrugged her thin shoulders. "One of Melodie's whims. A New England foliage cruise was her idea." Georgina snatched a wet rag out of an unseen sink and slapped it onto the shiny bar. "And you have no idea whom I'm talking about. Melodie and Bryce Fanning chartered the yacht. They're newlyweds, actually. They're celebrating their one-year anniversary. We arrived here at the marina early this morning. Next thing, I'm pulling together a party for twenty people."

Colin walked over to the bar. "Where are the Fannings now?"

Georgina waved a slender hand vaguely toward the stairs. "EMTs took Bryce out on a stretcher. Melodie's going with him. She's sick, too, but she's rallying. The EMTs and local police have been great. I'm just…dazed, I guess you'd say. I can't believe this is happening." She abandoned the rag and added more dishes to the tray. "We were supposed to leave late this afternoon and make stops in Camden and Bar Harbor, but who knows what will happen now. I don't know why the police are here. I don't know what made people sick, but it's nothing criminal, I assure you. And it's not due to anything I prepared."

Colin wasn't surprised at her defensiveness. He'd done a few food-poisoning checks on various types of boats and ships during his marine patrol days, and rarely did anyone want to lay claim to causing it. "Could someone have brought contaminated food on board?"

She seized on that one. "Yes, absolutely. I wouldn't necessarily have noticed. I was in the galley most of the time. It's so easy to make a mistake with food, especially when you're transporting it. People think they know what they're doing, and they don't."

"Happens all the time," Kevin said.

She flicked the wet rag back into the sink. "One of the passengers took off down the stairs. He looked terrible. I think he was bolting to his cabin to be sick. I hope he didn't pass out on the stairs or something. Would you mind taking a quick look for him? I'd feel better knowing he's okay, or that the EMTs found him. I just..." She gulped in a breath, her eyes wide, her pale skin ashen. "I don't want anyone to die."

She grabbed a fresh tray and set off from the bar to a cluster of chairs.

Colin followed Kevin down the narrow stairs. They didn't run into anyone until they reached the guest cabins on the lower deck. A man lay sprawled on his side across the threshold of a small, well-appointed cabin. He had one arm clamped on his lower abdomen, his teeth clenched in agony. A pool of orange vomit was soaking into the cream-colored carpet by his head. He was in his late forties, trim, fit, with gray-streaked dark hair.

When they were open, the sick man's eyes were pale gray.

Colin swore under his breath and knelt next to the man he knew as Jeremy Pearson. Might be his real name, might not be, but it wouldn't be the name he was using aboard Bryce and Melodie Fanning's chartered yacht.

The scars on his hands and face attested to his decades with the SAS, MI6 and now MI5, but they could be explained away. Car accident, bar fight, cooking mishap.

"Hold on, Kevin," Colin said. "Stand back."

Colin scanned Jeremy for any signs he wasn't experiencing some kind of ordinary food-borne illness. Excess saliva—classic foaming at the mouth—or effusive sweating. Pinpoint pupils. Convulsions. Delusions. Unresponsive. All could point to a neurotoxic reaction characteristic of exposure to a chemical weapon, one of Jeremy's areas of expertise.

"It's just food poisoning," he managed to mutter through clenched teeth.

"You need medical attention," Colin said.

Jeremy tucked his knees up as he was obviously seized by severe abdominal cramping. "I need a bloody coffin."

Colin looked up at Kevin. "Can you fetch the EMTs?"

His brother nodded. "You'll wait here?"

"Yeah."

Kevin hesitated half a beat, long enough for Colin to get the message. His brother knew something was up, but he said nothing as he rolled off to get help.

Once Kevin was out of earshot, Colin shook his head at his British friend and colleague, pale and writhing in agony. "I hope to hell you've expelled whatever's nailing your sorry ass, because, damn it, I need answers."

"Don't blow my cover. I'll explain once I'm done dying."

Jeremy moaned, curling up into a ball in obvious agony. Colin knew he didn't have much choice. He'd have to wait. That meant Kevin would, too, and he wasn't patient, either. Patiently waiting for answers wasn't a Donovan strong suit.

"What is your cover?" Colin asked.

"Art consultant."

What the hell? Colin got out of the way as Jeremy rolled out of his tight ball, tried to get up on his hands and knees and hurled again. No question the EMTs would decide to transport him to the emergency room for assessment and treatment.

Jeremy finished puking and collapsed. The guy was a mess. "Guess you had more to expel," Colin said. "I'll get you fresh clothes for the hospital. You're going to need them."

He stepped past Jeremy and entered the small, well-appointed cabin. He glanced around for any obvious indications that could explain why a senior MI5 officer—a friend—had slipped into his wife's hometown—land of the Sharpes—as an art consultant. As far as Colin knew, Jeremy Pearson's knowledge of art was limited to the *Mona Lisa*.

He got a change of clothes from a closet, keeping an eye out for any evidence that might explain what the sick MI5 officer was up to on the Fanning yacht. He didn't expect to find anything before Kevin returned with the EMTs, and he didn't.

Just that his British colleague was a boxers guy.

EMTs got Jeremy Pearson onto a stretcher and loaded him into an ambulance. Colin had shoved his friend's things into a laundry bag hanging in the closet and used it as an excuse to follow the ambulance to the ER.

Kevin didn't say anything until they were back in his truck, en route to the hospital. "You going to tell me what's going on?"

Colin watched out his window as the truck wound through the pretty village of Heron's Cove with its weathered-shingled shops and restaurants, another world from Rock Point. "I don't know what's going on," he said finally.

"The guy just now. William Hornsby. British art consultant. Sharpe world?"

Hornsby. So that was Jeremy's cover name. "I need room to maneuver, Kevin."

His brother sucked in a breath. "Okay. Do your thing. For now."

Colin debated asking Kevin for a list of everyone on board for the party, everyone who'd gotten sick. Passengers, guests, crew. He wanted names, addresses, phone numbers. Whatever he could get. But food poisoning wouldn't necessarily trigger that kind of response. So far, he had no evidence it wasn't what it looked like—accidental.

Kevin slowed for an elderly couple crossing the street. Summer was the busiest season for Heron's Cove, but fall was a close second, the village center crowded with leaf-peepers. "I bought apples yesterday."

"Apples," Kevin said. "Right. Good, Colin."

"Cortlands. Emma says Cortlands are good for pies. They're still in my truck. She likes to bake pies to relax." He paused, wondering why the hell he'd brought up the apples. "The biggest decision I expected to make this weekend was whether to add a dash of nutmeg to the pie or leave it out. That's a thing with her."

"Would you notice one way or the other?"

"Doubt it. You?"

Kevin shook his head. "No."

"I bought the apples at a local orchard. I made Mike stop on the way from the airport. He stayed in the car."

"You were away for a good spell. Apples and autumn. Nostalgia."

"I guess."

Kevin sped up when they got onto the highway, the ambulance long since leaving them behind. "If I hadn't dragged you to Heron's Cove, you could be peeling apples with Emma right now."

"I don't think so," Colin said.

Kevin glanced sideways at him. "What?"

Colin held up his phone. "Just got a text from her. Oliver York is in Rock Point."

"Our cheeky art thief."

"You're not supposed to know that."

"But I do."

"Henrietta Balfour is with him. They're an item these days. Grew up together."

"She was involved with that business in August."

Colin nodded without comment. *That business* included an opioid overdose in London that Henrietta, Oliver and Emma's grandfather had navigated, and then Tim Sharpe's death in Maine. A hell of a blow that had been.

"I'll save my questions," Kevin said. "We'll get this sorted out. One step at a time."

Some of the tight knots in Colin's stomach loosened. Whatever was going on with his and Emma's British friends, he wouldn't have to deal with it on his own. He wasn't in the midst of a solitary undercover mission. He was home. He had Kevin, Mike, Mike's fiancée, Naomi, his folks, Finian Bracken, and he had Emma.

3

Colin slipped through curtains into Jeremy Pearson's private treatment room in the ER. Jeremy was hooked up to an IV and heart monitor, stable and done, apparently, purging whatever toxin he'd ingested. He moaned under his thin hospital sheet.

A real moan or not, Colin had marginal sympathy given Jeremy's unannounced presence in Maine. "Pretending to be asleep?"

"I'm afraid I'll hurl again if I open my eyes."

"Warn me. I'll step out."

"You're a heartless bastard, Donovan. Always have been. Wasn't you? You've been wanting to poison me for months."

"It wasn't me. Doctors suspect it was something you ate at the party. It came on fast, so it probably wasn't salmonella. Any ideas?"

"No."

If their roles had been reversed, Colin had no doubt Jeremy would have jumped in the ambulance and interrogated him between episodes of the toxin evacuating his system.

"A dozen people on board got sick. Abdominal cramping, vomiting, diarrhea—"

"Stop." Jeremy lifted his hand without the IV. His voice was hoarse, ragged from vomiting. "I was there."

Colin glanced behind him, but the curtains were shut tight, any medical personnel on the other side busy with their work. Solid walls on three sides prevented anyone else from listening in.

He shifted back to Jeremy, who'd lowered his hand and was lying still now, probably to keep nausea and cramping at bay. "Why are Henrietta Balfour and Oliver York in Rock Point?"

No reaction from the ER bed.

"Emma's having tea and cookies with them and Finian Bracken at the rectory."

Jeremy shut his eyes. "Wedding cookies?"

"In the shapes of pumpkins, acorns and leaves."

"Autumnal. That was your brother with you on the yacht? He's not today's groom, I hope."

"Kevin. Groom's Andy."

"The lobsterman brother."

"Yeah. How did you know about the wedding?"

"Because I was trying to avoid crashing it." He opened his eyes. They were red-rimmed and bloodshot, and he was pale, a greenish cast to his skin. Despite how sick he was, he focused with a seriousness more typical of the hard-ass intelligence officer Colin knew. "I was going to alert you this evening."

"Alert me to what?"

"My presence on your patch. My name—"

"William Hornsby. You're an art consultant from London." Colin managed to keep his irritation in check. The guy was sick, after all. "What's going on? Why are you here?"

"Let me die first. Then I'll come to you in a dream and answer your questions."

"You're not dying." Which Jeremy knew. "Are the Fannings on your radar?"

Two doctors and two nurses pulled back the curtains and gave Colin a pointed look. He got the message and left. Jeremy had faded, anyway. "Food poisoning" covered a lot of territory but wasn't as alarming as a synthetic boutique nerve agent. Biological and chemical attacks weren't his specialty, but he did know the drill—the symptoms, dangers, protocols and a few of the potential players. The stuff of nightmares if he was the type to have nightmares.

Four people from the yacht were sick enough to be transported by ambulance to the ER. All but a handful of the partygoers had been infected, including guests who'd arrived at midday. That meant whatever had made people sick had turned up today and hadn't been stewing for a day or two. Otherwise only passengers and crew would have been affected.

Despite Georgina Masterson's protestations, the food she'd served was the likely source of the nasty bout of gastroenteritis.

Colin spotted her by the ER exit with a fair-haired man in his mid-to late thirties, also in the crew uniform of navy polo shirt and khakis.

"Agent Donovan," she said when Colin approached them. "I didn't realize you were still here. This is Nick

Lothian. He's Captain Hillier's right-hand guy, master of all things on a yacht, from operations to mechanics to people."

Nick grinned. "You know what they say, jack-of-all-trades, master of none."

"Nick, this is Special Agent Donovan with the FBI. He happens to be in Maine for his brother's wedding."

Colin figured one of the local cops must have told her. He hadn't, and Kevin wouldn't have. Nick crossed his arms on his chest. "FBI. Cool. Messy, nasty day, huh? Bet you wish you'd stayed at the wedding. Sorry about the drama. We're doing what we can to help out here."

"Everyone will be okay," Georgina added. "Fortunately, none of the crew got sick."

"I thought I might at first," Nick said. "Probably sympathetic nausea from seeing so many people turn green at once. It was like a massive chain reaction. I wonder if some people puked just because other people were puking."

"I'm going to be fired," Georgina said half under her breath.

Nick gave her a quick, brotherly hug. "No, you won't. It's more likely one of the guests brought food and won't come forward now that people got sick." He lowered his arm. "One of the guests who wasn't sick drove us here, but I'll see about renting a car. The marina's letting us stay as long as we need to. They've got the space. In August, they wouldn't."

"What about guests who dropped in just for the party?" Colin asked.

Nick fielded the question. "Obviously the rest of the cruise is canceled. The Fannings and crew are staying on board. I don't know yet about Bill Hornsby. He's a passenger. Everyone else will head home if they haven't already. They're all from the Northeast, so it's not a big hassle. We'll provide any help needed."

Georgina drew in a deep breath. "This doesn't get easier."

"It'll be fine, Georgie," Nick said. He turned to Colin. "We need to clean and disinfect everything. Most of the barf mess is confined to the sundeck and cabins. I've been working on boats since my teens, and today was as bad a case of chain puking as I've seen. I'm glad everyone will recover."

Georgina stared past Colin at the ER's busy main desk. "Everything came together fast. We had to scramble in the kitchen, but that had nothing to do with why people got sick."

Colin didn't have enough information to argue with her. "Why Heron's Cove?"

She seemed relieved at the change in subject. "Melodie Fanning is an avid art collector, and she and Bill Hornsby decided they wanted to see Heron's Cove because a famous art detective has offices there—next to the marina, in fact."

"His name's Wendell Sharpe," Nick said. "I don't know if he was invited to the party. I didn't handle the guest list."

Colin decided to keep his connection to the Sharpes to himself. "Who did handle the invitations?"

"Melodie invited people personally," Georgina said. "She only gave me an approximate number. I don't know the names of any of the guests. I'm new to the Fannings. Nick and Richie have crewed for them for a couple of years. I don't plan to make a career of being a chef on yachts. Not that it wouldn't be great." She made a face. "I'm talking too much."

She and Nick excused themselves to check on the Fannings and renting a car. Colin knew nothing about the Fannings, except they'd moored their yacht in spitting distance of the Sharpe Fine Art Recovery offices and they had an undercover British intelligence agent on board.

He went through the automatic doors to the ER admitting and waiting area. Kevin was chatting with two state detectives Colin recognized. He walked over to a trio of vending machines. The last time he'd been in this ER, his father-in-law was being treated for a heart attack. Tim Sharpe had never come around. A fall into the cold Maine ocean water had triggered the attack. He was already in the water when Colin had arrived with Kevin on the rocky headland by the Sisters of the Joyful Heart convent. They'd done everything they could, but Tim had been living on borrowed time, information he and his wife had kept not only from their son-in-law but from their two adult children.

Kevin pulled away from the detectives and joined Colin as he examined the offerings of the candy vending machine. He finally punched a button for a box of Junior Mints. Quick sugar, and the mint would counter all the barf and excrement he'd encountered since boarding the yacht.

"How's your friend?" Kevin asked.

"Sick."

Kevin rolled his eyes but didn't comment.

"And I didn't say he was my friend," Colin added.

"Right," his brother said.

A short ball-of-fire of a nurse flew out of the ER and

stormed to them. It took half a beat, but Colin recognized her as Kevin's sort-of girlfriend. He couldn't remember her name. She glared at Kevin. "What the *hell* is going on?" She kept her voice to a whisper that did nothing to make her seem less agitated. "I thought we were in the midst of a full-scale WMD attack."

An exaggeration, but Colin let Kevin deal with her. She'd moved to Rock Point recently but had grown up in Portland. The big city in comparison. She was smart, attractive, not easily intimidated. Kevin could do worse, and had.

The nurse—hell, why couldn't he remember her name?—informed them two men who'd been "poisoned" were being admitted. She addressed Kevin. "Bryce Fanning and an Englishman—I don't know his name. He's the one your brother pestered in the ER." She glanced at Colin. "He's had a setback. It's not dangerous, but he's not to have visitors."

An admonishment to him for sure. Colin didn't blame her. Jeremy Pearson, aka William Hornsby, *was* sick. Colin had no choice but to give the poor bastard a chance to get well enough to talk to him about what was going on. He thanked her but didn't explain his interest in the ER patient. "What can you do for him?"

"All the victims are being treated symptomatically, with supportive care as needed. That means we treat whatever symptoms patients present—vomiting, diarrhea, dehydration—and keep them comfortable until the toxin exits their system."

"Ride it out, in other words," Kevin said.

"If you want to put it that way. You two didn't have to go to the yacht, did you?" She shook her head in answer to her own question. "No. Of course you did.

You're Donovans. It's not how you're wired. Even you, Kevin, supposedly the easygoing brother. I've lived in Rock Point long enough to know Donovans don't ignore anything. You're lucky you weren't exposed to a toxin yourselves."

"The medical teams got there ahead of us," Kevin said mildly.

She scowled at him. "The symptoms of common, generally nonlethal food-borne toxins can mimic those of deadlier toxins that require full hazmat protection. Sarin, Ebola or—well, lots of options."

Kevin grinned at her. "No kidding."

"I'm serious," she fired back. "Make fun of me all you want."

"No one's making fun of you, Beth."

Beth. That was it. Beth…what? Colin couldn't remember her last name. He wasn't sure he'd ever known it. He gave her a reassuring smile. "The ER response was flawless."

Beth exhaled, some of the tension in her shoulders visibly easing, the fight going out of her. "I wasn't trying to be alarmist or overly dramatic."

"You weren't," Kevin said.

Since he'd had similar concerns given Jeremy's presence, Colin couldn't fault her, either. Kevin went with her back into the ER. He obviously didn't like this situation—particularly given Colin's silence about the sick Brit and his request for room to maneuver.

Teeth clenched, Colin tore open his mints and poured out a handful as Melodie Fanning emerged from the ER and walked over to him. He'd spotted her with Bryce, her husband, earlier. She had long, straight dark hair, pulled back neatly despite the chaotic scene on her yacht and, apparently, her own bout with food poisoning, if not as serious as her husband's. She wore a close-fitting black dress that smelled faintly but noticeably of stale vomit.

"Sorry," she said, touching a slightly trembling hand to her mouth. "I'm not going to throw up again. I promise. Am I still green?"

"Not too bad," Colin said. He held up his box of mints. "Want some?"

"Gross. No. I'm never eating again." She attempted a weak smile. "But thank you. I can't believe what's happened. You're one of the officers who boarded to help, aren't you? We took you away from—a wedding?"

"My brother's wedding. Reception was winding down."

"The man you were with—"

"Another brother. I'm Colin Donovan. He's Kevin Donovan. He's with the state marine patrol."

"And you?"

"FBI. I tagged along."

She gave a faint smile. "I'll assume there were other factors at work than a dull wedding. I'm Melodie—well, you know who I am, don't you?"

"I do," he said.

"It's been an awful afternoon. It's difficult to have so many people get sick at virtually the same time. I've never witnessed such a thing. I don't know if it qualifies as mass food poisoning. It's not like hundreds were affected, but a dozen? That's a lot of people."

"How's your husband doing, Mrs. Fanning?"

"He's utterly miserable, but he'll recover in time." She slipped a credit card into the vending machine and punched the code for an energy drink. Colin got it out, opened it and handed it to her. She took a tentative sip. "Don't worry. I won't throw up on your shoes."

"If you're feeling ill, I can get a nurse."

"I'm not," she said quickly. "I'm just shaken and upset. Bryce is being admitted overnight. He has some underlying health issues and lost a lot of fluids, so the doctors want to keep an eye on him." She motioned vaguely with her bottle. "I'll head up to his room once he's had a chance to get settled."

"Do you have any idea what made people sick?"

"Not specifically, no. Something Georgina served, obviously. I suspect the mini tacos. I had one and ran to the bathroom and spit it out. I gagged and threw up twice, but it was more a reflex reaction than anything—I don't think I swallowed any of it. It had a bitter taste. I saw what I took to be some kind of mushroom in red spice. I thought it was just my sensitive palate. Who knows. We'll sort it out. It's nothing nefarious, I assure you."

Colin wondered if Jeremy would agree. "Sorry your visit to Maine started out this way," he said.

"I am, too. Thank you. Food poisoning can strike anyone. It's unfortunate it struck us, at a party on a beautiful fall day aboard a yacht stopped in an adorable Maine village."

"I understand you were interested in meeting the Sharpes."

"Wendell Sharpe in particular," she said, no hint she was aware of his connection to Colin. "I'm not an art professional and haven't worked with him, but I know him and Sharpe Fine Art Recovery by reputation. Wendell is based in Dublin, but Bill Hornsby thought he might be in town. Heron's Cove wasn't on the itinerary, but Bryce and I like to keep things fluid and spontaneous when we can and rarely stick to a tight schedule."

"So you started calling friends to meet you?"

"It seemed like a good idea at the time," she said. "Not everyone we contacted could get to Heron's Cove on such short notice, but a number did. We offered a wide range of food and let everyone relax and enjoy themselves. It was informal. Fun." She swallowed more of her energy drink. Its raspberry color stained her lips, helped her look less pale and sickly. "I'm sorry people got sick. Georgina is distraught—not sick but truly distraught. She might be in denial right now, but deep down she has to know she's culpable."

"We met," Colin said.

"Oh. Right. Of course. Nick was with her. It's a small crew but they're fantastic. Richie Hillier is handling the emergency brilliantly as captain. I knew zip about yachting and was actually afraid of it until I met Bryce. We chartered this yacht, but we're in the process of buying one of our own." Melodie tossed her empty drink bottle in a recycling bin. "I've wasted enough of your time, Agent Donovan. I should go see about Bryce. You'll head out soon, won't you? It's not as if a crime's been committed, thankfully."

Colin shrugged. "Waiting for Kev."

She smiled, relaxing slightly. Her eyes were bloodshot, presumably from vomiting. Colin felt a touch of sympathy for her as she spun away from the vending machines and headed toward the elevators. He opted against more mints and tossed the box in the trash.

He decided not to wait for his brother. Kevin had given him the key to his truck, figuring Colin would leave first, and said he'd find his own way back to Rock Point.

Colin left the ER, welcoming the fresh, cool autumn air.

He wasn't a big puke fan.

One of Kevin's marine patrol buddies could drive him home. Maybe Beth the ER nurse. Hell, what was her last name? Colin gritted his teeth. Why couldn't he remember—why didn't he know?

Because you haven't been home in weeks.

Because you haven't even thought of home in weeks.

He'd thought of Emma during his time pretending to be someone else.

Always.

Of the four brothers, Kevin had the tidiest truck, and also the newest, biggest and fastest. Not a man to underestimate, his baby brother. As Colin backed out of the parking space, he saw Georgina Masterson waving wildly and realized it was at him. He stopped as she leaped to the driver's door.

He rolled down the window. "What can I do for you, Ms. Masterson?"

"Sorry. I feel slightly hysterical. I've been debating whether to say anything. Oh, and it's Georgina. Please." She gulped in a breath. "Did you happen to see a painting in Bill Hornsby's cabin? A mounted but unframed canvas. It wouldn't have been hanging on a wall. He was going to take a look at it."

"I didn't see a painting. Who owns it?"

"It's mine, as it happens. It's a recent present from my father. He's—he's not well. I had it in my quarters but it's not there. At least it wasn't when I stopped in just before Nick and I headed here. I assume Bill Hornsby grabbed it before he got sick." She waved a hand, looking tense. "Never mind. Sorry to trouble you. I'm sure it's somewhere on the yacht."

"No trouble."

"I shouldn't have said anything. I just…" Another gulp of air as she hesitated. "Someone said your wife is a Sharpe." She waved a hand vaguely toward the hospital. "In the ER. One of the police officers, I think. Maybe. I don't remember. The Sharpes specialize in art crimes, and I thought maybe—I don't know what I thought. I'm getting way ahead of myself."

"Is it an original painting, a print—"

"It's an original watercolor landscape by an Irish artist, Aoife O'Byrne. It's stunning."

Colin felt his jaw tighten. Aoife O'Byrne. He hadn't expected her name to crop up. He and Emma knew Aoife personally, and so did Oliver York—and their mutual friend Finian Bracken, Rock Point's own Irish priest. Colin wasn't sure if Henrietta knew Aoife, but he doubted it was a coincidence she and Oliver were in Rock Point, having tea and cookies at St. Patrick's rectory.

And Jeremy Pearson? Did he know Aoife O'Byrne? Colin wouldn't be surprised.

"Sounds like a nice gift," he said. "If you're concerned the painting's been stolen, I suggest you talk to the police. My brother Kevin's in the ER. Talk to him, or to a local officer or state detective. They'll help you."

She shook her head. "I'm not going to do that. I don't want to involve the police."

Colin studied her. Did she not realize he was a law enforcement officer?

Georgina reddened, as if she'd just tuned in to her

mistake, mumbled a goodbye and about-faced, walking quickly back to the ER.

Colin debated following her but didn't. A missing Aoife O'Byrne painting. An art thief at the rectory with Emma, an art crimes expert. A yacht full of sick people moored by Sharpe Fine Art Recovery.

And a friend, colleague and man he'd trusted with his life had asked him not to blow his cover. If Kevin could give his FBI brother room to maneuver, couldn't Colin give Jeremy Pearson the same courtesy?

He'd see what was up at St. Patrick's rectory in Rock Point.

Then he'd decide.

4

Henrietta insisted on a tour of the church, and Finian Bracken had obliged her. Emma Sharpe looked less enthusiastic but went with them, and Oliver wasn't the least bit enthusiastic and let it show, to the point Henrietta scowled at him. He got the message and went off on his own while she, Emma and Finian continued through the unprepossessing church. A rummage sale was planned for next weekend. Parishioners had dropped off bags of items and were sorting them on tables. Between his apartment in London and his farm in the Cotswolds, Oliver had plenty of rubbish of his own to sort at some unspecified point in the future.

He heard voices outside and went to the window in Finian's office. The trio were crossing the lawn to the rectory. Oliver would join them in a few minutes. They planned to make sandwiches to serve with tea and the cookies from the wedding, and to await Colin's imminent return from checking on the food-poisoning incident on the yacht in Heron's Cove.

Oliver looked around the office. It was a sad little room, wasn't it? Not because of the old, faded furnishings, never of good quality, but because it had no personality. It was as if Finian Bracken had never moved in. Most of the books on the shelves appeared to have been there for decades, as did the wooden crucifix and the framed print of Rock Point harbor on the wall. For that matter, so did the grayed sheer curtains in the single window. Even the stapler, scissors and paper-clip holder might have been purchased when Oliver was a tot. He could appreciate tradition and continuity, if Finian had added his own books, prints and such and made the place radiate with his amiable personality, his ready Irish wit, his depth of knowledge and experience.

Oliver couldn't put his finger on how to describe his mood. Curious? Annoyed? Filled with foreboding? Unsettled, yes, but why? No doubt his FBI friends and their powers of arrest had something to do with it.

And his MI5 handler, a man he knew primarily as Jeremy Pearson but also, just in the past week, as William Hornsby, a London art consultant. He'd sunk his teeth into Oliver a year ago and had yet to let go. Oliver was putting his particular skills and knowledge to use for UK intelligence services, and, as luck would have it, occasionally the FBI.

He was in the dark about most of this trip to Maine, but he suspected his crusty MI5 handler had been on the yacht with the outbreak of food poisoning. Henrietta had shared few details with him on their long flight across the Atlantic. He'd known from the moment she'd told him to pack for Maine this wasn't a fun, impromptu visit with friends. Was that even possible with MI5 and FBI agents?

Oliver went around to Finian's chair, with its duct-taped tears and creaky workings. It predated Finian's arrival in Rock Point. Oliver would have replaced it straightaway, but his Irish friend hadn't expected to stay in the dreary little fishing village past his one-year appointment.

"Best-laid plans, my friend."

Oliver sat, imagining himself a priest. Saying Mass, visiting the sick, burying the dead, hearing confessions, running suppers and rummage sales to raise money. A year ago, on Oliver's first trip to Rock Point, Finian Bracken had struck him as reasonably content in his role as a small-town parish priest, far from home in Ireland. Maybe content was too strong. Dedicated. Committed.

He noticed a thick book on the Iveragh Peninsula on the corner of the desk, a photograph of iconic Skellig Michael on the front cover. Well, then. *Something* Finian must have added. Oliver wanted to go to Skellig with Henrietta one day. He'd never toured its medieval Christian settlement, nine miles off the southwest Irish coast. He was fairly certain Henrietta hadn't, either, but he left room to be corrected, as one did not just with her but any Balfour.

She knew all his shortcomings and misdeeds and yet loved him.

And he loved her, pretty, smart, irrepressible Henrietta Balfour, the fresh-faced girl next door when he was growing up in the Cotswolds—the orphaned boy raised by his grandparents. Her parents would drop her off with her great-aunt down the lane while they flitted off to Paris, Rome, Sydney. She'd followed in her grandfather's footsteps and joined MI5, secretly, of course, but these days her heart was at least as much in garden design.

You don't deserve her.

A persistent inner voice, and an attitude that would only annoy her.

Oliver creaked back in the chair and noted the ceiling needed a fresh coat of paint. No posting at a historic cathedral for Father Bracken. As a newly minted priest, he'd found his way here to the shores of southern Maine. Meant to be, perhaps. A lonely, isolated man, his Irish priest friend.

Or was that jet lag and his own unsettled mood at work? Oliver snapped the old chair forward and sat up straight. The man in the Mayfair London art gallery a week ago had also struck him as lonely and isolated.

Jeremy Pearson had set up the meeting. He'd found Oliver having breakfast alone at Claridge's that morning. *I'm sending a friend to you at the gallery. Talk to him. Answer his questions.*

Who is this friend?

His name's Robin Masterson. He's a newly retired scientist. He's indulging hobbies and interests he didn't have time for when he was working. His daughter might show up with him. They know me as William Hornsby, an art consultant.

I see.

Keep this between us.

Henrietta?

She's digging up dahlias in the Cotswolds, isn't she?

Indeed she had been. She wanted to dry the tubers over the winter and then move them to a sunnier spot. Just as well, perhaps. Oliver had withheld his many questions, his usual practice when Jeremy Pearson contacted him. He finished breakfast, took a long walk in St. James's Park and resisted ringing Henrietta to say good morning. He didn't want to lie to her, or have her sniff out he wasn't telling her something. He skipped lunch and arrived at the small, upscale gallery fifteen minutes ahead of Robin Masterson, who did have his daughter with him, Georgina, a chef in her early twenties. Oliver introduced himself. He'd assumed the daughter would say hello and leave her father to his chat, but she lingered, transfixed by three paintings in a new woodland watercolor series by Aoife O'Byrne.

Oh, Dad, to be able to paint something like this. How wonderful. Are you familiar with her work, Mr. York?

Oliver had stolen one of Aoife's early paintings in his first heist a decade ago, an unsigned Irish landscape and the only work he hadn't returned—because she didn't want it back. *It's where it belongs, Oliver.* She hadn't told him outright she knew he was the elusive thief the Sharpes and various law enforcement officers around the world had chased for a decade, but he didn't doubt she knew. Aoife O'Byrne was a beautiful, talented woman. She was also in love with the priest whose hospitality Oliver was now enjoying.

He stood up, restless, uncertain. A Mayfair art gallery a week ago to here, in this musty church office in a struggling fishing village…

He'd given Georgina Masterson a vague answer, and after sighing longingly at the Irish scenes, she kissed her father on the cheek and left to shop and visit friends. Robin Masterson had then turned to Oliver with an awkward smile. *She'd rather I'd been an eccentric art-*

*ist than an eccentric scientist. Shall we find a pub and
have a pint while we chat?*

In his early sixties, balding, dressed in a well-tailored
but old and rumpled jacket and trousers, the man oozed
eccentricity and loneliness. He and Oliver walked to a
nearby pub and took a booth in a quiet corner. *I appreciate Bill Hornsby setting up this meeting, and you for
being here. I'm a neurotoxicologist, by the way. I specialize in the study of the effects of synthetic toxins on
the nervous system.*

How can I help you?

*I want to talk to you about the use of various poisons
in myths, folktales and legends.*

Not what Oliver had expected. Advice on authenticating a Monet still-life, perhaps. *Do you have any
particular myths or poisons in mind?*

*I'm a forager. I gather wild edibles. It's been a passion of mine for several years, and now that I'm retired,
I can indulge myself. Suppose we start with poisonous
plants? I could do my own research on the internet,
but I prefer to consult an expert. This way I can ask
questions and get pointed in the right direction for any
follow-up research.*

That last had sounded perfectly reasonable to Oliver.
Over the next two hours, he offered Robin Masterson a
wide-ranging crash course on the unusual topic. Oliver
regarded the scientist across from him as eccentric but
sincere, and he couldn't imagine how an ancient tale
of hemlock poisoning had anything to do with his own
work for MI5. But the man was a neurotoxicologist, and
given his association with a senior MI5 officer, Oliver
guessed his work involved the intelligence services.

Finally, Robin Masterson collected his umbrella and

waxed-cotton jacket and got to his feet. *Thank you for your time, Oliver. I remember reading in the papers about what happened to you and your parents. I'm sure they'd be proud of what you've done with your life.*

Rarely rendered speechless, Oliver had struggled to say goodbye. He'd watched as the scientist stopped at the bar to pay for their pints and then exited, unfurling his umbrella as he walked out into rainy London. Oliver ordered fish and chips and a coffee, and collected his thoughts. He seldom ran into anyone these days who commented on his past. At eight years old, he'd witnessed the murder of his parents in their London apartment by two handymen they'd trusted. The men had then kidnapped him, taking him to isolated ruins in a remote part of Scotland.

He escaped to safety, and his paternal grandparents raised him on their Cotswolds farm, dying within months of each other when he was at Oxford. He abandoned his formal studies, and day by day, year by year, he isolated himself, finally turning to stealing art in various cities around the world—including, unfortunately, the UK and the United States. Hence, MI5 and the FBI in his life.

A slight exaggeration, perhaps. Oliver smiled to himself and went back to the window. The sheers had snags and pills in addition to that grayish cast. They had to go. He'd put an order in himself and have new ones sent.

With Robin Masterson on his way, Oliver had eaten his late lunch–early dinner and concluded the odd little neurotoxicologist had nothing to do with him personally—with his life in London, his work, his past misdeeds, his affection for Scotch or his love for Henrietta Balfour. No, the meeting had to do with Jeremy Pearson—his work, his life and perhaps his misdeeds.

As he was finishing his coffee, his MI5 handler sat across from him, rain dripping off his hair and scarred hands. He took a napkin and dabbed at the moisture.

How was your chat with Robin Masterson?

He's fascinated by poisons, isn't he?

Aren't we all?

Oliver had offered to repeat their conversation, but Jeremy was a big-picture sort and hadn't required details.

Except about the daughter.

How did she strike you, Oliver?

I only saw her for a short time—

And? What was your impression of her?

We have similar taste in art. She admired the new Aoife O'Byrne series at the gallery.

All right. Continue to keep this between us.

Still dripping, Jeremy left the bar. No explanation of the strange meeting. That was his MI5 handler, wasn't it? It wasn't as if Oliver had any sway over him. He was an asset. Someone to be used as Jeremy Pearson saw fit. The truth was, Oliver hadn't wanted Jeremy to confide in him about his relationship with the Mastersons. He'd wanted to pull up dahlias with Henrietta. But he had amends to make, and it was his duty to make them, no matter the inability of prosecutors to present a legal case against him.

He sucked in a breath when he spotted Colin Donovan walking toward the church, straight to the side entrance that led to Finian's office. He had the purposeful gait of a man on his turf, confident, strong and in no mood for obfuscation. Oliver was a master at obfuscation.

He heard Colin's steady thump up the stairs. They'd met a year ago in Boston, where Oliver had been working under an alias he'd used as a mythology consultant for films and television. A murder investigation had eventually led Colin and Emma to uncover—without too much effort—Oliver Fairbairn's real identity. They and their humorless boss, FBI Special Agent Matt Yankowski, had come to Oliver's apartment in London. They'd figured out he was their elusive art thief, and also that they could never prosecute him due to lack of evidence and jurisdictional issues.

Over the winter, he'd returned all the stolen art, intact—and without getting caught. It'd taken some doing, but it was done. And now he was putting his skills, contacts and knowledge to use for the UK intelligence services.

Colin would cuff him in a heartbeat given the opportunity. Emma wasn't a pushover, but Oliver knew she liked him better than her husband did.

He turned from the window as Colin arrived in the office doorway. "Hello, Oliver."

"Special Agent Donovan."

Oliver could see the FBI agent, still in the suit he'd worn to his brother's wedding, wasn't in the mood for small talk. Not that they'd ever engaged in much small talk.

"I didn't expect you and Henrietta here today," Colin said, entering the small office.

"Next time we'll text you as well as our Father Bracken."

"Good idea. What do you know about a British art consultant named William Hornsby?"

Oliver checked any obvious reaction. "He was one of the food-poisoning victims?"

"Uh-huh. He'll survive. He's being kept overnight at the hospital." Colin glanced out the window, as if to force himself to take a moment to collect his thoughts, and then narrowed his gaze on Oliver. "You know who he is, don't you?"

No point in dissembling. Oliver nodded.

"Did you go on board the yacht?" Colin asked.

"When people became ill?"

"At any time, ever."

Oliver shook his head. "No."

"What about Henrietta?"

"She can answer for herself, but no, she didn't."

"Then you didn't steal a painting off this yacht."

Oliver knew Colin was watching him for his reaction. Could he guess how little Oliver knew about what was going on? But that was what the FBI agent was gauging—how in the dark Oliver was about the man they both knew as Jeremy Pearson.

Finally, Oliver shook his head. "I did not steal a painting."

"Did anyone ask you to steal a painting?"

"No." Oliver motioned to the door. "You have a lot of questions. Perhaps we should go find Emma and Henrietta."

"We'll do that," Colin said. "Did you know our mutual friend was on board the yacht, posing as an art consultant?"

"I'm on a need-to-know basis, Agent Donovan. It's never otherwise with your lot."

Not the faintest smile from Colin. "Wonder why that is. What's your cover story for being in Maine?"

"Henrietta and I are here to visit friends," Oliver said.

Colin rubbed the back of his neck. "Does our friend recovering from gastric distress know you're here?"

"I haven't spoken with him."

"Do you know Bryce and Melodie Fanning?"

"They own the yacht in question? No, I do not."

"Heard of them?"

"No."

"What about a young chef named Georgina Masterson?"

Oliver was caught off guard by that one. "Did she prepare today's ill-fated food?"

"Apparently. Don't think I haven't noticed you aren't answering my questions."

"I've learned the hard way you notice everything."

Colin walked over to the desk and touched its worn wood. "All right." He straightened, visibly tired. "Let's find Henrietta. I gather she knows things about today that you don't know."

"The devil, I hope so," Oliver blurted. "Last I saw her, she and Emma were on the way. To the rectory to prepare tea. You look as if you could use a nice cuppa and a pumpkin-shaped biscuit."

This time, Colin managed at least a faint smile. He motioned toward the open door. "After you, Oliver."

5

"So these are bean holes." Henrietta peered into one of four three-meter-deep holes in the backyard of the church. "Fascinating. And these bean-hole suppers are a fund-raiser for the church?"

"That's right," Emma said, standing. next to her. "They're a Maine tradition."

Henrietta seemed genuinely interested, but the sudden urge to see the bean holes stemmed from her obvious desire to keep an eye on Colin and Oliver at the church. Emma didn't mind. With Finian on the tour of the church, she'd held off on questioning Henrietta and Oliver about the real reasons for their presence in Rock Point. Now she'd wait for Colin and Oliver to join them.

Henrietta moved to another of the bean holes. "I saw the flyer on the table in the rectory and wondered what in heaven's name is a bean hole? As I see now, it's as described. One digs a hole, makes a fire in it and adds pots for the slow-cooking of baked beans." She grinned. "I'm still a bit mystified, although not as much as I would have been an hour ago."

"The menu hasn't changed in decades," Emma said.

"Baked beans, roast pork, coleslaw, applesauce, etcetera, etcetera. Do you and Colin contribute?"

"When possible. I like to bake pies. The rummage sale is part of the weekend festivities."

"I love a good rummage sale." Henrietta stood straight, her rich reddish curls catching the fading light. "I donated bags of Aunt Posey's clothes for one at home. I didn't save a single thread she'd worn. She was a brilliant gardener, though."

Emma had been to the Cotswolds house Henrietta had inherited from her great-aunt. Posey Balfour's death a year ago had prompted Henrietta to launch a new career as a garden designer. Or at least appear to, Emma thought. Henrietta could have pretended to exit MI5 as a ruse to keep an eye on her neighbor. Over the summer, she and Oliver had surprised themselves—and probably her MI5 superior and his MI5 handler—by falling for each other.

Henrietta smiled. "The lure of life in the country. Do you and Colin ever dream of moving here full-time, quitting the FBI, leading a quieter life?"

"Colin toys with becoming a tour boat captain."

"Whale watches, puffins, seals? That sort of thing? I don't know if it'd be quieter, but I could see it. Oliver would say he'd have to learn to be a bit more—what's the word he uses? Charming? I suppose he could play the role of the curmudgeon Maine sea captain."

Emma laughed. She liked Henrietta but didn't underestimate her. Her amiable personality no doubt helped with everything she did, whether as a garden designer or an MI5 officer.

With dusk fast approaching, the cloudless sky was easing from its vibrant blue to a soft gray. Henrietta sighed wistfully. "I love a scoop of baked beans at breakfast, or on toast for a quick supper. Are they better if buried and baked over—how long?"

"At least a day," Emma said. "They are good."

"Perhaps Oliver and I will go to the supper if we're here next weekend. We can help sort things for the rummage sale. What do you suppose there is? Pilled hand-knitted jumpers and mittens, old juice glasses, chipped pottery, I imagine. I've found several incredible flowerpots at rummage sales."

Emma smiled. "Of course."

Henrietta took a deep breath. "What fantastic air after planes and cities. I like what I've seen of Rock Point thus far. It's not a biscuit-tin village. It's real."

"Did you get a chance to stop in Heron's Cove?"

"We drove through Heron's Cove and took the ocean route to Rock Point. All was quiet at the Sharpe offices. I assume we were there before the partygoers were struck ill." Henrietta looked past Emma. "It gets dark earlier now we're into October, but it's been a brilliant day for my first visit to Maine. Oliver's been here, of course."

"When did you arrive in the US?"

"Last night. We stayed at an airport hotel in Boston."

"Why didn't you get in touch with Colin or me?"

"Oliver texted Finian this morning. When he mentioned the wedding, we came on up without getting in touch with you and Colin. It seemed like the right thing to do at the time."

Not a trace of guilt but Emma hadn't expected one.

Henrietta tightened her arms around her middle. "It's downright chilly." She nodded toward the church's side entrance. "Here come Oliver and Colin now."

The two men strode to them. Colin and Henrietta exchanged a warm greeting, and he kissed her on the cheek. "We've been examining bean holes," she said.

"If you've never been to a Maine bean-hole supper, you're missing out. Best baked beans anywhere." His amiability faded quickly, and he steadied his gaze on Henrietta. "Did you know Jeremy Pearson is in Maine, posing as William Hornsby, a British art consultant?"

"How is he?" Henrietta asked softly.

"He'll recover."

She shivered in a gust of wind. "I want to see him, Colin."

"No visitors until morning."

She nodded, more in acknowledgment of his words, Emma thought, than agreement. "Did you speak with him?"

"Barely. Henrietta, did you know Jeremy was on board that yacht?"

"It's complicated."

"No, it's not. It's a yes-or-no question."

"And I can't provide you with a yes-or-no answer." She stepped back from the bean hole. "I'm sorry. I need to speak with him first. I'm sure you understand."

Emma could see that remark didn't sit well with Colin, but he said nothing. Oliver looked as if he wouldn't mind jumping into one of the bean holes. "I suspect Finian is waiting for us," she said.

They went into the rectory kitchen through the back door. Finian had a teapot, sandwiches and cookies set out on the table. He grabbed the kettle off its stand and poured boiling water into the teapot. The electric kettle was one of the few additions he'd made to the simple kitchen. The entire rectory needed updating, but he would never complain. One of his three sisters in Ireland had sent him a traditional oilcloth cover, decorated with flowerpots, for the table. A touch of home, perhaps. He'd said little since he'd returned to the rectory with Emma. She suspected he knew more about Henrietta's and Oliver's true backgrounds than he let on—or perhaps could let on, given his vows.

He returned the kettle to its stand. He looked awkward, as if he were expecting trouble—a hazard, Emma understood, of his friendship with her and Colin, never mind with Oliver and now Henrietta. He must have expected a quieter life when he'd agreed to leave Ireland to serve the little Maine church.

"I'll leave you to catch up with each other," Finian said, moving away from the counter. "I have a few things to do in the den. Shout if you need me."

He withdrew into the hall, and Henrietta sat next to Oliver, across from Emma. Colin stayed on his feet. Henrietta reached for the wedding cookies, arranged on a plate in the middle of the table. Emma had already had one. They were buttery, melt-in-the-mouth sugar cookies in the shape of pumpkins, acorns and oak leaves, decorated in autumn colors. Henrietta grabbed a leaf-shaped one. "I suppose I should start with a sandwich, but I can't resist."

Oliver helped himself to a triangle of a cheese sandwich. "I understand today's happy couple is off to Ireland for their honeymoon. Excellent choice."

Emma agreed, but she wasn't going to let him or

Henrietta sidetrack her. Oliver set his sandwich on a small plate and poured tea into the four cups Finian had set out, anticipating Colin's arrival. Colin had taken off his suit jacket and must have left it somewhere, because he didn't have it with him. Since he and Kevin had responded to the call about the yacht in Kevin's truck, she assumed he'd walked from wherever the truck had ended up.

"Do you know why the chef, a young woman named Georgina Masterson, has a painting by Aoife O'Byrne, and does it have anything to do with Jeremy's presence on the yacht?"

"That's multiple questions. Best to stick to one at a time."

A faint smile from Colin. Emma caught her breath. Given Henrietta's and Oliver's presence, she'd anticipated Jeremy Pearson, aka William Hornsby, might be involved, but Aoife? Colin glanced at her and before he shifted back to Henrietta, Emma saw his apology, but she knew why he hadn't given her much of a heads-up. He wanted to see Henrietta's and Oliver's reactions to the mention of Aoife O'Byrne in comparison to hers. As slick as Henrietta and Oliver were, they weren't entirely surprised at mention of the Irish artist.

Henrietta picked up her teacup. "I have a feeling I'm going to regret not packing wool socks. Colin, Emma, I appreciate you want answers, but I need to speak to Jeremy as soon as possible. Then we can talk."

Colin gave her a half smile. "Sure, Henrietta. We'll let you call the shots. Did any of you—Jeremy, Oliver, you—contact Wendell or Lucas Sharpe, or the Sharpe offices?"

Oliver grabbed another half a sandwich, leaving Henrietta to field Colin's questions. "No idea," she said.

"Who pulled the strings to keep your arrivals in the US quiet?"

"You're assuming someone did."

"Yes, I am."

"I'm sure you understand my position. We would in similar circumstances with you."

Colin shrugged. "If you two want to play games, that's your call. I'm trying to find out what happened to a friend and colleague I found in a pool of his own vomit a few hours ago."

Henrietta met his gaze with an equally steely one of her own. "Understood." She pushed back her chair and smiled. "Why don't we find Father Bracken? He mentioned he wants to open a new Bracken Distillers pot-still."

"Happier words never spoken," Oliver said. "Shall we?"

But Henrietta kept her eyes on Colin. "Apparently, our good father has been saving the pot-still especially for you, Special Agent Donovan."

There was a knowing undertone to her words, suggesting she had an idea of where he'd been the past few weeks. Even so, Emma saw some of Colin's tension ease. He nodded. "After you, Henrietta."

"Brilliant." She stifled a yawn that seemed to come out of nowhere. "It's bedtime at home in England. It's been a long day." She adjusted the waistband of her skirt. "No more traveling in long skirts on flights. I kept getting twisted up in the bloody thing."

With that, she took Oliver's hand and changed the subject to bean holes as they headed to the den. Colin hung back in the kitchen, touching Emma's hand. "I don't know much more than what I just told them. Fin's in the dark?"

"So far. He's not the type to listen at keyholes."

"He's the type. He just resists."

Emma smiled at the welcome touch of Colin's sense of humor. "He likes Henrietta and Oliver."

"Who doesn't? Come on. Let's see if Bracken Distillers' latest loosens their tongues."

The den was as simple and faded as the rest of the rectory with its wood paneling and sturdy, cozy furnishings. Sofa, club chairs, a lounger Finian had adopted for himself. A bookcase filled with a wide range of reading material—theological, Maine guides, kayaking and cross-country skiing instruction, wildlife manuals and novels, most Emma recognized as favored by Father Callaghan, Finian's predecessor. Finian had collected whiskey glasses from the dining room and had them lined up on the coffee table. "A *taoscán* each," he said genially as he poured the Bracken Distillers eight-year-old pot-still. *Taoscán*, Irish for "imprecise measure," was the word he preferred to a dram or a splash of whiskey.

He handed out the glasses and raised his to his guests. *"Sláinte."*

They responded in kind.

"It's gorgeous," Henrietta said after her first sip.

Even Oliver, who tended to prefer Scotch, agreed. "No wonder Bracken Distillers is winning awards."

"It's Declan's doing," Finian said, referring to his twin brother. "But I did help put this one into the casks in the dark days after Sally and the girls went to God."

Emma was no whiskey expert, but she liked the pot-still. Neither she nor Colin had known Finian eight years ago when he'd lost his wife and daughters in a sailing accident. He and Declan had launched Bracken Distillers in their early twenties, on a shoestring, with more hope than anything else. She noticed his eyes, warm with nostalgia but not, she thought, the rawness of grief. He'd never get over the loss of his family, but he'd achieved at least some peace over the years.

She and Colin sat next to each other on the couch. He crossed one leg over the other, almost touching her. She felt his intensity. He'd gone with Kevin to provide moral support, and he'd ended up discovering a friend and colleague sick and getting him into an ambulance. Then her text that Henrietta and Oliver were in his hometown.

And an Aoife O'Byrne painting.

Henrietta turned to Finian. "I'd like to take my whiskey upstairs and get settled. I'm dead on my feet, and I'm sure Oliver is, too."

"No problem at all," Finian said politely. "I didn't have a chance to see to the guest rooms, but everything should be in order. We keep them ready for the odd unexpected guest. Let me know if you need anything."

She thanked him. Oliver nodded. "We'll be no trouble. I'd like to pop into the kitchen for another sandwich and cookie, if you don't mind."

Finian smiled. "Of course not. Help yourself. There's plenty. I'm afraid the rest of us filled up at the wedding."

"Excellent," Oliver said. "Henrietta?"

"I'll go with you to the kitchen and see if I'm tempted."

Emma thought Colin might balk at their ducking out

early, but he settled next to her with his whiskey. "We'll talk tomorrow, then."

"We're having breakfast at Hurley's. Join us if you'd like." Henrietta beamed Colin a smile. "Oliver's raved about Rock Point's favorite watering hole. It's good it keeps fishermen hours and opens early. We'll be up at dawn given the time difference."

They said good-night and took their glasses with them out of the den. A quick visit to the kitchen, and then Emma heard them on the stairs, confirming they were doing as they said and not trying to slip out of the rectory under her and Colin's noses. Not that they wouldn't go out a window, Oliver in particular.

Finian sat on his usual chair by a small table with the whiskey bottle, his breviary and a mystery novel. He cupped his glass in both hands. "Help yourself to more whiskey if you'd like."

"Thanks, Fin," Colin said. "Sorry for the intrusion."

"FBI business?"

Colin savored a sip of whiskey, swallowed as he leaned forward and set the glass on the coffee table. "To be honest, Fin, I have no idea what's going on. Have you been in touch with Aoife O'Byrne recently?"

"Aoife? No, I haven't." Finian glanced down at his whiskey, as if trying to decide whether to follow up with Colin for more information. Finally, he looked up. "Why do you ask, can you say?"

"Apparently one of her paintings was on the yacht today." Colin waited a moment. "Is she in Dublin?"

"I don't monitor her whereabouts, Colin."

"But Kitty, Sean—you're in regular touch with them. Have they said anything about her? What she's up to, any travels, openings?"

Finian glanced at the pot-still bottle with its distinctive black-and-gold label. For the first time since Emma had arrived at the rectory after the wedding, he looked uncomfortable, not typical for a man so centered and thoughtful. She didn't know if Colin noticed. They'd both met Aoife and her older sister, Kitty, the owner of a boutique hotel in the tiny Irish south coastal village of Declan's Cross. Kitty was engaged to Sean Murphy, the Irish detective who'd investigated the tragic, accidental deaths of Finian's wife and daughters. Since then, he and Sean, who owned a farm in Declan's Cross, had become close friends.

Aoife, though.

Last fall, she'd as much as told Emma that Finian Bracken was her forbidden love—the man she couldn't have but wanted. Whatever was between them, they had unfinished business about their relationship.

Finian placed his glass on the side table, next to his black-bound breviary. "I spoke to Kitty last week. She mentioned Aoife's decided to give up her studio in Dublin altogether and move to Declan's Cross."

"She holed up in a cottage near Sean's farm over the summer to paint," Emma said. "Maybe she's tired of city life and wants to be closer to Kitty."

"I don't know. I didn't ask."

"Is Aoife in Declan's Cross now?" Colin asked.

Finian shrugged, his midnight blue eyes lost in the shadows. "I have no idea. What's this about? Is she in danger? Should I ring Sean?"

Colin shook his head. "I have no reason to believe she's in any danger, Fin. I'd have called Sean myself if I did."

"The painting you mentioned. Did you see it yourself? Is it a new one of Aoife's paintings?"

"I didn't see it," Colin said. "Fin—"

"But this yacht and Henrietta's and Oliver's visit are related," he said, not making it a question. He picked up his whiskey glass. "Henrietta and Oliver aren't the average houseguests. That's why I grabbed Emma at the wedding."

Emma took a last sip of the pot-still and set her glass on the coffee table. "If you have any concerns about them staying here—"

"I don't. I rather enjoy their company." Finian smiled. "You two aren't the average friends, either."

"Same goes for you as a priest, Fin." Colin got to his feet. "Thanks for the whiskey. Call if you need us. Don't hesitate."

A faint smile from Finian. "You're not going to offer to sleep on the sofa, are you?"

Colin grinned. "Only if Emma joined me. I've been away for weeks. But think of Franny Maroney walking in here and finding us."

Finian laughed, his eyes sparking with genuine humor. "We'll be fine here. I trust you'll tell me what I need to know about what's going on."

"I guarantee the two Brits upstairs know more about what's going on than I do."

Emma followed the two men into the entry. Colin opened the solid-wood door. "Call us if they leave."

"Should I try to stop them?" Finian asked.

"No. Let them do what they want." Colin shrugged, matter-of-fact. "They will, anyway."

"I do seem to have independent-minded friends these days."

"You barely know Henrietta."

Finian nodded thoughtfully. "I have a feeling most people barely know Henrietta."

"No argument from me," Colin said. "Good wedding today. Andy and Julianne will enjoy their Irish honeymoon. It was generous of you to offer them the cottage."

"My pleasure. I hope they have a grand time." Finian held up a hand as if he'd just remembered something. "Hang on."

He disappeared down the hall, returning quickly with a small paper bag. He handed it to Colin. "Sandwiches and cookies. Take them. Enjoy your evening despite the mysteries of the day."

"We will," Colin said. "Thanks, Fin."

He watched from the doorway as they headed out to the sidewalk. Emma glanced back as he stepped inside and shut the door behind him. "Ireland's home for him," she said. "It always will be."

Colin stayed close to her as they walked past the church. "Can you see him ditching the priesthood and moving to Declan's Cross himself? Hooking up with Aoife, maybe."

"There's something there between them. He'll sort it out."

"You quit the convent."

"Quitting the priesthood is different. I left the Sisters of the Joyful Heart as a novice, prior to making my final vows. Finian is an ordained priest."

"You could have quit after you made final vows. He can quit, too."

"He'll figure out what his purpose is," Emma said.

Colin slipped his hand into hers. "Right now I can't

think much past a beer and a couple of these sand-wiches."

"And cookies. Don't forget the cookies."

"I never forget cookies."

"What did you tell Kevin?" Emma asked when she and Colin turned up the street toward their house. It was dark now, the air cooler but not uncomfortably so.

"Nothing but he knows something's up with our British art consultant. I'm glad I had the foresight to drop off his truck at his place and walk to the rectory. If I'd left it at the house, he'd have picked it up and had a chance to grill me."

"One needs to be cautious with a Donovan on your case."

Colin grinned at her. "Do I look nervous?" But he turned serious. "Kevin won't bug us tonight. He'll give us room to maneuver. We have no evidence a crime's been committed, and I'm not going to get anything out of Jeremy until he's feeling better."

"It must have been difficult seeing him so sick."

"It wasn't fun, that's for sure."

"We won't get anything out of Henrietta and Oliver until after they speak with Jeremy—at least until after she does."

"They're holding back," Colin said.

"From each other, too, I suspect." Emma felt Colin's hand warm in hers. It wasn't the postwedding evening they'd expected, but he was here with her and that was good. "What about the Aoife O'Byrne painting?"

"I told Georgina Masterson to talk to the police, but she balked. She was in a state. Even if the food poisoning was just one of those things—bad luck, whatever—she feels responsible as the chef."

They passed houses lit up for the evening, teenagers playing street hockey, a couple walking their yellow Lab. Colin greeted them—he knew most everyone in the neighborhood. Emma was getting there, but she hadn't grown up in Rock Point. Even through his years with the FBI, working deep-cover missions and away for long periods, Colin had always considered his tight-knit fishing village home.

"I don't like guessing," he said. "But if I had to guess, I'd say Jeremy is keeping Henrietta and Oliver in the dark, if not about everything."

"Would that be like him?"

"Oh, yeah."

He hadn't hesitated. Emma had learned Colin wasn't one to waver when his gut told him something. He was naturally a man of instincts, but he had the training and experience to know what he could trust and what he couldn't—when he needed to hold back and not rush in. His independent thinking was one of the qualities that made him a good undercover agent, but he was always professional.

They crossed a quiet intersection, their house just up the street. Colin was good at compartmentalizing, but Emma could see the events of the day were still on his mind.

He handed her the bag of cookies and sandwiches. "I need to fetch apples out of my truck."

"When did you buy apples?"

"Yesterday on my way from the airport with Mike. We stopped at a local orchard. I figured we could make a pie together. You know. Relax. Have a normal weekend. They're Cortlands."

"Cortlands?" Emma smiled. "They're perfect for pies."

He returned her smile. "I remember."

While he fetched the apples from his truck, she went inside through the front door and headed to the kitchen. She grabbed two beers out of the refrigerator and arranged the cookies and sandwiches on two plates. Colin came in through the back door and set the bags of apples on the counter. They took the beers and plates to the front room. He got a fire started in the fireplace, and they sat on the floor with their simple meal.

"I spent the past month picturing a night like this," he said, kicking off his shoes, undoing a few buttons on his shirt. "I could have done without the afternoon with the barfing and the sneaky Brits."

Emma started with half a ham-and-cheese sandwich. "What can you tell me about your relationship with Jeremy Pearson?"

"We met on my first undercover mission. He was looking into the same network of arms traffickers. That was five years ago now, and he'd done it all even by then."

"Were you in danger together?"

Colin stretched out his legs and leaned against the base of a chair. "We met at Thames House, but we ran into each other in the field. We got into it with a low-level, violent thug who made the mistake of trying to kill us both at the same time."

"The thug was part of the arms trafficking network?"

"Periphery."

And the incident had occurred before she and Colin had met. She'd entered the FBI after he had. Matt Yankowski, now their boss, then Colin's contact agent, had recruited her. Yank had looked her up at her convent, but he'd been in Maine specifically to meet with Colin about that first undercover mission. Last fall, he'd shoehorned Colin into HIT, the small, Boston-based team that was Yank's brainchild. Short for high impact targets, HIT focused on elusive criminal enterprises with international reach and virtually unlimited resources. Its future remained uncertain while Yank recovered from the bullet wound he'd suffered the same day Emma's father died.

"Did you tell Yank about today?" she asked.

Colin drank some of his beer. "Texted him. He's not happy." He winked at her. "We complicate his life."

"He'll be back at his desk full-time soon."

"Yeah."

She could hear Colin's fatigue. They ate their sandwiches, drank some of the beer and watched the fire as it took hold, crackling, warming up the chilly room. She'd learned early on that Colin didn't like to turn up the heat until he had no choice. It was something they had in common.

He set his beer bottle on the floor next to him. "Do you think Oliver could have slipped on board the Fanning yacht without Henrietta's knowledge?"

Emma considered a moment. "Could have, but would he?"

"If Jeremy told him to do it."

"It's time Oliver put his past behind him."

Colin got up and went to the fire. "I wonder how much he helped British intelligence before we figured out who he was. Maybe Jeremy's known about Oliver longer than any of us realizes."

"I've wondered that, too."

"Oliver's wily. Jeremy's devious. Anything is possible with them." Colin grabbed a log out of the wood box, pulled back the fireplace screen and placed it on the hot coals and flames. "It's good no one died today."

He sat next to Emma again. She placed a hand on his thigh. "It must have been rough seeing Jeremy that way. Alone, undercover. Did you think it could be you one day?"

"Who says it hasn't been me?"

"There's that."

She leaned against his shoulder. "Would you ever pose as an art consultant on a yacht on a foliage cruise?"

"I haven't. That doesn't mean I wouldn't. You could pull it off given your background." He paused, his gaze steady on the fire as it consumed the fresh log. "I don't know what's going on, Emma, but Jeremy could have contacted me and he didn't. He let me find him in a pool of barf."

"Have you been in contact recently?"

Colin shook his head. "He and I cleaned up some rough arms trafficking network, but there's always another."

"But it doesn't always have to be you unraveling it."

"That became Jeremy's thinking. Always had to be him. It's not mine. Not yet, anyway."

"There are other jobs you can do, with the FBI or not."

"Ah. So you want me to become Captain Colin."

She smiled. "I'm with you whatever you decide."

He put an arm around her and pulled her close, kissed the top of her head. "You're the best."

They took their plates and scraps into the kitchen. "I

hope Kevin's having chowder and whiskey with Beth at Hurley's. You remember her?"

"No-nonsense ER nurse new to Rock Point."

"We ran into her at the hospital. She was irritated Kevin didn't invite her to the wedding."

"She said so?"

"Not in so many words but it was obvious."

"To Kevin?"

"Doubt it. He's got rocks in his head when it comes to his romantic life." Colin shut the dishwasher and winked at Emma. "Another Donovan trait."

"No argument from me," she said with a laugh. "You all weren't sure Julianne and Andy would ever get together, and now they're on their way to Ireland for their honeymoon."

"Then there's Mike and Naomi." Colin moved toward her, slipped his arms around her. "And us. The burned-out undercover agent and the ex-nun art crimes specialist."

"But here we are."

"Yes." He pulled back, just a little, enough for Emma to know his mind was on the events of the day. "The Fannings stopped in Heron's Cove at the last minute. Supposedly Melodie Fanning and our British art consultant wanted to see the Sharpe offices."

"We need to know if they or any of the passengers, crew or guests got in touch with the offices, or directly with my grandfather or brother. The Aoife O'Byrne painting by itself would make me wonder."

"It's late in Ireland now."

"I'll get in touch with Lucas and Granddad first thing in the morning."

"Meantime?"

She tossed her head back and smiled at him. "I thought you might have energy to burn off and could carry me up the stairs?"

"I like how you think."

6

The rectory's two guest rooms were separated by a shared bathroom. When he took their bags upstairs, Oliver had opted for the bedroom overlooking the back garden for Henrietta. It was quieter, and it had flowers. He could see the bean holes from his room.

He stood in her doorway, watching her plop her suitcase onto the double bed. "You didn't tell me things so I wouldn't get in trouble with our friends in the FBI or have to lie to Finian Bracken," he said mildly. "Or you didn't tell me because you know Jeremy has me in his clutches and you're after him for some reason."

"You're overthinking, Oliver."

She unzipped her soft-sided suitcase with more force than was necessary. It was lilac, not a color he'd expected until he'd been confronted with it and had thought...*yes, it suits her.* Her room was small and sparsely if adequately furnished with the bed, a single bedside table, dresser and wood chair all painted in co-ordinating shades of turquoise, presumably given the rectory's coastal location. Cheerful, anyway. The walls were decorated with two prints of seagulls, rocks and ocean, a mirror with seashells embedded in its frame and a small wood crucifix.

Henrietta took a small pile of lingerie from her suit-case. Oliver noticed a sports bra, a lacy bra, a tank top—he stopped there and focused on her movements as she placed the pile on top of the dresser and opened a drawer. She smiled and withdrew a linen sachet. "Lav-ender. How lovely."

"Not Finian's doing, I suspect. A previous guest, perhaps?"

"A gift from Ireland, I think. He does have a brother and three sisters there, and a host of friends. I wouldn't be surprised if all or most of them want him back."

"So send lavender sachets?"

"Reminders of home," she said.

Oliver heard a catch in her voice, but it could be jet lag at work. He didn't always trust his first impressions with her.

She put the lingerie in the drawer and placed the sachet on top of it. She returned to her suitcase for another stack of clothes. "I always unpack, even if I'm only staying in a place for one night. I feel more settled. I sleep better."

"A good Scotch helps me."

"It might help you fall asleep, but it won't help you stay asleep. And don't be cheeky with me, Oliver York."

He smiled at her. "I do love you, Henrietta, no matter your MI5 secrets and sneakiness and all the rest."

"Put like that…"

But she laughed, placing the pile—more lingerie—in the drawer. He hadn't known that about her unpacking rule before they'd started seeing each other over the summer. They'd known each other since they'd been young children, before his parents were murdered in front of him, reshaping not only his life but, in unexpected ways, hers, too, and the lives of so many others in their small Cotswolds village. Amazing, the things he'd learned about her in these past few months. He'd thought he'd known everything.

She shut the drawer, grabbed actual clothes from her suitcase. One of her ubiquitous skirts, a couple of tops. She opened another drawer, shoved them in, shut the drawer with her knee. "I know you have questions, Oliver. So do I. But we must remember it's okay for me to hold back on you. I have…restrictions. It's not okay for you to hold back on me."

"Even if Jeremy tells me to?"

"Right now, under the circumstances, especially if he told you to."

Being here—knowing as little as he did—reminded Oliver of his inferior position. Henrietta and Jeremy were MI5 officers, and he was an asset, someone they had by the short hairs and would use and discard once they'd played him out.

Henrietta had corrected him on his terminology. *Release* was her word of choice, not *discard*.

All in all, toeing the line with MI5 was preferable to prison.

"In his own way, Jeremy *is* your friend, Oliver," she said. "Remember that, won't you?"

"Don't tell him he's my friend."

"Jeremy is his own authority. Not many people tell

him anything." She sighed audibly. "Now I'm over-thinking. Nothing positive comes of a combination of jet lag and overthinking. Speculating is the enemy of good judgment, not to mention good sleep."

"I've rarely struggled with insomnia. Nightmares? Another story."

"Has Jeremy been in touch with you, Oliver?"

"Since—"

"In the past month, in particular the past week, including today."

"I'm not supposed to discuss our contacts."

"Is that a yes? Just tell me when, where and why he's been in touch." But he didn't answer immediately, and she inhaled through her nose, blew out the breath forcefully. "Oliver." She waited. "All right, then. I won't ask."

"Are you going to tell me how you knew Jeremy was on board that yacht?"

"You're assuming I did know."

"You did, Henrietta."

"I'll say this much. I don't need the details of how you returned the art you stole, or how you stole it in the first place. You don't need the details of every bloody thing I do in my work."

"Stealing art isn't my work."

She held up a hand, apologetic. "I'm sorry, Oliver. I truly am. It's not what I meant."

"What I was isn't who I am, but it's contributed—and I want to be the man my grandparents and parents wanted me to be. I want to use everything I did and learned in positive ways. I can help. I have helped."

"Jeremy wasn't wrong in thinking you could, and would help—and are helping."

"No, he wasn't. Henrietta, why are we here?"

He saw her swallow, bite her lower lip before she spoke. "We're visiting friends and seeing the New England autumn foliage."

"*Friends* includes William Hornsby. You're worried about him, aren't you? Could this be his last hurrah with the service?"

"I suspect it could be mine, too."

"MI5 doesn't know you're here?"

She didn't respond. Instead, she pulled her cosmetic bag out of the suitcase and set it atop the dresser.

Oliver walked across the small room to her, touched her wild hair. "You're trying to save Jeremy from himself," he said.

"I don't know what I'm trying to do. Get answers. That would be a good start." She put her arms around his waist and kissed him softly, then looked up, her blue-green eyes filled with emotion. "We both need to get some sleep. Good night, Oliver." She smiled. "A full American breakfast in the morning, I think, and something with wild blueberries."

He'd told her about wild blueberries on their long flight yesterday, when they'd avoided talking about what was really going on. He glanced behind him, but the stairs were dark, no sign Finian was coming up. But it was earlier in the evening for him. Oliver wasn't hungry after their snack, and neither was Henrietta. Jet lag put meals at odd times.

"You'll love Hurley's." He eyed Henrietta, though. He could see that mind of hers working. "You want to get onto the Fanning yacht, don't you?"

"Could you manage it?" she asked, skirting his question. "Without being seen, of course."

"Are you asking me to, Henrietta?"

"Absolutely not. We're in enough hot water with your FBI friends as it is."

"I like how you use the plural. Colin would object."

"He likes you. He just doesn't trust you." She pulled the last of her hair from her clip and set the clip on the dresser. "Rock Point is a ragged place in comparison to Heron's Cove, but I like it so far."

"You've been here less than twelve hours."

"I did say so far, Oliver. Now, off with you. I'd love for you to stay but it would be rude to abuse Father Bracken's hospitality. Let's talk at breakfast, shall we? We'll visit Jeremy and get things sorted. I'm sure Finian can hear us whispering."

Oliver traced the line of her jaw with one finger, saw her eyes soften as he leaned toward her. "Good night, love." He kissed her, a quick, sweet peck of a kiss. "Sweet dreams."

"You, too."

Oliver regretted having stepped foot in Henrietta's room. They'd had whiskey, for one thing. "Never try to speak to her when we have a good Irish pot-still in our systems," he muttered to himself, shutting his bedroom door behind him.

The small room had similar furnishings to the one down the hall, but this one had framed photographs of Ireland—he recognized both scenes. One was of the old, abandoned distillery the Bracken twins had purchased as lads almost twenty years ago. Tucked in the Killarney hills, the stone ruins had required imagination, heart, grit and hope to create a thriving distillery out of them. Finian and Declan Bracken had succeeded, even before the sailing accident that had claimed Finian's family.

The second photograph took Oliver's breath away. It was of three Celtic stone crosses on the headland above the tiny Irish village of Declan's Cross, on a grassy hilltop above the sea. He sank onto the edge of the bed and choked back tears. It was as if whoever had taken the photograph had known it would reach into his heart and draw him back to a place he loved, and to a time he didn't want to revisit. A cold, rainy November night…alone with his stolen loot…unable to fathom what he'd done, why he'd done it…certain the Irish police would find him and arrest him, and he'd be in a jail cell and the art returned to the O'Byrne family by noon.

But none of that happened, and so he'd continued.

Bolder, cheekier and never caught. Technically, that last held true today.

He'd first encountered Jeremy Pearson a year ago, around the time Emma and Colin had pegged him as the elusive international art thief Wendell Sharpe and a variety of law enforcement entities had been chasing for a decade. Jeremy had turned up on the farm, on a public trail that went past a dovecote Oliver's grandmother had converted into a garden shed. A few years after her death, Oliver had added a secret stone working studio. He'd become quite a competent carver, polisher and engraver. He'd perfected engraving small polished stones with a simplified Celtic cross like the one he'd lifted from the O'Byrne house in Declan's Cross. Once world-renowned art detective Wendell Sharpe set after him, he'd send a cross to the old man in Dublin after every heist. Taunting him. Energizing him in his later years. Amusing himself. Asking to be caught, perhaps.

Jeremy had stopped at the dovecote that rainy late-autumn morning. *The taunting was immature, Oliver. The stonework is quite good, however, although Michelangelo you'll never be. Close up shop. Get yourself straight with your stolen works. Then we'll see about making amends. You know a lot. Interesting people, places, methods. Art, mythology. You can kick ass with your martial arts training. We couldn't have trained you better ourselves for what I have in mind for you.*

We?

That grim smile Oliver had come to know so well. Jeremy had pointed his walking stick toward the lane. *How far to the main road?*

A ten-minute walk that I've no doubt you can do in five.

You see? We know each other already.

And so Oliver had become an MI5 asset and Jeremy Pearson his handler. *Bad things will happen, Oliver. We can't stop them all, but we can stop some of them.*

He'd never asked how much Henrietta knew about their arrangement, their work together. He never had the full picture of what Jeremy was up to, only a few crucial pieces of a larger mosaic of an investigation within the scope of the UK intelligence services.

Oliver looked up at the photograph of Declan's Cross. To be there now, walking with Henrietta, the sea breezes whipping through her curls and her smile reminding him he was no longer alone.

Instead, they were in Maine, and Jeremy Pearson was in trouble. And possibly Henrietta, too.

Oliver had told himself he didn't want to know what his chat with Robin Masterson had to do with his MI5 handler. He returned to his Cotswolds farm on Sunday as planned. He'd expected to confer with Henrietta on what needed to be done with the flower beds before winter. She'd promised to guide him on mulching and pruning and such since, of course, he had no clue.

When he arrived at the farm, he discovered Henrietta had left a message with Martin Hambly, first Oliver's grandparents' assistant and now his right-hand man—if not always a deferential one. But he counted on Martin's clarity, didn't he? They'd never discussed the thieving. They never would. In his fifties, never married, close-mouthed and particular, Martin had guessed Henrietta was MI5 before Oliver had.

In his understated way, Martin explained Henrietta was unexpectedly detained. *She said you should feel free to pull the dahlias and place their tubers on the worktable in the garden shed to dry out over the winter. She welcomes your opinions on where to move them. It's too shady where they are now.*

Did she say how long she'll be detained?

No.

Did she say why she's detained?

No.

Martin, help me out here.

She also said the dahlias in the pots aren't worth saving and you can toss them into the compost bin.

Oliver had done nothing of the kind—he found gardening mind-numbing unless he had Henrietta with him—and occupied himself rooting out any books in his library on the subjects he'd discussed with Robin Masterson, and digging into what was up these days with foraging. Quite the explosion in interest, apparently.

He'd noticed various wild things popping up on his plate at restaurants but hadn't given them much thought.

Henrietta finally turned up Thursday evening. *Find your passport and pack your bags.*

We're going somewhere?

We fly to Boston and then drive to Maine.

When?

First thing tomorrow.

Should I tell—

No one, Oliver. You tell no one.

Only after they'd landed in Boston had she released the tiniest bit of information. *We're making a surprise visit to your friends in Maine. I thought we could stay with Finian Bracken.*

Not Emma Sharpe and Colin Donovan, Oliver noticed. *Does Finian know we're coming?*

Not yet. If he's busy or out of town, we can book a room at an inn.

He won't be out of town. We exchanged emails last week. He has a wedding tomorrow. Colin's brother Andy is getting married.

Balderdash. That means he and Emma will be in Rock Point, too.

Only Henrietta could pull off such a word as *balderdash* without sounding ridiculous, and it was likely on the tip of her tongue because she'd been going through her grandfather's opera collection. An MI5 legend, Freddy Balfour had died when she was five but had been quite the opera buff, a form of relaxation for him. Oliver wasn't an expert, but he recalled a few operas involved poisons.

He noticed his bedside light created eerie shadows.

He supposed they were eerie given his mood. On another evening, they might strike him as romantic.

He tugged off his clothes, and when he got into bed and switched off the light, he could see himself on the headland above the tiny Irish village of Declan's Cross...he could feel the soft, wet ground among the ruins of a church and its gravestones and Celtic crosses...and he could hear the sheep in the dark fields and taste the sea on the breeze.

He heard Henrietta enter the bathroom, and then, after a half minute, the rush of water as she turned on the shower. She hadn't fallen straight to sleep, had she? She'd leave the bathroom steamy, smelling of shampoo and soap. He listened to the water, imagining the possibilities of their lives together. Not now, perhaps, with Jeremy Pearson up to something and Henrietta preoccupied with whatever it was. But someday.

What were the odds it was ordinary food poisoning today? Oliver had learned not to operate according to odds. Georgina Masterson was Robin Masterson's daughter, and he was a neurotoxicologist and she was a chef. They could figure out how to make people sick but not kill them, couldn't they?

Where was Robin Masterson now? Had something happened to him?

Oliver wanted to ask Henrietta, but to ask her meant explaining to her how he knew about him—and that would have to wait until tomorrow, once they had a chance to see Jeremy Pearson.

Where had Henrietta gone when she'd left him to the dahlias? Wherever it was, it had to do with Jeremy

Pearson, Robin Masterson and his daughter, an Aoife O'Byrne painting and, very possibly, at least, poison.

Oliver realized he hadn't finished the pot-still. He sat up, propped against pillows, and watched the shadows and drank the Irish whiskey as he listened to Henrietta turn off the water and pictured her stepping out of the shower.

Finian Bracken finished his whiskey in the den, in the ridiculously comfortable lounger. He took his time with the eight-year-old pot-still, savoring its smoothness, its notes of sherry, chocolate, elderberry and oak. With the Maine wind buffeting the rectory windows, he nonetheless thought of Ireland. He could see himself and Declan as lads, hiking the Kerry hills, shearing sheep, working in the garden and plotting—always plotting—their own whiskey distillery. Few believed it would ever happen, or succeed if it did.

He smiled at the Bracken Distillers label on the pot-still. He and Declan had done it, hadn't they? Against the odds, they'd found backers, bought a hundred-year-old distillery in ruin in the Killarney hills, refurbished it, put their first whiskey in casks and held on as those first casks matured. In the meantime, they produced a popular gin, put together marketing plans, launched a whiskey school and prayed it would all work out.

And it had, until he lost Sally, Mary and Kathleen. He'd abandoned Bracken Distillers, his twin brother, their sisters, in-laws, nieces and nephews, and, eventually, Ireland itself.

Not abandoned, he reminded himself. He'd responded to a call to God that had led him away from grief and drunkenness to seminary and now here, to the southern coast of Maine, his struggling church and his friends with dangerous jobs and adventurous lives.

He sipped the last of his whiskey. It wasn't regrets about the Brackens and the distillery back in Ireland that preoccupied him now. They were a distraction, a way for his mind to divert him from the real matter at hand.

He hadn't expected Aoife O'Byrne's name to come up.

He could see her in Declan's Cross, in the dark days between his family's deaths and his call to God. It was as if he had transported himself back to that cold, tormented November so long ago. Caught together in her uncle's wreck of a house on the south Irish coast, now her sister's boutique hotel, he and Aoife had lost themselves in each other's arms. She was the up-and-coming painter, beautiful and wrapped up in her work. He was the tortured widower, the grieving father, a man who had found no solace anywhere in the months since a freak sailing accident had robbed him of his wife and their daughters.

He should have been with them. He'd been meant to be with them. For that rainy weekend in the O'Byrne house, he'd let himself stop thinking as he'd made love to the only other woman he'd ever been with besides his wife. It was a weekend that never should have happened, but it had. He could hear Aoife's whisper now, years later, as if he were another man.

I don't want strings, Fin. I don't want attachments. You're dedicated to your work.

*I am. It would be easy to fall in love with you, if I
were inclined to romantic entanglements.*

Her words had suited him. They'd parted after that
weekend. Aoife had returned to her life and work in
Dublin. Her star was on the rise, and she knew what she
had to do. He'd returned to his whiskey bottles and the
little stone cottage he'd shared with his wife and their
girls. Seeking oblivion, racked with grief and guilt, he'd
expected he'd die there. But he hadn't. He'd experienced
a spiritual awakening, and now, seven years later, he
was serving a small church in Rock Point, Maine.

Finian considered Aoife a dear friend, but was that
truly possible, given their history?

It hadn't been just sex that November weekend in
her uncle's house. They'd had long talks by the fire
and in the rain, and they'd cooked together in the ram-
shackle kitchen. A couple of years earlier, a thief had
relieved the upstairs drawing room of two valuable west
Ireland landscapes by Jack Butler Yeats, an unsigned
local landscape by an unknown artist now believed to
be Aoife, and a silver wall cross carved with symbols
depicting Saint Declan, an early medieval Irish saint
who'd settled in the area.

The thief was upstairs in a rectory guest room. He'd
returned the stolen items last fall, except for the local
landscape.

Finian smiled, thinking of cheeky, wily, irrepressible Oliver York. The unreturned landscape depicted
a church ruin and crosses on the headland above Declan's Cross, a place of special meaning to the lonely
man who'd taken it.

That was all before Finian's call to the priesthood—

to this life he had now. *The priesthood isn't a prison sentence, Fin. If you want to leave, you can.*

His friend Colin, not long ago. Finian smiled. Colin wasn't a man who minced words. Finian didn't know what Aoife believed, but he didn't want her to use their brief interlude as a crutch to avoid a romantic life for herself. He was the forbidden love, the man she could never have—the soul mate who'd rejected her for the priesthood and a vow of celibacy. Meanwhile she could immerse herself in her work and think of nothing and no one else.

On a book shelf was a photograph of the cottage where Andy and Julianne would enjoy their honeymoon. It was constructed of stone, with thick walls and a loft. Finian was glad to have the means to keep it, and he enjoyed loaning it to friends—as he had this very day. He'd refused to let Andy and Julianne pay him. "This is my gift to you," he'd told them.

Over time he'd shifted from thinking the cottage as a place of sadness and loss—a place he'd succumbed to drunkenness and rage in his immeasurable, unimaginable grief and pain in the immediate aftermath of the sailing tragedy that had claimed his family and changed his life forever. Now he thought of the smiles and laughter and love he'd experienced there, and of the happy memories others were creating in this little cottage that had meant so much to his small family.

He got up abruptly and took his breviary, switched out the lights and went upstairs. He'd wash his whiskey glass in the morning. His guests—an art thief and a British intelligence officer, regardless of what anyone admitted—had settled down for the night, no lights under their bedroom doors or the bathroom door.

In his days as a whiskey man in the Kerry hills, Finian had never known spies, thieves and FBI agents.

Was Aoife involved in today's crisis aboard the yacht? In the reasons for Henrietta's and Oliver's presence on Rock Point and Colin's and Emma's stern looks?

He knew it wasn't his concern, reminded himself it wasn't—warned himself it wasn't. Yet as he got ready for bed, he could see Aoife that late autumn in Declan's Cross so long ago…her dark hair and translucent skin, her sea-blue eyes and bright smile. Intense, brilliant, troubled, racked by her sensitivities and her dreams and ambitions, she'd needed oblivion as much as he had. His because he was lost in the past. Hers because she was caught up in the unknowns of the future.

He'd entered seminary and begun an intensive process of discernment and study, never imagining he'd find himself in a small church in a Maine fishing village, a friend and confidant to men and women with tough jobs to do in a scary and unsafe world.

He itched to text Aoife and ask her about the yacht.

Colin would strike him dead for interfering in an FBI investigation.

An exaggeration, perhaps, but only a bit of one.

When he climbed into bed, Finian realized he was aching for home. It wasn't Oliver's and Henrietta's mysterious arrival and its connection to the food poisoning aboard the yacht in Heron's Cove. It was today's wedding, the love between Andy and Julianne, that of their friends and family. For the first time in many weeks,

Finian hadn't felt a part of things in Rock Point but, rather, a man apart, isolated and alone.

He opened his breviary and placed it on his lap.

All was well in his life. He just had to accept it was so.

7

Georgina Masterson hung out in a small waiting area down the hall from Bryce Fanning's room. He and William Hornsby did end up being the only two admitted after today's disastrous lunch, and she tried to tell herself that was a positive outcome, all considered. No one had died. Everyone would recover, if hating her.

Nick was getting food in the cafeteria for Melodie. Georgina didn't want anything to eat. When Melodie was ready to leave, he'd bring the car around to the lobby entrance, so she wouldn't have to trek out to where he'd parked. Georgina would like nothing better than a good walk. She could have gone back to the yacht but she was hoping to see Bill Hornsby. So far, the nurses insisted he wasn't to have visitors until morning and wouldn't let her into his room.

She exhaled, trying to get a firm grip on her emotions. How could she make sense of today? A dozen people sick due to something they'd eaten.

The Aoife O'Byrne painting...

Why had she asked the FBI agent about the painting? *Why?*

She wasn't one to blurt things. What if someone had stolen the painting and used the food poisoning as cover—as a distraction to smuggle it off the yacht?

But that was a leap. Georgina knew she had to calm down and apply logic to the situation. She had zero evidence to suggest anything criminal had occurred today.

Kevin Donovan spotted her and joined her in the waiting room. A nurse was with him—Beth from the ER, Georgina remembered. Beth had her coat on over her uniform, obviously finished with her shift and heading home.

"You okay?" Kevin asked.

Georgina smiled and nodded. "Yes, fine, thanks, but it's been a horrid day."

"It's not going to help if we told you it could have been worse?"

His easy manner helped her throttle back on her nervousness, frustration and sense of general dread. She was used to an adventurous life as a yacht chef and tended to keep her emotions in check. That they were driving her now was unsettling.

"Have you been in to see Bill Hornsby?" she asked. "Do you know how he's doing?"

"He's hanging in there," Kevin said.

"I'd like to see him."

"He's had a rough day," Beth said. "Best to let him rest. Are you family?"

"No," Georgina said, almost too quickly. But it was

true. She wasn't family. "If you tell him I'm here, he'll want to see me. He's in the US alone."

"I'd wait and see him in the morning," Beth said. "He has a good prognosis. He's likely to be discharged tomorrow."

Georgina wasn't about to argue, but she cringed at the thought of waiting. "Melodie Fanning thinks some type of mushroom in the tacos made people sick. It's possible, I suppose, but I have no idea how it could have happened."

"People make mistakes," Beth said.

"I didn't prepare tacos or anything else with mushrooms, at least not knowingly. There were a lot of people around today, and I put together a delivery of local vegetables. It didn't include mushrooms, though. I'd have noticed."

"Did you have help in the galley?" Kevin asked.

"People were in and out, but I'm in charge of the food. I'm not trying to shirk my responsibility. I'm just trying to figure out what happened."

"If mushrooms are your culprit, the rapid onset of symptoms is a good sign," Beth said. "The more dangerous mushrooms tend to take longer to produce symptoms. Do you have a ride back to the yacht? I'm dropping Kevin off in Rock Point. We can take you to Heron's Cove first."

Georgina glanced from Beth to Kevin. She didn't want to answer more questions, but she didn't want to wait for Nick and Melodie, either. She preferred to drive back to the yacht with two first responders. Once the stress of today settled in, Melodie could start looking for someone to blame for the embarrassment of her party turning into a disaster. Georgina wanted to stay out of her employer's line of fire, at least until she had concrete answers to give about the source of today's illness.

"It's not out of our way," Beth said.

Georgina decided to seize on the invitation. "I'd appreciate a ride, thank you."

"How do you know Mr. Hornsby?" Kevin asked as they walked to the elevators.

He was so casual and pleasant, it was hard to think of him as a state law enforcement officer. "He and my father are friends. My father's a retired scientist. Art's a hobby for him. That's how he and Bill Hornsby got to know each other." Georgina paused, wondering if she still believed that any longer, given the sensitive nature of her father's work. "He's sick. My father. Mr. Hornsby—Bill—had business in Boston and stopped by the marina as we were preparing for the cruise. The Fannings invited him to join us." Georgina followed Kevin and Beth onto the elevator. "I'm sure now he wishes he'd stayed in London."

Beth's car was parked in the employee lot. Georgina welcomed the cool early-evening air, but she felt a surge of panic at the prospect of getting into a car with these two strangers. Beth seemed to sense her agitated mood and opened the front door. "Hop in. Kevin will jump in back. Just pull your seat up a bit so he doesn't bang his knees into it." She smiled easily. "Small car, long legs."

Georgina could see how Beth managed the intensity and unpredictability of her work as an ER nurse. She'd have flamed out on her first day, not because of the emotions but the frenetic atmosphere, the hierarchy, the protocols. Her life as a chef was simple by comparison. *Just don't poison people.*

Work as an ER nurse turned out to be the perfect

subject for the drive to Heron's Cove. Instead of talking about food-borne illnesses and their unpleasant symptoms, Georgina asked Beth how she'd become a nurse, was she from Maine—nonintrusive, innocuous small talk.

Then Georgina stepped into a sensitive area, asking about the wedding today. She saw her mistake immediately when Beth hesitated before answering. "I don't know much about it," Beth said. She glanced into her rearview mirror at Kevin in the back seat. "I wasn't invited."

"Look at all the excitement you'd have missed," he said with a grin.

Beth bit back a laugh and sighed at Georgina. "That's what we call a tone-deaf remark."

But it *had* made Beth at least want to laugh. Georgina smiled. A budding romance, she thought, feeling a spark of cheerfulness for the first time in hours.

Heron's Cove was quiet when Beth and Kevin dropped Georgina off at the marina. She thanked them and promised if she discovered the source of today's food poisoning, she'd let someone know. "I'll look into Melodie's mushroom theory. Whatever happened, though, I assure you it was an accident."

Kevin didn't look convinced, but she reminded herself he was a police officer and decided she shouldn't read anything into it. She thanked them again and cut past the marina's main building down to the docks.

Once on board the yacht, she went straight to the galley. The crew had cleaned it while she'd been at the hospital. She dragged her finger across the edge of the stainless-steel sink.

Richie Hillier entered the galley. He was from Nassau, in his fifties, dark, silver-haired and slender, his entire life spent on boats of one sort or another. He'd taken her under his wing since she'd joined the crew. Trusted her. "Hey, Georgina. Welcome back."

"Thanks. You never got sick?"

"Nope. No one else did, either. Whatever it was, it was in and out, thank you, ma'am. Miserable experience but quick." He made a face. "Unless some poor guest is puking his guts out at home as we speak."

"It's hard to say with food poisoning. I'm really sorry about today, Richie."

"I had every inch of the yacht cleaned and disinfected, including in here."

"I see that. Thank you." She attempted a smile. "I could tell by the smell of disinfectant. It's reassuring."

"Assuming it kills whatever made people sick. Has anything jumped out at you that could have caused the illness today?"

She shook her head. "Not yet."

"I heard it could be mushrooms," Richie said. "Not ones that went bad but the wrong ones."

"That's Melodie's theory."

"Aren't you a mushroom expert?"

"I wouldn't call myself an expert, no. I'm an amateur forager. I would never serve any wild mushrooms I'd picked myself to anyone but myself, no matter how certain I was they were safe."

"Good to know."

"I take what happened today seriously, Richie. I know it can't happen again. Food poisoning, whatever the source, reflects badly on the entire crew, not just me."

"You'll tell me once you figure out what did happen?"

"I will. Promise."

He left without further comment. Georgina wanted to leap off the yacht into the river and swim away. She wasn't a good swimmer, and it was a chilly night. She wouldn't get far before someone plucked her out of the water, she got tired and swam to shore or she went under and drowned. But the urge to flee was real, and it perfectly reflected her emotions.

She looked around the gleaming galley. It had high-end appliances but was designed for efficiency rather than showing off, or for a host cooking while guests looked on, visited or helped. It was her domain. Had someone slipped in here and unwittingly added contaminated food or inedible mushrooms to one of her dishes? To the bloody *tacos*?

Did today's chaos have anything to do with the Aoife O'Byrne painting, with William Hornsby—with her father?

She didn't want to ask Melodie or any of the crew about the painting, not yet. Bringing it up now would only call attention to her, and she absolutely didn't want that. It was a valuable painting, at least by her standards. Hornsby had gone to some trouble to bring it to her and wanted her to have it, a gift from his friend, her father.

On the other hand, maybe he'd been so aggravated at getting sick on food she'd prepared, he'd thrown the painting overboard.

She groaned. "Silliness."

She ran down to the lower deck. The door to Hornsby's cabin was shut but not locked. She went inside and switched on the light. Like the rest of the yacht, the cabin smelled of disinfectant and deodorizer. She could see a slight stain on the soft, expensive carpet where her father's friend had been sick.

The furnishings were lovely but simple, and it took only a moment for her to do a quick search.

Colin Donovan hadn't been lying. There was no painting.

She looked for anything that could help her understand why her father had sent his friend to Boston with the painting. Was it true he'd had business in Boston? She'd given her father the name of the marina. He'd asked, idly, for details of the cruise, and she'd been ridiculously pleased to tell him—he'd seldom shown that kind of an interest in her life. It wasn't that he didn't care. She knew that, at least when she was more herself. He just didn't know *how* to care.

Your father asked me to bring you a gift...

Not for a single second had Georgina anticipated the gift would be the stunning woodland watercolor by Aoife O'Byrne. Bill Hornsby had it with him when he got out of his taxi at the marina. It was in its packing materials. For most of her life, her father hadn't remembered her birthday or acknowledged special occasions. He'd do all right at Christmas, but he lived in his head— he was all about equations and formulas and such, anything to do with neurotoxins. He was always willing to talk about the dangers of mixing bleach and ammonia. As a teenager, she'd deliberately get him going by mentioning how one could make a potent chemical weapon from ordinary garden supplies.

She wasn't to joke about such matters, he'd tell her. Then he'd bang on about how, indeed, one could do exactly what she'd proposed. But it wouldn't be easy to accomplish or stable, and a delivery system was problematic…none of which interested her. She'd only been pretending, to rile him up—to see what he was like when he was interested in something, since he wasn't interested in her, at least not in the same way.

They'd shared a passion for foraging for wild edibles.

Bill Hornsby knew about that. *I talked to your father before he got sick, and he told me he had a grand time hunting wild mushrooms with you on Sunday.*

I hope he'll recover soon and get back to enjoying his retirement. Are you interested in foraging, Mr. Hornsby?

Not in the least I'm afraid. Will you fly back to London?

I'm in wait-and-see mode.

She hadn't wanted to abandon the Fannings at the last minute. The cruise was only for a few days, and they were staying close to the Maine coast. She'd figured she could leave if her father didn't bounce back quickly and be all right.

Your father ingested a highly toxic mushroom…

The doctor who'd spoken with her on Tuesday had wanted to make sure she hadn't consumed the same mushroom and was at risk, too. But she hadn't. They hadn't eaten any mushrooms together.

Georgina realized now she'd been in shock and denial. She wished she'd left for London the moment she'd found out he was sick. The Fannings would have had time to find another chef. Between them, Richie and Nick knew everyone in the yacht world.

Maybe the replacement chef wouldn't have poisoned anyone.

She pushed that thought aside. She'd refused to take

the painting out of its packaging and have a look at it until the yacht was underway. By then, Melodie had invited Bill Hornsby on the cruise. Irritated, not quite understanding why, Georgina had finally shut herself in her claustrophobic cabin and liberated the painting from its bubbles, cardboard, brown paper and duct tape.

She'd known already it was an Aoife O'Byrne work. Hornsby had meant to keep it a surprise until she opened it, but she'd insisted he tell her. She didn't want a surprise. *I'm busy, just tell me.*

By the time she'd sat the painting on her bunk and propped it against the wall, she'd wanted to hate it. She'd wanted it to demonstrate how out of touch her father was with her and what she liked, wanted, needed in her life. But she'd looked at the simple Irish landscape that in Aoife O'Byrne's hands was nothing short of miraculous. Her chest tight with unfamiliar, indescribable emotion, Georgina felt as if it had been painted just for her, as if it spoke to her soul. It was so incredible, so breathtakingly perfect, she'd burst into tears.

Not like her. Not at all.

She'd decided she wouldn't—couldn't—keep it. The painting was extravagant, an obvious attempt by her father to curry her favor. They'd never been close, but they'd never been at total loggerheads, either. He didn't need to win her over, ingratiate himself—spend all that money. She would return the painting to him, and he could decide what to do with it.

If he died, she would inherit his entire estate—he'd told her as much—and the painting would come to her, anyway. Ingrate that she was, it'd serve her right, wouldn't it?

"Georgina?"

She jumped at Nick's voice and flew around, hand on heart. "Oh, wow, you startled me. My mind was a million miles away. I didn't realize you were back from the hospital."

"What are you doing? You okay?"

"I was going to grab clothes for Bill Hornsby. I forgot the FBI agent already did that." She motioned at the floor where Nick stood. "Richie had the rug cleaned."

"Nothing like the faint odor of barf and disinfectant."

"Did Melodie come with you, or do you have to go back to the hospital?"

"She's here. She's gone to bed. She was beat. She says we've all been gems. Her word. Gems. Works, huh?"

He was being polite, Georgina knew, and trying to make her smile. Melodie surely hadn't meant to include her chef in her compliment. *Not me...a total mess, useless.* Georgina cleared her throat, dismissing her obsessive negative thoughts. They'd gripped her hours ago, and except for the occasional tiny respite—with Beth the ER nurse, for example—they'd refused to let go. She simply didn't know how to handle such overwhelming emotion.

She followed Nick out of the cabin. "How's Bryce?"

"He's weak and his blood pressure's up, but he's still expected to make a full recovery. It'll take longer than he wants. Five minutes would be longer than he wants. We'll likely stay here a couple of days. Melodie wants to be sure he won't need to go back to the hospital."

"I can understand that. And you—how are you feeling?"

"Me? I didn't get sick. I'm fine. Melodie's doing okay, too. She's more worried than she wants to admit to Bryce. He's already on meds for high blood pressure, and he could lose a few pounds. I guess this ordeal will help with that."

"He is stable, though, right?"

Nick nodded, looking unconcerned. "Yeah, no worries. He got dehydrated and his electrolytes are out of whack. Who knows, maybe this'll motivate him to take better care of himself. I've had a few cruises short-circuited by one thing or another during my years at sea. It happens. Put it behind you."

Georgina stifled a prick of irritation. She wasn't ready to take the full blame for today, even if it was her responsibility. But Nick meant well. "I'm sure I could find something if you're hungry."

"Richie's having lobster rolls delivered. Why don't you join us?"

"What, you don't want to risk food in the galley in case it's tainted? Richie had all the food from lunch tossed."

"We didn't want to bother you or go out," Nick said, patient, no hint he'd been stung by her comment. "Come on. Join us. Relax. Meet on the sundeck in ten?"

She forced a smile. She knew he was right. "Sounds like a plan."

"Richie picked up recovery food, did he tell you? Saltines, Gatorade, ginger ale, white rice, that sort of thing. All good to have on hand under the circumstances. It's in the fridge and cupboard, ready when anyone wants it. Melodie said she can't face anything right now, but maybe in the morning." Nick pointed up the stairs. "I'm off. See you soon."

Georgina waited for him to get well ahead of her. She started to shake, a delayed reaction, perhaps, to getting caught sneaking into Bill Hornsby's cabin. She hadn't told anyone about the painting.

Only the FBI agent.

She groaned to herself. *Stupid.*

She headed up the stairs, past the master suite, its double doors shut tight.

When she reached the sundeck, she took several deep breaths in a row, relishing the fresh air, the sea breeze and the starlit sky. Nick and Richie were at the bar, digging lobster rolls, fries and onion rings out of a bag and setting them on plates. They'd ordered more than enough. She appreciated their bullet-dodged approach to the day. She wanted to look at it the same way but couldn't, not yet. Despite the short notice, everything had gone perfectly at the party, until the first person—an older woman who owned a second home in Kennebunkport—had leaped up, sick to her stomach.

Richie made martinis for himself and Nick. "Don't tell me they don't go with lobster rolls."

"Tonight, martinis go with anything," Nick said cheerfully. "Make mine dry as can be."

"I'll pass, thanks," Georgina said.

Nick handed her a plate with a lobster roll—chilled lobster chunks, mayonnaise and celery tucked in a grilled, buttered hot-dog roll—and a smattering of fries and onion rings. "Relax, Georgie. No one thinks you poisoned anyone on purpose." He grinned at her. "Whoa, that didn't come out right."

Richie dropped a couple of olives in a martini glass. "I'll say."

But Georgina found herself relaxing, as she often did with Nick's easygoing, outspoken nature. They gathered at a table under the awning. The temperature had dropped with nightfall, but they didn't bother with the heat lamps as they ate dinner. Although a serious-minded skipper, Richie could throttle back, enjoy the quiet moments that his job offered. They should have been serving dinner to passengers and whatever guests had stayed on through the evening. With the foliage cruise now a disaster, they had the sundeck to themselves.

Georgina ate most of her food and was glad for it. Richie got up to make another round of martinis, but she excused herself and went over to a cushioned bench. She stretched out on it and shut her eyes, focusing on the feel of the breeze, the sounds of the tide washing onto the river's pebbled beach down the docks, past the Sharpe offices.

Why had Bill Hornsby wanted to stop here? Did he know the Sharpes? Who was he, really?

Was he responsible for today?

She squeezed her eyes more tightly shut, fighting tears. She and her father were stiff-upper-lip sorts. She'd told his doctor she'd get there as soon as she could. Had she meant it? She hadn't booked a flight yet, had she? She'd told herself she was being sensible. He was receiving the medical attention he needed. That was all that mattered.

"Don't you care, Georgina?"

She couldn't hear her whisper above the wind and tide. She *did* care. But she wasn't a normal daughter, and Robin Masterson wasn't a normal father. Would the police want to know about his condition? Did the FBI agent already know? Her father was, after all, an expert in deadly neurotoxins.

Chemical weapons, she thought.

She bolted upright, jumped to her feet. Nick and Richie were deep into their second martinis. The doctor had promised to stay in touch and let her know if there was any change in her father's condition. She felt paralyzed. She didn't know what to do. What should she make of his getting sick so soon after her visit? He'd always been pleased to see her but he'd never objected to her leaving, or meddled in what she chose to do with herself—schools, work, her romantic life. He had his interests, his life. She had her interests, her life. He hadn't been thrilled when she'd decided to become a personal chef on yachts, but he hadn't interfered.

Nick's and Richie's raucous laughter broke through her obsessing. She shivered, cold now. She headed down to her quarters, a small cabin she had to herself.

The water in her Yeti was ice-cold. She drank some, dribbled some on her head, as if it could help her think—help her to make sense out of all the bits and pieces of the past week that kept swimming around in her head.

Her father had handed her an empty mesh bag after breakfast on Sunday. *The chanterelles are fantastic this year. Why don't we go to the park and see what we can find? I'd love to grill some for dinner.*

And off they'd gone, foraging for one of nature's treats. It had been one of the best mornings she'd ever spent with him. She'd left for Heathrow before they'd had a chance to grill the chanterelles they'd picked. Her father being the man he was, in the profession he was in, hadn't limited himself to chanterelles. He'd helped himself to a range of inedible and even a few dangerously poisonous mushrooms. To further his knowledge, he'd said. Chanterelles were easy to spot, but some mushrooms were more difficult to distinguish between a harmless, tasty edible version to one that could sicken or kill.

These are death caps, love. Stay away from them.

Georgina was familiar with the deadly mushroom. In its early growth, it could be mistaken for an innocuous puffball, but she would never make that mistake. Neither would her father. They took a methodical, careful approach to identifying mushrooms—or any wild edible—and didn't rely on gut instinct, experience or just one or two traits.

Had her father made a mistake?

She got out her laptop and did a search for flights to London. Lots of options out of Boston. But would booking a flight now make her look guilty?

Best to wait, figure things out and talk to her father's art-consultant friend when he was well enough. Maybe everything would make more sense tomorrow.

8

The south coast of Ireland

Lucas Sharpe started up the hill from the small, popular village of Ardmore at a slower pace than he might have on his own, but he quickly realized he needn't have bothered. His grandfather had no trouble keeping up with him. In his early eighties, Wendell Sharpe, world-renowned art detective, was a keen walker, and he loved Ardmore with its beaches, cliffs, sea views and ancient stone ruins. Lucas appreciated how damn good his grandfather looked, even as he coped with the searing loss of his only son.

Ah, Dad...

Lucas felt a tightness in his throat he had come to expect. His father had been an avid walker, too, and would have loved to have joined them today. Was he watching his father and son from one of the puffs of white clouds above the glistening sea, just to their left, down a tumble of cobbles and boulders? Lucas liked the image, a metaphor, maybe, as he, too, coped with Tim Sharpe's untimely death.

The sidewalk hugged the shore as Lucas continued up the steep hill with his grandfather, toward Sheep's Head and its marked cliff walk. They were both fair and lanky, and fit, if to suit their fifty-year age difference, but Lucas was fine with their measured pace. He had Emma's voice mail on his mind. He hadn't noticed it until after he and Wendell had finished brunch at a popular restaurant in the village center.

What had his little sister got him into this time?

He hadn't told their grandfather about her call. He needed to collect his thoughts first. Emma rarely did anything idle or out of the blue, and her cryptic voice mail was no different.

Lucas could feel his brunch roiling in his stomach. Oh, but it'd been good. Decadent, and just what he'd needed after four days with his grandfather. There was no hiding from grief with his father's father right there with him. Tim Sharpe would never see his eighties. Or his sixties…

Lucas cleared his throat. "I'll go for a run this afternoon. I had too many carbs."

His grandfather gave him a sideways glance. "No one forced you to have both toast and scones."

"Don't forget the brown bread."

"Or the Irish butter."

"Butter's okay on a low-carb diet."

"What's the point of having butter if you can't have bread?"

Sort of what had crossed Lucas's mind when he'd dived into the bread basket at brunch. He'd dived into the Irish whiskey orange marmalade, too. And everything else.

"Good point," he told his grandfather. "Dad used to say if you're going to sin, sin boldly. Did he get that from you?"

"All on his own. Your grandmother and I taught him not to seek out sin."

"Ha. Right."

Lucas appreciated his grandfather's wry humor. He was more himself since the early days after his son's death. Having just been in Maine, he hadn't flown back for the funeral, but Lucas had video chatted with him once or twice a week since then. His pragmatic, clear-eyed grandfather had seemed to turn old overnight, the lines in his face deeper, his color off. He would drift away even when they were talking Sharpe Fine Art Recovery business. His time with Emma walking the southwest Irish hills had helped in those early days of shock and loss. It had helped Emma, too. Now it was Lucas's turn, and he was glad to be here with their grandfather—for his grandfather's sake and for his own.

At home in Dublin, Wendell would have joined the "lads" after Mass for a full Irish breakfast, but he and Lucas had driven to the south coast yesterday for a short break. His grandfather's idea. Lucas didn't think the impromptu getaway had anything to do with Emma's voice mail, but it could. Wendell Sharpe wasn't always forthcoming.

Lucas had legitimate Sharpe Fine Art Recovery business in Ireland, but he'd also wanted to spend time with his grandfather. He had no deadline to get back. He could work from Ireland, and he had a capable, if small, staff in Heron's Cove. Just in the few days since his arrival in Dublin, he could feel himself starting to come to terms with his father's death. He'd handled his chronic health issues his way. Lucas accepted that, but it didn't ease his grief, didn't fill the gap that his father's death had created.

He choked back a sudden wave of emotion. It'd be like that for a while, he knew. Maybe forever, since his father would never be far from his thoughts.

He paused and looked out at the rocks and sea. Two kayakers were paddling with the tide toward the crescent-shaped beach down to his left. He patted his stomach. He didn't think he'd gained any weight, but he would if he kept eating like he had at brunch. "I should have at least skipped dessert," he said.

"That meringue you had looked good, and it had fruit. Had to be more keto friendly than my sticky toffee pudding."

"Sticky toffee pudding is its own glucose tolerance test."

"Delicious, though."

No argument from Lucas. His meringue had been delicious, too, filled with whipped cream and topped with fresh-cut fruit. He didn't delude himself into thinking resisting sticky toffee pudding had been much of a victory, but he'd been pleased to see how well his grandfather ate. He'd lost weight since August. He insisted it was due to all the walking he'd done with Emma in September, but it wasn't. It was grief.

Walking did seem to help him make peace with his loss. It was definitely a Sharpe thing. Lucas could tell his grandfather had benefited in the weeks since his son's death from his long solo treks in the heart of Dublin where he'd lived the past sixteen years, then with his granddaughter on the Kerry Way and now with his grandson, here in Saint Declan country.

They resumed climbing the hill, small houses and shops across the narrow road on their right. Wendell sighed. "Are you going to tell me what Emma wants?"

Lucas could hear the suspicion in his grandfather's voice. The old man did have sixty years of experience as a private art detective. "How did you know—"

"You had that 'Emma's on the phone' expression. She's in FBI mode?"

"Isn't she always? It was just a voice mail. I didn't speak with her. She had a few questions for us."

"Like what?"

"She wants to know if we've been in contact with Oliver York or Aoife O'Byrne recently. I haven't. Have you?"

Wendell slowed his pace. "Define recently."

"She didn't get specific. Why? Have you been in contact with them?"

"I haven't been in touch with Oliver since Emma was here. Aoife, though. She dragged me to a cocktail party at her studio in Dublin on Tuesday—the night before you got here. As much as I like her, I didn't want to go. I knew I'd be up early to greet you, and I just wasn't in the mood. You're better at socializing than I ever was. It's part of the job, I know, but you're single. I was already engaged to your grandmother when I got into this business."

"How did Aoife 'drag' you?"

"She sent a car."

Lucas held back a smile. "Was it an art-related party?"

"It was a going-away party for her. She sold her studio and plans to buy a place in Declan's Cross. She's been renting a cottage down here. All her arty friends were at the party, but no one cornered me to talk stolen vases or anything, if that's your next question."

Given Emma's mention of Oliver York, it wasn't a unreasonable comment. "Is Aoife still in Dublin?"

"She cleared out on Wednesday. It's all these paintings she's been doing lately of laundry hanging on clotheslines and chickens and sheep and wildflowers. She's turning homey."

Lucas knew some of the works to which his grandfather referred. In Aoife O'Byrne's hands, with her technical skill, artistic sensibility and unwavering eye, they were anything but mundane and cutesy. "They're amazing pieces, Granddad."

"Of course. All her work is amazing, and popular."

"Oliver wasn't at the party, then?"

"Not that I saw, but you know how he is. He could steal your socks off your feet and you wouldn't know it."

True enough, Lucas thought. The pair had an interesting relationship given their past as art thief and private art detective. Hunted and hunter. Now they were... well, friends. Lucas didn't pretend to understand. "What about Henrietta Balfour?"

His grandfather stopped dead in his tracks. They'd come to the Cliff House Hotel, a five-star landmark built on the rock face between street and sea. Lucas thought they might stay there, but his grandfather had opted for the O'Byrne House Hotel in Declan's Cross.

"Granddad? What's up?"

"Henrietta's an interesting character. Oliver says she's sorting through her grandfather's opera record collection. I gather old Freddy Balfour was quite the opera buff, when he wasn't chasing Nazi and Soviet spies." Wendell paused, catching his breath, his cheeks red with exertion. "One says vinyl these days, though, not records."

"But has she been in touch?"

"Not in touch, no."

Lucas bit back his impatience. It wasn't his grandfather's age at work. It was his nature. Technically he'd retired, closing up his Dublin office. Lucas had spent days with him over the past year, prying tidbits that he'd stored in his head, not in any official company files. He'd decided what Lucas needed to know. Although his father had suffered chronic pain from a fall on black ice, Lucas wouldn't be surprised if his reluctance to get too involved in Sharpe Fine Art Recovery had to do with its founder's closemouthed ways. Most days, Lucas and his grandfather worked fine together. But they did have their moments.

"I can't swear for certain, Lucas," Wendell said finally.

"You don't need to. Just tell me what came to your mind."

His grandfather took a folded red bandanna from an inside pocket in his lightweight jacket and wiped beads of sweat from his upper lip. "Henrietta was at Aoife's studio in Dublin on Tuesday night. I was avoiding small talk and looked out the window, and there she was on the street."

"Did she attend the party?"

He shook his head. "Not while I was there. I went down to invite her up for a drink, but she was gone by the time I got there. You remember the studio. It's on the second floor of a refurbished mill."

Lucas remembered, but he didn't know Aoife as well as his grandfather and sister did—or Henrietta and Oliver. Best that way, he'd figured. "You're positive it was Henrietta?"

"I wouldn't swear to it, but, yeah, I'm confident." Wendell nodded up past the hotel entrance. "Keep going?"

"Sure. Do a bit of the cliff walk?"

"I'm up to doing the whole thing if you want."

"You're red as a beet, Granddad."

"It's a sign the heart's still pumping. Let's go."

The street dead-ended at a gate onto a rough, dirt trail that wound along the edge of the headland, past dramatic cliffs with stunning sea views, and eventually looped back to the village. They walked in silence past the lichen-splotched stone ruins of an ancient church and holy well, a reminder this part of the south Irish coast was Saint Declan country. More than a thousand years ago, the early Irish saint had established a Celtic Christian settlement in Ardmore. Lucas wasn't up on all his Irish history, but he knew that bit.

They continued on the trail, taking in the expansive view of the sea, glistening under the late-morning sun in a myriad of shades of blue and blue-green. Lucas gave them both a moment to appreciate the scenery— and catch their breath—before he returned to the topic at hand.

"Did you get in touch with Henrietta after you saw her at Aoife's studio?" he finally asked.

His grandfather shook his head. "I didn't."

"And Oliver? Where was he?"

"No idea. I wanted to spend time with you. If those two want to see me, they know how to get in touch. I wasn't in the mood for any of their drama, to be honest."

That was concerning. Lucas felt his own mood shift. Normally he'd soak up the views and the sounds of wind and birds, and relax and enjoy the walk. That wasn't happening now. Bloated with his carbohydrate overload, he couldn't work up much energy after the trek up from the village, but his elderly grandfather was billy-goating it ahead of him on the rough trail. He was walking too damn fast for a man in his eighties. If Lucas said anything, it'd just piss him off. Wendell was in great shape but he was pushing hard. Did he want to trigger a heart attack of his own, join his son in the great beyond?

Nah, Lucas thought. Not Wendell Sharpe's personality.

He finally stopped, breathing rapidly, his entire face red now, not just his cheeks. "What else did Emma have to say?"

"Henrietta and Oliver are in Rock Point for a surprise visit. They're staying with Finian Bracken at the rectory. Emma didn't elaborate in her voice mail."

Wendell dug out his bandanna again and wiped his brow, forehead and the back of his neck. "Oliver is fond of Emma, and he's taken with Father Bracken. Colin, however. I think he might be warming up to Oliver, don't you?"

"Anything's possible with Oliver, but Colin's a tough hurdle even for a wily guy like him. Any idea why Henrietta was in Dublin?"

"None. I didn't follow up. Anything else?"

"Emma asked if we'd heard from a Bryce or Melodie Fanning, or anyone at a yacht party yesterday at the marina next to the offices."

"Fannings? I don't know them. Do you?"

Lucas shook his head. "I might get more out of Emma when I call her back."

"Or you might not."

True. Lucas eyed his grandfather. "But you didn't hear from anyone?"

"Not a peep." He waved a hand, looking less winded. "We're at the halfway point. Might as well keep going rather than double back."

They weren't halfway back to the village, but Wendell clearly wanted to complete the loop. Lucas realized he did, too. They'd pass the twelfth-century round tower that rose above the village, and more Saint Declan ruins. He smiled. "I'm not going to quibble. What difference does a few minutes make either way?"

"Good attitude. You can burn off that meringue. Will you have lettuce for dinner?"

"Nothing. I'm fasting until breakfast."

"It's called intermittent fasting. I read an article about it. I used to skip dinner or breakfast once in a while. Well, fasting will allow you to rationalize diving into another bread basket at breakfast."

"With Irish whiskey marmalade, I hope."

"That's my boy."

Wendell drained a bottle of water on the drive to the picturesque village of Declan's Cross, not far from Ardmore. Lucas had rented a car, and had no intention of letting his grandfather do any of the driving. For once, he didn't argue. They parked at the ivy-covered O'Byrne House Hotel, situated on a scenic stretch of coast within walking distance of the village shops and restaurants. Kitty and Aoife O'Byrne had inherited their uncle's sprawling, run-down house, but it was Kitty who'd seen to transforming it into a popular boutique hotel. Lucas had booked two rooms with water views for himself and his grandfather.

They found Kitty O'Byrne, fortyish, dark-haired and blue-eyed, busy behind the bar. "Aoife's here if you'd like to say hello." Kitty gestured to the tables in the lounge area. "Can I bring you something to drink?"

"Sparkling water with lime," Lucas said.

His grandfather shuddered and then smiled at Kitty. "A pint of Guinness for me, Kitty, dear."

Lucas had no idea where he'd put it but said nothing.

They found Aoife seated on a softly cushioned chair facing the fire. Dark-haired and striking, she was an artist with a growing reputation for her moody paintings of ordinary Irish scenes, anything but trite in her hands, with her unafraid, unabashed blend of drama, reality, fantasy and emotion. Her work was approachable, and brilliant.

She spotted them and smiled brightly, sliding to her feet. "I heard you were here," she said, greeting them each with a kiss on the cheek. She motioned to the cluster of chairs and small sofa. "Please, join me."

They all sat, the fire crackling but not roaring on the cool but beautiful early afternoon. Kitty delivered the sparkling water and pint but didn't linger.

Aoife pointed to a glass on the side table next to her chair. "I'm having Dingle Gin and tonic. I'm indulging myself. I was out walking all morning and landed here. I didn't take my phone. It's wonderful. I do screen-free

Sundays, but I might make it screen-free weekends. Kitty says you've been to Ardmore. How was it?"

They engaged in friendly small talk for a few minutes. Finally, Lucas asked how her move to Declan's Cross was going.

Aoife sat back, crossed her legs. She was in black leggings, a sapphire-blue tunic and worn walking shoes. "I don't miss Dublin but it's not been a week."

"Granddad tells me he was at your going-away party."

"Did he also tell you I had to twist his arm? But we had a fantastic time, didn't we, Wendell?"

"He mentioned he saw Henrietta Balfour outside your studio," Lucas said. "She didn't come in?"

"No, I had no idea she was in Dublin."

Lucas noticed her frown at what must have struck her as an out-of-nowhere comment and smiled. "I was just thinking about her because Emma called earlier. Henrietta and Oliver York are visiting Maine. They're staying with Finian Bracken, as a matter of fact."

"At the rectory?"

"Apparently."

Aoife gazed up at the marble fireplace, a silver Celtic cross on display on the mantel. Fifty years ago, John O'Byrne had unearthed the sixteenth-century artifact when he'd renovated his back garden. It was among the items a thief had stolen eleven years ago this coming November, in a brazen heist that still, publicly, remained unsolved. The stolen cross and two Jack Butler Yeats paintings were mysteriously returned last fall, intact, presumably by the thief himself.

Oliver York, of course.

Lucas, his grandfather and Aoife knew the truth, but they couldn't prove it, and perhaps didn't want to.

"I remember studying the cross as a child," Aoife said quietly. "I was fascinated by its Celtic carvings, their possible meaning—who'd done the work hundreds of years ago. My uncle never thought twice about it. He grew up here, walked the ground. He was delighted when it was discovered, but to him, the cross was a part of everyday life rather than a valuable work of art."

"The art of the ordinary," Wendell said.

"I like that. I like it a lot. I miss my ordinary life." She swept her gin and tonic off the coffee table and took a sip. "One of my last acts in my studio was to sell a painting of a scene here in Declan's Cross. I took that as a sign I'm merging my two lives into one, and all is as it should be."

Lucas considered the timing. "When was this?"

"On Monday. It's not my usual approach to sell a painting myself, not nowadays, but this man said he was in Dublin for the day and was taking his chances. He was a Brit—he'd flown in from London. I was clearing out my studio, and I was in the right mood."

Wendell eyed her. "Did he have a particular painting in mind?"

"A particular series—my new one of a woodland here in Declan's Cross, up on Sean Murphy's farm on Sheep's Head. He was hoping I had a painting from that series available. We met in the gallery in the same building as my studio. He said his daughter had seen three paintings in the series in London and fell in love with my work. Those paintings had sold already. As it happens, I had finished a fourth. He bought it on the spot."

"Did you show the painting to him first?" Lucas asked.

"He said he didn't need to see it. I insisted. I didn't invite him up to my studio. I brought it down myself, and he gave it a quick look and said it was perfect. That was that. He wasn't particularly chatty but he was amiable." She hesitated, cupping her glass in both hands. "After he left, I wished I'd let the gallery handle him and stayed in my studio and cleared bookshelves. I can't pinpoint why."

Lucas picked up his water glass. "What was his name, do you recall?"

Aoife's vivid eyes narrowed. "Why would that matter?" She shook her head. "No, don't answer." She reluctantly dug her phone out of her jacket pocket, tossed on the arm of her chair. "You'd think I could manage one day. At least I had the walk." She tapped the screen. "Robin Masterson. I assumed he'd have me ship the painting, but he took it with him. I wrapped it myself for travel, and he was on his way. It might have been a pair of shoes."

But, of course, it wasn't a pair of shoes, Lucas thought. It was a painting by a rising star in the art world, and this man—Robin Masterson—had made a special trip to see Aoife and buy a painting for his daughter.

"Kitty mentioned you had brunch in Ardmore," Aoife said, awkwardly changing the subject.

"We ate everything in sight," Wendell said. "Lucas is fasting tonight."

"Maybe forever," he said with a grin.

Aoife smiled, but her blue eyes were distant. "It's impossible not to overindulge at brunch. It's one of life's rules." She slipped her phone back into her jacket pocket. "But you're not going to tell me what's going on, are you?"

Lucas appreciated her question—her suspicion, given his mention of Emma, and Henrietta and Oliver. "My sister might want to talk to you, Aoife."

"In her capacity as an FBI agent?"

"As she'd tell you, she's always an FBI agent."

Aoife jumped up, her black hair shining as she grabbed her jacket. "Excuse me," she mumbled. Lucas could see she was agitated, needed to move. She burst through the French doors out to the terrace.

He touched his grandfather's arm. "Stay put. Enjoy your pint. I'll go talk to her."

He followed her outside. A gusty wind caught the ends of her hair as she stood with her arms crossed tightly on her chest and stared at the garden and sea. "It's not you, Lucas. I'm restless these days. I'm adjusting to the move—to giving up Dublin. Figuring out what's next for me. Sorting through lots of uncertainty, unknowns, hopes, fears, dreams. Shadowy dreams, dreams I daren't go near."

Lucas stood next to a large stone flowerpot dripping with colorful begonias, a contrast to Aoife's dark mood. Farther to his left, a few guests had gathered at one of a half dozen outdoor tables, enjoying glasses of wine and the quiet, attractive surroundings. Pebbled paths wound through the lush garden of flowering shrubs, raised herb and flower beds and stretches of green grass.

"I hope we didn't upset you," Lucas said.

She cleared her throat and turned to him, her blue eyes shining with tears. "I'm ashamed of myself, whining to you when you've just lost your father. I'm so sorry

for your loss, Lucas." She lowered her arms to her sides.
"This man—Robin Masterson. He didn't seem upset or
anything. He knew what he wanted."

"Did he mention any names?"

"Not that I recall. He didn't mention Heron's Cove,
Sharpe Fine Art Recovery, Wendell, Boston, Maine,
the FBI. Oliver. Henrietta." She paused. "Finian." She
sniffled, glancing away. "I'd remember if he had."

"But his visit was unusual," Lucas said.

"Yes." The wind whipped a strand of hair into her
face; she brushed it behind her ear and turned to him
again. "Sean Murphy is at his farm. You know what he's
like, Lucas. He'll sniff out any trouble, particularly if it
involves Kitty and me."

Lucas had met the garda detective, and he couldn't
argue with Aoife's assessment. But he'd be vigilant and
suspicious just with two Sharpes in the village, even
without his personal connection to the O'Byrne sisters.
Given Emma's voice mail, Lucas couldn't deny the possibility of some sort of trouble. He needed to talk to her.
He'd call after he finished talking with Aoife.

She touched a bright red begonia blossom as she
thought a moment, then finally looked back at Lucas.
The emotion had gone out of her expression, an act of
willpower, he suspected. "Oliver and Henrietta arriving in Rock Point complicates things for Emma, doesn't
it?" She didn't wait for an answer. "She has my number.
Please tell her she can call anytime."

"I'll do that." Lucas glanced back to the lounge and
saw his grandfather was almost finished with his pint.
"I should go inside. I don't know if he needs rescuing
but he looks intense."

Aoife managed a small laugh. "Good luck." She mo-

tioned toward the garden. "I'll take the back way home."
She caught herself, her laugh fading. "Home. It rolled
off my tongue, didn't it? Another good sign, I hope."
She touched Lucas's arm. "You'll stay in touch, won't
you?"

He promised he would, and she glided off the terrace onto a pebbled walk.

Lucas went inside, and his grandfather got stiffly to
his feet. "Brunch, a walk, a pint—I'm going up to take
a nap. You'll call Emma? Keep me posted."

"Will do, Granddad."

"When you report back to me, don't hold back anything, Lucas. Tell all."

He nodded. "No problem."

"That means everything I need to know, want to
know and should know."

"Got it. Need, want, should."

He seemed satisfied, and Lucas watched him head
out of the lounge. His bony shoulders were slumped
and he wasn't billy-goating it now, but all in all, he
looked okay.

Lucas headed to the bar. He could replenish his sparkling water, or he could give it up and have a pint of
Smithwick's before he called his sister.

The pint won out.

9

Emma was dressed and awake when Kevin Donovan came in through the back door and set a box of doughnuts on the kitchen table. It was just after seven, not that early by Rock Point lobstering standards. "I ran into Franny Maroney at Hurley's when I was buying the doughnuts," Kevin said. "She told me Henrietta Balfour and Oliver York are staying at the rectory. I let her think she'd gotten a jump on me. She was thrilled. She's right in a way, though. I am clueless about what's going on."

Colin grinned at him. "It's a good thing you're the easygoing Donovan. Mike wouldn't have brought doughnuts. Sorry, Kev. I appreciate the breathing room. Figures Franny beat me to the punch."

"She should have been a spy."

"Who says she isn't? Emma and I don't know what's going on with Henrietta and Oliver. We had no idea they were in the US never mind in town until they turned up at the rectory with their bags."

"That doesn't reassure me. Do they know this hospitalized Brit—Hornsby?"

"Yeah. A friend of theirs. They planned to get together on the yacht's stop in Heron's Cove. All I know."

"Or it's all you're going to tell me." Kevin tore open the doughnut box. "I got a mix. Emma, you like Hurley's doughnuts, don't you?"

"Who doesn't?" She eyed the tempting array of glazed, plain, chocolate-covered and apple-cider doughnuts. "A dozen is a lot of doughnuts, Kevin."

"It's revenge for holding back on him," Colin said.

"I'm not that passive-aggressive. If I wanted revenge, I'd have left them on the back steps for the raccoons."

"Wouldn't blame you. Any word from the hospital?" Colin asked.

"No. I haven't checked. I'd know if anything had gone wrong overnight. I gather you haven't checked, either. We suspect it was some kind of inedible mushroom that makes you sick but doesn't kill you. Lots of candidates. We can consult a mycologist, but it's not necessary medically. That's an expert in mushrooms, in case you didn't know."

"I didn't." Colin helped himself to a glazed doughnut. "Any evidence it was deliberate?"

Kevin shook his head and took an apple-cider doughnut out of the box. "It looks as if the chef made a mistake with mushrooms and doesn't want to admit it. Turns out the fast onset of symptoms was a good sign. A longer latency period—six hours, even days—would have indicated a more dangerous species might be involved." He leaned against the counter with his doughnut. "Sprinkling mushrooms onto food at a party isn't the most effective way to target an individual."

"You don't necessarily know who's going to eat what," Emma said, continuing to resist the doughnuts.

"I suppose someone could have intended to cause a stir—create a smoke screen for something else."

"We have no evidence of that," Kevin said. He polished off his doughnut and looked at his older brother. "Except for your mysterious art consultant, we have no reason to push this thing and investigate further."

"I don't know anything about mushrooms, Kevin," Colin said.

"Fair enough."

Emma poured coffee. She held up the pot at Kevin, but he shook his head. He'd have ordered some at Hurley's, with the doughnuts, listening to Franny's gossip about the local priest. "If an inedible wild mushroom is responsible for yesterday's incident, I can see it happening given the popularity of foraging." She set the coffeepot in the sink and added half-and-half to her mug. "There are strict protocols for identifying wild mushrooms. You don't want to make a mistake."

"Noted," Kevin said. "Thought you might like to know the Sisters of the Joyful Heart delivered fresh vegetables to the yacht yesterday before the party."

Emma's former convent. "They don't grow mushrooms, and wouldn't include wild mushrooms in an order."

"Still, if it was mushrooms yesterday—and it looks as if that's the case—they came from somewhere. I'd want to know where if I were serving people on the yacht or eating their food. Then again, I eat at Hurley's without thinking about it."

Colin rolled his eyes at Kevin's stab at humor. Emma wasn't surprised the Sisters of the Joyful Heart had provided vegetables to the yacht. They specialized in art conservation and education, but they were self-sufficient and had extensive gardens, selling and giving away surplus flowers and vegetables. This time of year, that would include winter squash, brussels sprouts, carrots, potatoes, spinach, leaf lettuce—a wide variety of vegetables that didn't include wild mushrooms. It was too easy to make a mistake.

Kevin shifted to Colin. "I'm heading to the hospital soon. Do you plan to go back up there?"

"At some point. Beth on today?"

"She didn't share her schedule with me. We gave Georgina Masterson a ride back to Heron's Cove last night. She was in a state. Colin, Emma—if you're aware of any cause for concern for the safety of the passengers and crew on that yacht, I need to know." Kevin stood straight and nodded at the box of doughnuts. "A dozen didn't seem like that many with Franny Maroney breathing down my neck. Now it seems like a lot.

"Emma and I will make a dent in them," Colin said.

"Yeah. I should get rolling. Any word from Andy and Julianne in Ireland?"

Emma thought she saw a touch of wistfulness, if fleeting, in Colin's expression. He shook his head. "I don't expect to hear from them. They should pulling into Fin Bracken's cottage soon."

"Guess I wouldn't want to be in touch with my brothers on my honeymoon. Mike, Andy and I didn't hear from you, either." Kevin took another doughnut. "See you soon."

He left through the back door. Emma finally suc-

cumbed to temptation and took the last glazed doughnut. She broke it in two roughly equal pieces, keeping
one and returning the other to the box.

Colin drank some of his coffee and leaned close to
her. "How long are you going to give yourself before
you eat the other half?"

"What if I resist?"

"Do you want to resist?"

She sighed. "No, I want the other half, and I want a
chocolate-covered one, too."

"We're supposed to meet Henrietta and Oliver at
Hurley's."

"Doesn't mean we have to eat anything." She polished off the doughnut half. "I'll head to the convent
after breakfast. Sister Cecilia is into wild mushrooms."

They decided to split up. Emma would drive to the
convent on her own and then meet Colin at the hospital. She knew he didn't want to delay getting in to see
Jeremy Pearson and get him to talk.

She took the second half of the glazed doughnut
with her to her car and the short drive to the harbor.
The crisp, clear autumn morning only accentuated that
her weekend hadn't turned out as planned. Colin pulled
in behind her in the small lot that served the working
docks and Hurley's. The popular rustic restaurant was
set up on pilings, the tide lapping under its floorboards.
Somehow it managed to stay open year-round, in part,
Emma thought, because Rock Point had so few options
and no one complained about drafts and cold feet.

They found Henrietta and Oliver at a round table in
back, by windows overlooking the harbor, sparkling in
the early-morning sun. "We were up at dawn but only

got here a few minutes ago," Henrietta said. "This place is perfect. Quintessential Maine, isn't it?"

Emma smiled, sitting across from them. "A lot of people think so."

"I wish Father Bracken could join us, but he's seeing to his church duties," Oliver said. "I debated attending Mass this morning. I've never seen Finian in the pulpit."

Colin took a seat, his back to the windows. "Neither have most people in town, but he's beloved by those who do attend church."

"Especially the women, I imagine," Henrietta said. "Or shouldn't I say that?"

Oliver laughed. "You can say anything you'd like— and you will." He turned to Emma. "I first noticed Henrietta on a rainy Sunday at our little Cotswolds church. She was four and I was seven."

Henrietta snorted. "I remember that. You sat behind me and pulled my hair."

Oliver's parents and grandparents were buried in the church's cemetery, and Freddy Balfour, Henrietta's legendary spy grandfather, and her great-aunt, Posey. Emma had been to the old graveyard with Colin. It was a lovely spot, shaded and green—quintessential Cotswolds, Henrietta would say.

"I'm famished." Henrietta glanced at the menu in front of her on the table. "My stomach's reminded me it's lunchtime at home. I'm ordering everything."

She practically did, telling the waiter she wanted fried eggs, bacon, sausage, home fries, orange juice, a blueberry muffin and tea. "Hot tea, not iced tea. I understand it's best to specify."

Oliver was slightly more modest, leaving off the sausage. Emma stuck to coffee, but Colin ordered scrambled eggs in addition to coffee. "Does either of you know anything about wild mushrooms?" he asked casually as their drinks arrived.

"Foraging for wild edibles is gaining in popularity in the UK," Henrietta said. "I imagine it is here, too. Mushrooms are particularly tempting, but I prefer mine from the grocer. It's too easy to make a mistake."

Oliver lifted the lid to his stainless-steel teapot. "I forgot how pathetic tea is in this place. Finian hasn't reformed them, I see. A small price to pay for everything else, I suppose. In any case, I'm not sure I'd trust my friends to bring me wild mushrooms."

Henrietta poured her tea without complaint. "Is that what happened yesterday? Did your partyers ingest poisonous mushrooms?"

Colin shrugged. "Possibly."

"I know a bit about mushrooms, but I'm more familiar with flowers, trees and shrubs in my garden work." She picked up a small pottery pitcher and poured a dollop of cream into her tea. "Any word on the condition of the two hospitalized?"

"I checked with the hospital on my way down here," Colin said. "Fanning and our William Hornsby—they should both be discharged today."

"Well, that's good news," Henrietta said, clearly relieved. "I'm sure they'll be pleased to put yesterday behind them. I know it was a difficult day, and our presence—not great timing, to say the least. We aren't here to cause trouble."

Colin didn't touch his coffee. "But you're here because of trouble."

Oliver grinned at him. "I'm here for wild blueberry

muffins." He turned to Emma. "You seriously aren't going to have anything to eat?"

"Kevin Donovan stopped by the house with doughnuts," she said.

"The other Donovan in law enforcement." Oliver gave a fake shudder. "You need protein, Emma. I can share my breakfast with you. I'm not as hungry as Henrietta. You don't want to get irritable. And you, Colin? I can't tell. You naturally look a tad irritable. Then again, you're having eggs. That's good."

Colin ignored him. He was more indulgent of Oliver's cheekiness than he'd been when they'd first met last fall, but he had his limits. Emma usually was more tolerant, but she'd noticed since her father's death her patience was more easily frayed than it used to be. "I might nibble on a piece of bacon," she said.

Henrietta drank her tea. "Oliver will be less exasperating once he's fed." She glanced at him. "Won't you, love?"

He grinned at her. "Am I exasperating this morning?"

Their breakfast arrived, steaming and tempting, but Emma could tell with their first forkfuls of eggs they weren't going to say anything substantive until Henrietta, at least, spoke with Jeremy Pearson. Colin, obviously reaching the same conclusion, didn't object when they changed the subject to autumn lobstering.

When he finished his eggs, he pushed back his chair. "I'm heading to the hospital. Do you two want to ride up there with me?"

"We'll drive up on our own," Henrietta said. "That way we can stay flexible and take our time, not tie you down."

"Makes sense. We'll talk later, then." He got to his feet and kissed Emma on the cheek. "Say hi to the sisters. I'll see you soon."

Oliver frowned but said nothing. Henrietta watched Colin cross the worn wood floor to the main door before she turned to Emma. "The sisters?"

"At my former convent. They provided fresh vegetables for the party yesterday."

"I see," Henrietta said.

Emma didn't elaborate. She knew they had questions, but right now, that wasn't her concern—which Henrietta would appreciate perhaps more than Oliver. Emma paid for their breakfasts on her way out, and by the time she climbed into her car, she wished she had more than doughnuts and coffee in her system.

She saw she had a message from Lucas in Ireland. She tried calling him but got his voice mail again. Phone tag, she thought in frustration. "It's Emma. Call me, or I'll try again in a bit. Talk soon."

Oliver eyed Henrietta as they left the rustic restaurant after their delicious breakfasts. He took a moment to appreciate the colorful autumn leaves reflected on the sparkling harbor water. He doubted Henrietta noticed their surroundings. Something Emma or Colin said had thrown her.

"You know, Henrietta, you're as focused and intense when it comes to your MI5 work as you are with a rosebush that hasn't been pruned in a decade. It's your nature. In their own ways, Freddy and Posey were the same, he as a spy catcher, she as a master gardener."

She frowned at him. "What are you talking about, Oliver?"

He smiled. She'd made his point for him. "We're on tricky ground here, Henrietta."

"Yes, I'm afraid we are."

He could feel her frustration, but he didn't think she was annoyed or upset. She bit off another sigh and resumed walking, shoulders back, hair tangling in the breeze off the water. She'd opted for another of her long flowered skirts today. It didn't seem to get in her way, but Oliver didn't know much about such matters. The skirts suited her complicated swirl of a personality.

She squinted at the harbor with its working boats bobbing in the tide, docks stacked with lobster pots, ropes and other bits and bobs of a fisherman's life. "Did you sneak aboard that yacht yesterday, Oliver?"

Her question didn't take him entirely by surprise. Henrietta Balfour wasn't one to ask direct questions unless she was positive she wanted an answer, whatever it was. Her wild curls were already tousled and tangled from their windy walk from the rectory for breakfast, and he doubted the fresh gusts could do more damage.

"Oliver. Speaking about it hypothetically as we did last night is one thing. That's not what I'm doing now. I need to know. Did you sneak aboard that yacht?"

"Even Colin didn't ask me that."

"Because it complicates his life if he asks, whether you lie or tell the truth." She paused, her blue-green eyes warm with love—and suspicion, he noted. "If you did it, I know when it happened. It was when we stopped to admire the ocean view up from the Sharpe Fine Art Recovery offices. I dozed off due to jet lag. You walked down to the rocks by the water, you said."

"It was a convenient nap, Henrietta."

She scowled. "For you to do Jeremy's bidding."

"And for you to let me do it if he had instructed me to do so. But he didn't, and I didn't."

She raked a hand through her hair. "Then you didn't steal that bloody painting."

Oliver hadn't considered what to do if his MI5 handler slipped into the US without telling Henrietta and ended up out of commission and leaving him to deal with her on his own. Not to mention the FBI, a town filled with Donovans—*and* a local priest with a strong bond with the Irish artist responsible for the painting now apparently missing from a private luxury yacht.

Henrietta came to an abrupt stop when they reached the rectory. A few but not many more cars than usual were on the street, and a handful were in the small church lot. Mass would end soon. Oliver wondered if she'd interrogate Father Bracken, too. She was in that sort of mood.

"Do you suppose the locals are called Rock Pointers?" he asked her.

She glared at him. "Oliver."

"No, Henrietta, my love, I didn't sneak on board the yacht while you were napping. I didn't then or at any other time." He bent down and scooped up two freshly fallen orange-colored leaves and tucked them behind her ear. He smiled. "They match your coloring."

She was undistracted. "Did you and Jeremy discuss his decision to pose as William Hornsby, fly to Boston and get himself invited onto the Fanning yacht?"

"No. I don't 'discuss' anything with Jeremy. He tells me what to do and I do it."

"Mmm. That straightforward, is it? By your standards, perhaps so—and please don't take that as an insult. You have a scholar's mind." She sighed—she'd been sighing since he'd had tea with her in the rectory kitchen at 5:00 a.m.—and tugged the leaves out of her hair. "They're pretty when they first fall to the ground. Eventually they turn brown and crumble to bits, or they get soggy and stick to one's shoes. Oliver..." She raised her gaze to him. "You're a well-regarded English mythologist who's helped William Hornsby with his work as an art consultant and happens to be in Maine visiting friends, and I'm your garden-designer friend. That's where we need to keep our focus."

He nodded. "Got it."

"All the best cover stories are woven with facts and truth."

Oliver had learned that himself during his time as an art thief and working as a Hollywood consultant under an alternate identity. As Henrietta marched up the front walk, he realized she'd said all she would say about what she knew about this excursion, and no amount of badgering would get her to say more.

Once inside the rectory, he jotted a note for Finian to let him know they were off to the hospital and placed it on the kitchen table where he couldn't miss it. Henrietta grabbed the key fob to their rental car, and they headed back out.

She sighed—another one—at the small church and its smattering of cars. "Thirty people at Mass, maximum, wouldn't you say? But I don't see our Father Bracken serving at a cathedral."

Oliver noticed two elderly women emerge from the side entrance, smiling, one with a cane. "He belongs here for now, if not forever."

She handed him the key. "You drive. I need to think."

She grinned at him. "You cheeky bastard. Don't look so relieved."

He grinned back at her but made no comment as they headed to the car. He absolutely, without question preferred to do the driving. Henrietta was a demon on the road, and driving on the right—he didn't need that madness on top of everything else. He knew few details about her work with British intelligence, but she didn't drive like a normal person. Her MI5 training, no doubt, but also her personality and the way she'd grown up, with parents who'd pawned her off as often as they could on her elderly great-aunt. She was self-sufficient, courageous and smart, and she loved puttering in her garden. If his parents hadn't been killed, would they have fallen for each other sooner, had a brood of children by now?

He started the car, an ordinary sedan, serviceable but not as fun to drive as his Rolls-Royce at home. Henrietta settled into her seat. "I suspect there's a personal connection between Jeremy and Georgina Masterson. If you know what it is, Oliver, I suggest you tell me."

"Or...what?"

The hint of a smile. "Or I'll let Colin and Emma get it out of you."

"Ah."

Her smile spread across her face, to her eyes. "And here I'd hoped I'd have you shaking in your boots. I suppose it would take more given your history. Do you remember the way to the hospital?"

He did, and as he pulled out onto the quiet street, he wondered what it would be like to be in Maine visiting friends for real—and to have Henrietta's trust as well as her love. Nonetheless, he *was* holding back on her about his meeting with Robin Masterson. Perhaps best to earn her trust.

10

Sister Cecilia Catherine Rousseau met Emma at the shaded main entrance to the Sisters of the Joyful Heart's convent, located on its own small peninsula that jutted into the Atlantic not far from the village of Heron's Cove. Emma had called ahead, after she'd left her voice mail for her brother in their ongoing phone tag. Wearing a simple black headband, dove-gray tunic and sturdy shoes, Sister Cecilia greeted Emma with a hug and a squeal of delight. They exchanged a few innocuous updates about their lives. Sister Cecilia was making progress on the biography she was writing on Mother Sarah Jane Linden, the convent's foundress and an accomplished artist in her own right.

"Mother Linden and your grandfather were such great friends," Cecilia said. "Do you think he might be amenable to an interview with me?"

Emma couldn't imagine anyone refusing to talk to the young religious sister, including her sometimes unforthcoming grandfather. "I've no doubt."

"Maybe I could visit him in Dublin and interview him in person. I'd love to see the Book of Kells while I'm there. It'd take some doing, but I bet I could figure out how to pull off such a trip."

Of that, Emma had no doubt. Once Sister Cecilia put her mind to something, she had a formidable knack for getting it done. She was an art educator, with truly a joyful heart, Emma thought, fully committed to her order and its dedication to art education, restoration and conservation. "Let me know when you decide for sure, and I'll be happy to help."

"That would be wonderful. Now, you want to know about the vegetables we delivered to the yacht in Heron's Cove yesterday—the one that suffered the food-poisoning episode."

"Yes, anything you can tell me."

"The chef came here to choose them herself."

Emma raised her eyebrows in surprise. "Georgina Masterson?"

Cecilia nodded. "She ran here from the marina in Heron's Cove."

"By herself?"

"Yes. She said so, and I didn't see anyone else with her. I met her here at the gate. She told me she takes the opportunity when in a port to go for a run and get out on her own. She's training for a half marathon. I took her to the shed where we keep the fresh-picked vegetables. She chose what she wanted and we put them in a box, and one of the sisters delivered them to the yacht. I walked her back here, and she asked if she could check the woods for mushrooms. She was hoping to find a few chanterelles."

"She specifically mentioned chanterelles?"

"That's right. I pointed her to the coniferous forest on the hill. Chanterelles love conifers. She said she'd have a look and then run back to the yacht. I was impressed, I have to say." She made a face. "I hate to run."

Emma didn't love it, but she did it to stay in shape. "What time was this?"

"About 9:00 a.m. Would you like me to show you where I told her to go?"

"Please."

Sister Cecilia ducked past a white pine to a trail along the outside of a black iron fence that enclosed most of the former Victorian estate the Sisters of the Joyful Heart had purchased in their early days as an order. The property had been in a state of disrepair and neglect, but, bit by bit over the years, the sisters had transformed it into a place where they could live, work and welcome visitors for retreats. On the convent side of the tall fence were wide, well-kept lawns dotted with shade trees and a variety of gardens. The trail on the other side of the fence curved along the top of a densely wooded hillside that plunged to the rockbound coast and sea.

After about fifty yards, Sister Cecilia stopped as the trail narrowed and made a ninety-degree turn and descended through pines and spruce trees. She was breathing hard but not, Emma knew, from exertion. In August, they'd followed the trail down through the woods to the water, where they'd discovered a man dead, his body wedged among rocks, in the cold tide. It was the same area where, a few days later, Emma's father had fallen into the water and suffered what had turned out to be a fatal heart attack.

Emma felt her own emotions rise, but she focused on the matter at hand. "Have you picked chanterelles out here?"

Sister Cecilia took in a breath, composing herself. "Oh, yes. They're one of my favorites. You can spot them by their funnel shape and yellow color. It's important, though, never to get complacent with wild mushrooms. You need to follow specific rules before confidently identifying an edible species. Sometimes it's difficult to distinguish an edible mushroom from an inedible one."

"What are some of the rules?" Emma asked.

"Stick to opened-cap mushrooms, especially if you're inexperienced. Mushrooms in the button stage can trip you up. Pay attention to where the mushroom is growing—its environment can help with identification. I avoid gilled mushrooms. Shape, color, texture, whether it's growing singly or in a cluster—I take note of everything." She shrugged. "That's a start on the rules, anyway.

"Thank you," Emma said. "Did Georgina have anything with her to collect mushrooms?"

"She had a mesh bag tucked into her running belt. She showed it to me."

Prepared, then.

"She only mentioned chanterelles," Cecilia added. "I don't know if she actually picked any, or if she picked any other mushrooms or other edible plants while she was here. I didn't stay with her. She said she's an enthusiastic forager."

"Was anyone else out here?"

"I didn't see anyone. We get a few people out here from time to time, but it's not easy to reach."

"Can you describe Georgina's mood?" Emma asked.

"Between the run and the foraging, I got the impression she wanted to be alone. She was quiet, thoughtful. She said she loved seeing Maine and the convent, especially this time of year with the changing foliage."

Emma noticed yellow birch leaves among the evergreens. She could see the appeal of running out here, doing a bit of mushroom foraging before a busy day. "Did you see Georgina again before she left?"

Sister Cecilia shook her head. "No, I didn't. I don't think anyone else at the convent did, either, but I can ask."

"That's okay." Emma had discovered her friend was naturally curious, and as a result never bored. "And there were no mushrooms in the vegetable order itself?"

"Not a one." No hesitation, no hint of uncertainty. "I'm the only one here who has any real interest in wild mushrooms. I'd love to collect chanterelles, but—I just haven't. Next year, maybe. It's been difficult for me to come out this way." She hesitated. "It's hard for you, too, isn't it?"

Emma nodded. "I expect it will be for a while. Colin and I haven't been to Maine in several weeks. I went to Ireland to be with my grandfather. It was good but it's a blur now." Emma pulled her gaze from the twisting path before she could go too deep into memories. "I didn't realize chanterelles are still in season."

"They're winding down now. I think of them as a September treat."

"And you didn't see Ms. Masterson pick them or any other mushrooms, take them with her—"

Sister Cecilia shook her head. "She said if she found any chanterelles, she wanted to grill them with garlic, olive oil and shaved Parmesan. That does sound wonderful, doesn't it?"

"It sure does," Emma said with a smile.

"Whatever made people sick yesterday, it wouldn't have been chanterelles. They're harmless, unless, of course, one is allergic or sensitive to them." She started down the steep trail, her breathing returned to normal. "There are some nasty mushrooms out here. Some toxic mushrooms are tricky to differentiate from nontoxic varieties. I don't feel confident enough in my wild mushroom skills to consume any I pick, much less include them in a vegetable order."

"What types of toxic mushrooms might you find out here?"

"A fair number, actually. There's toxic but not lethal and there's toxic and lethal. Some are gastrointestinal irritants that can give you unpleasant symptoms for a miserable day or two but are unlikely to kill you. Others are downright deadly."

Emma followed her down the shaded trail. "Can you give me an example?"

Cecilia stood on a protruding root and touched a bit of sticky pitch on the trunk of a gnarly pine tree. "Well…you definitely want to stay away from white Amanitas. There are a number of different species around the world. We have the eastern destroying angel. *Amanita bisporigera*."

"Do they grow out here?"

"I spotted several out here the other day. The most well-known and possibly the most dangerous Amanita is the death cap. *Amanita phalloides.* It's native to Europe but I understand it can be found in North America. Best to avoid any of the Amanitas."

Emma considered Sister Cecilia's words. "Destroying angel. Death cap. Aptly named, I take it?"

She nodded, spots of color high in her cheeks given the intense nature of the topic. "I'm not a medical expert, but the toxin in Amanitas attacks and can ultimately shut down the liver and kidneys, leading to coma and eventually death. Learning to identify Amanitas is critical for a mushroom enthusiast."

"Sounds like an understatement," Emma said, trying to lighten the mood. "Mushroom Hunting 101."

"Most certainly."

Emma noticed an attractive brown mushroom under the pine tree, not far from where she stood. She had no idea what it was. "What about mushrooms that aren't deadly but still can make you sick?"

Sister Cecilia hopped off the pine root and lifted a low-hanging branch, pointing to the ground. "See those red mushrooms? I haven't had a mycologist make a positive identification, but I believe they're the *russula emetica* species. They'd be my first candidate for yesterday."

"*Emetica?* Another one appropriately named?"

"Says it all, doesn't it. They're commonly known as the sickener."

"Not as terrifying as death cap and destroying angel, but it gets the point across." Emma took a closer look at the trio of mushrooms, indeed a distinct red color. "They don't look appetizing, and they certainly don't bear any resemblance to chanterelles."

"That's true," Sister Cecilia said, lowering the branch. "Symptoms after eating *russula emetica* typically develop quickly—within thirty minutes to two hours. Amanitas have a delayed toxicity. Symptoms don't appear for six to twelve hours after ingestion, and sometimes not for several days. Anyway, the gastrointestinal symptoms from eating sickeners are unpleasant but generally not lethal."

"How do they taste?" Emma asked.

"That's the rub in my theory. To make people sick, they have to be eaten raw. Cooking renders them harmless. But when raw, they have a strikingly bitter taste. You'd likely spit them out before the toxin had a chance to get into your system."

That had been Melodie Fanning's reaction to the mini tacos. "Could you mask the bitter taste?" Emma asked.

Sister Cecilia shrugged. "I suppose you could try. Maybe something spicy or as strongly flavored could get people to swallow enough to make them sick. You might not want more, but it'd be too late."

They returned to the path, their talk of toxic mushrooms a contrast to the smell of the evergreens, the sounds of the ocean down through the trees, and a few seagulls, somewhere in the distance. It was a beautiful spot to be talking about poisonous mushrooms. Had anyone else noticed a bad taste yesterday? Would passengers and guests be reluctant to mention it with the Fannings as their hosts?

"I'm not suggesting Ms. Masterson picked the wrong mushrooms out here." Sister Cecilia adjusted her headband, tucking strands of her fine brown hair back in place. "I don't know if she picked any mushrooms at all. I'm just providing information, and I'm an admitted amateur."

"I understand that," Emma said.

She regretted bringing up such a topic with her friend. They'd met last fall when a nun—Sister Joan Fabriani, Emma's former mentor in art conservation—was murdered at the convent. She'd been a brilliant woman, and she'd never believed Emma would remain a religious sister.

They continued up the path, but Sister Cecilia's breathing became rapid and shallow. Emma stopped and turned to her. "Are you all right, Sister?"

"Yes—thank you." She placed a hand on her upper chest and smiled. "It's not always easy to have you as a friend, Emma, given the nature of your work—of your family's work—but I'm so glad you are my friend. I don't want you to think you can't tell me anything, can't come to me when something is on your mind."

"I appreciate that."

Sister Cecilia cleared her throat, her breathing more normal. "There is one more thing. I don't know if it's of interest. When she was choosing her fresh veggies, Georgina Masterson mentioned her father is very ill in England. She asked us to pray for him. She said she isn't a believer herself, but she figured he could use any positive thoughts."

"Did she say what made him sick?"

"No, and I didn't feel comfortable asking. I was open to whatever she wanted to say, of course, but she changed the subject. I suppose it could go to her state of mind. If she made a mistake with the mushrooms, maybe she was just preoccupied with her father's condition." Sister Cecilia flushed, waved a hand dismissively. "Sorry. I know I'm jumping ahead of the facts and shouldn't speculate."

"You can do whatever you like, and I appreciate hearing your thoughts. Thank you for your help."

They said little as they walked back to the main gate. Through the tall fence, she could see a solitary maple, its leaves turning orange against the blue sky.

Sister Cecilia's color was better and she appeared more her usual cheerful self when they reached the main gate and parking area. "Are you painting?" she asked Emma.

"Some. Not much. Our apartment in Boston is on the waterfront. Lots of great scenes to capture, but I don't think I'll ever master painting boats."

"We can do another lesson."

Emma smiled. "That'd be great."

She opened her car door but took a moment to watch Sister Cecilia go back through the gate, taking the shaded paved walk to the motherhouse and her convent life. Emma could picture the gardens, the stone Victorian buildings and the rocky headland where she'd first spotted Colin a year ago. He was convinced she'd fantasized about meeting a rugged Maine lobsterman-turned-FBI-agent back in her days as a novice.

Maybe, deep down, she had, and she'd somehow conjured him.

But as she got in her car, she could see herself picking wild blueberries with her father on a hot August morning when she was still a postulant with the Sisters of the Joyful Heart.

Are you sure you want convent life forever, Emma?

He'd been direct and interested, and he'd encouraged her to talk to him. Her mother hadn't liked to discuss such things. She didn't understand, and she didn't want to understand. *I'm not going to lie to you, Emma, Sister Brigid, whoever you are now—I want my daughter back. I want grandchildren. This isn't* The Sound of Music. *You're not going to meet a rich, handsome sea captain.*

Emma had appreciated her mother's frankness and honesty. She was a widow now, visiting friends in Paris, but she and her father had both attended Emma's wedding to Colin. Her mother approved of him. He wasn't rich or a sea captain, but he was good with boats and ruggedly handsome.

Emma pulled her car door shut. People's lives didn't always take straight, easy roads. They had twists, turns, switchbacks and roadblocks, sometimes—maybe often—of one's own making. She couldn't remember all the details of what had drawn her to the Sisters of the Joyful Heart as a teenager, but she'd learned so much with them. She wouldn't be an FBI agent without that time. She wouldn't be with Colin without it.

She remembered that long-ago conversation with her father. *Whatever you decide, Emma, I'm your dad. I'm always here for you.*

I've never doubted that.

And if I go to God sooner rather than later—

Dad, please don't talk like that.

Remember that it's okay. Won't you? Carry on with your life. Be happy.

She got behind the wheel, pulled the door shut and jumped when her phone vibrated in her jacket pocket. She fished it out. Lucas. She answered, relieved at the distraction from where her thoughts had taken her. "Hey," she said. "Where are you?"

"Walking in the garden at the O'Byrne hotel. You?"

"The convent. Sister Cecilia and I were just talking about poisonous mushrooms."

"Oh, nice. Want me to call back?"

"No, we're done. I'm about to leave. Have the Fannings been in touch?"

"No, and no one else from the yacht. But Granddad and I talked to Aoife a little while ago. Do you know a Brit named Robin Masterson?"

"Georgina Masterson is the chef on the yacht."

"His daughter." Lucas sighed. "For what it's worth, Emma, he bought the Aoife O'Byrne painting. Made a special trip to Dublin to go to her studio on Monday. She sold it to him herself. She was in the midst of her move to Declan's Cross. The painting is a watercolor, part of a new series of Declan's Cross woodland landscapes."

"Okay. I didn't expect the father. We don't know who he is?"

"English is all I know."

Emma could tell from Lucas's voice there was more.

"What else, Lucas? Please—don't leave anything out, no matter how trivial it might seem."

"Henrietta Balfour was in Dublin the next day."

"Tell me."

Emma didn't interrupt Lucas as he related the rest of his conversation with Aoife and their grandfather. When he finished, she took a moment to collect her thoughts. "Did you get the sense Granddad told you everything about Aoife's going-away party and seeing Henrietta that evening?"

"I think so, but you know him, Emma. If he doesn't want to tell me something, he won't, and I'll be the last to know he's holding back. Doesn't surprise me that he and Oliver York get along as well as they do."

Nor Emma. She could picture her brother and grandfather in pretty Declan's Cross. "What's Granddad up to while you're in the garden?"

"He's having coffee on the terrace."

"How is he, Lucas?"

"Grieving. He misses Dad, but he carries on. He wants to take me out to the cliffs where he heard the banshee in the days before Dad died."

"It's gorgeous out there." Emma heard the catch in her voice even before she felt tears hot in her eyes. She sniffled, reminded herself these surges of emotion while sudden weren't unexpected. Part of grieving. She blinked back the tears and smiled. "I hope you don't hear a banshee."

"If I hear a banshee, Emma, I'm beating a path back to the hotel and the whiskey cabinet."

She laughed. "I don't blame you."

"Emma…" Lucas paused, probably taking a moment

to collect his own thoughts. "Can you tell me anything about why Henrietta and Oliver are in Rock Point?"

"I don't know why they're there, Lucas."

"You have your hands full, don't you? Get in touch if there's anything else I can do. How's Colin?"

"He got home on Friday, in time for the rehearsal dinner at Hurley's."

"Give him my best. I'll let you know if I learn anything else. I'm just here hanging out with Granddad."

"Don't underestimate his ability to walk forever."

"This I've learned," Lucas said with a chuckle as they disconnected.

Emma tossed her phone onto the passenger seat. Next stop was the hospital. Colin would give Jeremy, Henrietta and Oliver only so much time before he started pushing hard for answers about their presence in Maine, what they knew about the Aoife O'Byrne painting and the nature of their relationship with Georgina Masterson, the young chef responsible for a dozen people getting sick yesterday.

Probably from consuming inedible mushrooms.

Russula emetica, Emma thought, as she drove down the convent's tree-lined access road, her Sunday not even close to the one she'd planned. Except for the doughnuts. She and Colin would have had doughnuts before peeling apples, kayaking, taking a long walk on the water.

She took in a breath as she came to the main road. She'd missed Colin when he was away. She loved having him in her life. She wanted to get up with him and go to bed with him. She wasn't used to such feelings. Her life now was different from the one she'd had before she'd met him last September—certainly than the one she'd had as Sister Brigid with the Sisters of the Joyful Heart—but it was good.

Whatever was next for him—for her, for HIT—they'd figure it out.

Right now, though, it was on to the hospital and their British friends.

11

The medical types made Colin wait to see Jeremy Pearson, aka William Hornsby. The nurse explained their patient needed to rest after his previous visitors. Henrietta and Oliver hadn't beaten Colin to Jeremy. He'd let them go first, knowing he wouldn't get anything out of any of them until they'd had a chance to talk. He'd run into Henrietta and Oliver by the nurses' station. She'd suggested he meet him in the hospital cafeteria. Colin figured he knew where to find them if they took off. Unfortunately. It'd been their idea to stay at the rectory, but he felt guilty for bringing the pair into Fin Bracken's life. Not that Fin would complain. He even liked Oliver, and Henrietta was impossible not to like.

Finally, Colin got the all clear and went in. Jeremy had the double room to himself and was in the bed by the window, which overlooked not much of anything—

a parking lot, a playground, a few trees in full autumn color.

Colin approached the bed. "I see you're upright and awake."

"Progress." He held up his left arm, an IV taped to his hand. "Still have this, though."

"You lost a lot of fluids."

"Tell me something I don't know. Sorry about Henrietta and Oliver dropping into your quiet little village."

"Did you invite them?"

"No." Jeremy didn't elaborate. "Doctors say I should be able to get out of here later today."

"That's good news. You'll make a full recovery?"

"In time. We didn't get into how much time. I've never been so sick. Did you find the lung I threw up?"

"Tossed in the river."

He tried to laugh, but winced. "My abdominal muscles still hurt. I gather they will for a while." He licked his raw, chapped lips. "You're here to badger me, aren't you, Donovan?"

"I want to ask a few questions that you can answer as you're able." Colin filled a glass with water and ice from a pitcher on the wheeled tray table. He handed it to Jeremy. "I don't want to do anything to impede your recovery."

Jeremy snorted. "Glad you got that BS out of the way? Where's your brother? Did I hear you two mention doughnuts?"

"Kevin's checking on Bryce Fanning, and we did mention doughnuts. Why, do you want one?"

"You're trying to kill me. I knew it."

"We need to talk, my friend," Colin said. "Why were you a passenger on the Fanning yacht?"

"It's not their yacht, but they're buying one of their own. It'll cost more than you and I combined would make in multiple lifetimes. But good for them. Have at it. Enjoy. I hope never to step foot on another yacht."

"The yacht didn't make you sick, and you didn't answer my question."

"What question?"

Colin didn't respond. No need. Jeremy knew what question.

Jeremy shut his eyes for two beats. When he opened them, he was focused, serious. "Melodie Fanning invited me. I was in Boston on business."

"As Hornsby," Colin said.

"Correct. Melodie is already thinking about what art to buy for the new yacht."

"And I bet you come highly recommended."

"I do, in fact."

"What about Georgina Masterson?"

"I stopped by the marina where the yacht was moored to see her. That's how I met the Fannings. Georgina's father is an old friend." Jeremy tried drinking some of the water, but ended up dribbling it down the front of his hospital gown. "Bloody hell."

Colin took the glass and set it back on the tray table. "Sorry about that. I should have helped you."

"I don't need help. I need to get out of here. I can't hold up a fork and get out of bed on my own. Can you imagine if I have to ask Henrietta for help getting to the toilet? Or, God forbid, Oliver?" Jeremy shook his head, obviously with some effort. His eyes were still red-rimmed and bloodshot, if less so than yesterday, but as piercing as ever. "I told them they could talk to you."

"Good of you."

"It is. Otherwise you wouldn't get a word out of them."

"What do you know about an Aoife O'Byrne painting that was on the yacht?"

Jeremy yawned. "I can't stay awake. It's driving me mad."

"Georgina says you were going to take a look at it, but it's not in your cabin. Where is it?"

"Is she filing a complaint?"

"No. Backing off her story."

His British colleague blinked, a vacant expression on his face. "Painting—Colin, I'm sorry. I'm fogged in. I can't bloody think straight." He moaned and sank into his pillows. "I need to rest and get back on my feet. You understand."

No way was Colin getting anything else out of him. He knew the signs, and they had nothing to do with his recovery. "By the way, is Henrietta getting in touch with your wife?"

"I hope not. My darling wife wouldn't be disappointed I'm making it through this ordeal, but she wouldn't mind having me suffer a little."

"Provided she didn't have to clean up after you?"

"Precisely." Jeremy glanced out the window. He did look like hell, if not as out of it as he wanted Colin to believe. "I should rest. I want to be sure I can get out of here today."

"Where will you go once you're discharged?"

"Don't you have a guest room?"

"I turned it into a weight room. Emma wants to convert it into a proper guest room. Oliver sent us a sheepskin for it. You could sleep on an exercise mat but that wouldn't be very comfortable, and it's up a flight of stairs. I'm not carrying you."

"God forbid." Jeremy managed a weak smile when Emma entered the room. "Special Agent Sharpe. Welcome. Colin was about to get out the thumbscrews."

She greeted him with a warm smile. "How are you feeling?"

"Almost alive. It's good to see you, Emma. I'm so sorry about your father. I had the pleasure of meeting him in London. He was a wonderful man."

"Thank you. We miss him."

"How's your grandfather?"

"As well as can be expected. My brother's with him in Ireland. I just spoke with Lucas, in fact." Emma paused, eyeing Jeremy. He adjusted his position, wincing in what appeared to be genuine discomfort. "He and Granddad are in Declan's Cross. That's the village—"

"I know it," Jeremy said.

Of course he did. Colin said nothing. Emma approached Jeremy's hospital bed. She had something on her mind. Colin waited as she smoothed a few wrinkles in the white blanket at the foot of the bed. "Lucas spoke with Aoife O'Byrne. She's in Declan's Cross, but she was in Dublin earlier this week. She had a party at her studio there. My grandfather stopped in."

"Did he? We should all be so spry and alert in our eighties." Jeremy took in a shallow breath and shut his eyes. "I'm as weak as a kitten. Another…"

He drifted off before he could finish. Faking it, probably, but Colin knew he'd look like a total jerk if he shook him and he really was out. Especially since everyone thought their patient was a mild-mannered art consultant rather than a hard-as-nails intelligence operator.

"Let me know if you want me to get Finian Bracken in here to give you last rites. He makes regular rounds at this hospital." Colin waited ten seconds, but he didn't get any reaction from Pearson. "All right. Get well soon."

Emma frowned at him when they left the room and started to the elevators. "Colin, do you really think he was pretending to be asleep?"

"Probably not since he didn't give me the finger for bringing up last rites. Then again, he is good." He grinned at her. "Sorry to horrify you."

"The proverbial case of two peas in a pod."

"I'm younger and cuter. How's everyone at the convent?"

"I only saw Sister Cecilia. We had an interesting conversation about toxic and nontoxic mushrooms. Have you ever heard of destroying angels?"

"Not of the mushroom variety. Sister Cecilia's something. Watch out. Yank will be recruiting her out of the convent next."

"He won't succeed, but she does have natural investigative instincts."

"And there's more from Lucas?"

"Oh, yes."

Emma filled him in on the highlights of her conversation with her brother and her visit with Sister Cecilia.

"Mushroom lesson, Georgina Masterson and her mesh bag, Robin Masterson sick in London, and Henrietta Balfour in Dublin. Busy morning, Emma."

She smiled. "A good thing I had those doughnuts."

They reached the elevators. Colin pressed the down button. "Let's go find Henrietta and Oliver."

One of the elevators dinged and the doors opened,

letting out medical types and Kevin. Colin could see his brother wasn't in a great mood. Kevin waited for the medical types to disperse before he spoke. "Figured I'd find you two here. CID thinks I'm not telling them things. If you get me fired, Colin, you're going in with me on a sightseeing boat."

"Captain Kevin? Running whale watches and puffin tours is my backup plan, too. We could do worse." After seeing Jeremy Pearson, Colin wasn't kidding. But he appreciated his brother's concerns. "I'll run interference for you with your bosses if it'd help."

"Don't talk to them without my knowledge. Henrietta Balfour and Oliver York just spent twenty minutes visiting the British art guy, and now you two just visited him. I'm adding things up in my head. Where are Henrietta and Oliver now?"

"Having tea in the cafeteria, I expect," Colin said. "Emma and I are heading there now. What are you up to?"

"I'm going down to the ER to talk to Beth."

"Making up a reason or have one?"

Kevin ignored him. Colin noticed Emma hadn't said anything. Smart, since his younger brother wasn't mad at her. Why tempt fate?

Another elevator stopped and the doors opened to Beth Trahan. She and Emma exchanged a pleasant greeting, and Beth nodded to Colin. "Good morning, Special Agent Donovan."

"Hey, Beth. Kevin here's looking for you." Colin could feel his brother gritting his teeth next to him. "You must have read his mind."

Kevin turned to her. "What's up, Beth?"

"I ran into the yacht chef—Georgina—in the ER

lobby just now. She wants to see Mr. Hornsby. I told her she'd have to check with his nurse to see if he could have visitors. She seemed flustered. I thought you might like to know."

Kevin frowned. "Is she still in the lobby?"

"I don't know," Beth said.

"All right. I'll see what they have to say at the nurses' station."

"Okay, great. I'll meet you there in a sec." She waited for Kevin to start down the hall before she turned to Colin. "It's hard to know what to do. Kevin—he's good at his job, isn't he?"

Colin didn't hesitate. "Kev's the best."

"You sound sincere, Special Agent Donovan, but I hear you Donovans are a tight-knit lot."

You Donovans again. He smiled at her. "Colin."

"What?"

"You can call me Colin."

"Oh. Right. Fine." She didn't seem particularly self-conscious. "I was talking with some of the nurses. We think there's more going on here than you're letting on. I mean you plural. You, Kevin, Special Agent Sharpe, the sick art consultant, Hornsby, the Fannings."

"Emma. You can call Special Agent Sharpe by her first name. Right, Emma?"

"Of course," she said.

At first he thought Beth might kick him or swear at him, but she didn't. Instead, she shook her head and sighed. "I can't say I wasn't warned."

"I understand inedible mushrooms are the likely cause of yesterday's sickness," Beth said. "Last year a teenage girl ingested a destroying angel mushroom. She got to the ER early on and survived, but it was touch-and-go for a while. I'd rather pick apples, I can tell you that, but people do enjoy foraging. You have to be extremely careful, though." Beth slid Colin a cutting glance. "Not a Donovan trait, I know."

She hadn't struck him as particularly annoyed still with Kevin. Had she come to her conclusion about Donovan traits on her own and Kevin was basically doomed? Colin didn't need to go there.

But she wasn't finished. "I don't believe you're reckless, but you are shit magnets."

"You're an ER nurse." Colin winked at her. "Where would you be without us?"

She obviously didn't think that was funny at all.

Emma smiled at her. "You get used to the Donovan sense of humor after a while."

"That's okay. I'm sorry. I didn't mean... I wasn't criticizing." Beth straightened, shifting into her professional mode. "I have to get to work. Let me know if I can help in any way."

Colin thanked her. The elevator doors opened, and he and Emma got in. "Beth's no slouch, is she, Colin?"

"I wouldn't underestimate her."

"And Kevin?"

"He'd do better with puffin tours than I ever would." Colin kissed her on the forehead. "He'll be fine." He stood back. "Anything else from Ireland and the convent?"

"I can go into more detail on toxic mushrooms. One called the sickener is a good candidate for yesterday. It's not lethal but you wouldn't want to eat it raw."

"And our good sister knows these things?"

"She's a woman of many talents and interests. She asked me if I'm painting again."

Colin realized he didn't know the answer. He hated that. "Are you?"

Emma shook her head. "Not yet."

"But you will be," he said.

"Soon. Have you been in touch with Yank?"

"Sam Padgett. He's looking into the Fannings."

Sam was a rugged, dogged Texan as good with numbers as he was in the field. Colin hadn't been surprised Sam had been at the HIT offices on a Sunday morning. He'd do a thorough background check on Bryce and Melodie Fanning. Any alarm bells, he'd get a warrant and they'd go from there.

"Sam's been great since Dad died," Emma said. "He's solicitous without overdoing it."

"Still making bad jokes?"

She laughed. "Of course. He didn't stop being Sam."

As promised, Henrietta and Oliver were at a table in a quiet corner of the cafeteria with their ubiquitous pots of tea in front of them. They sat next to each other, allowing them both a view out the floor-to-ceiling windows at the hospital's meditation garden. Colin wasn't in the mood for soothing flowers and grasses or a chat over tea. Kayaking, hiking, peeling apples with Emma. After weeks working undercover, that was the Sunday he'd had in mind. He sure as hell wasn't in the mood for a runaround, and after her conversations with Sister Cecilia and Lucas, he doubted Emma was, either. He sat next to her, across from Henrietta and Oliver.

Oliver raised the lid on his one-person metal teapot and peered inside. "This isn't tea. It's tea-flavored barely hot water."

Colin shrugged. "Here we go again. Isn't that what tea is?"

"Not proper tea. Henrietta isn't as particular as I am. I do know one can get proper tea in the US, just not where I've been lately. But this is fine. No complaints." Oliver shut the pot lid and poured the tea—it was steaming, Colin noted—into his cup. "You've seen our mutual friend? He looks ghastly, doesn't he?"

"Not as bad as yesterday," Colin said.

"Any improvement is positive, I suppose. At least his system has settled down."

Henrietta hooked a finger onto the handle of her teapot and dragged it closer to her, as if it were the most important thing she had to do. "We're waiting to see when he'll be discharged. After lunch, we think. He won't be able to travel for a few days, at least, but Father Bracken said he could stay at the rectory."

"There's always the Donovan family inn," Oliver said. "I've stayed there. It won't be long before Jeremy will be in the mood for your father's soon-to-be-legendary wild blueberry muffins."

Colin wasn't worried about his folks handling the likes of Oliver York or Jeremy Pearson, or Henrietta Balfour for that matter. His father was a retired Rock Point police officer. Not much got to him these days. Not much had ever gotten to his mother.

Henrietta lifted the lid to her teapot. "It looks fine, Oliver. You just miss Martin. He doesn't travel with you, though, does he?"

"Only to London," Oliver said. "Even that's less often now that Alfred is at the farm."

Alfred being a wire fox terrier puppy as independent and stubborn as his owner. Colin noticed Emma smile, but he wasn't surprised. She was easier on Oliver than Colin ever would be. That the elusive art thief her grandfather had chased for a decade had turned out to be Oliver York—cheeky, charming, wealthy, intelligent, haunted—had been a relief, in a way. The thief could have been a lot of things besides a wealthy mythologist with a tragic past.

"Autumn is a wonderful time to be in the Cotswolds," Emma said. "Alfred is doing well with his training?"

"When Martin is with him." Oliver tore open a packet of sugar and emptied it into his tea. "He's an unruly little sod with me."

Henrietta, who exuded tension, softened slightly. "Don't listen to him. He adores Alfred. I brought him to Aunt Posey's house one rainy afternoon, and he was completely incorrigible. Alfred, I mean. Not Oliver. He shredded an old shawl of hers. When we went out, he tramped through every puddle and muddied himself from head to toe. I'm not as stern with him as I should be, I suppose." She finally turned to Colin next to her. "Now, what can you tell us?"

Colin bristled. "We're here for what you can tell us."

Her eyes cooled. "All right, then. What can we tell you?"

"Let's start with Robin Masterson, the father of our yacht chef."

"How much do you know already?"

"Assume we know nothing."

Colin glanced at Oliver and realized it wasn't the case with him. But he let Henrietta respond. "He's a recently retired neurotoxicologist. He was a lecturer and consultant, and happy to turn the page on his work life. He's an expert in synthetic neurotoxins."

"Chemical weapons," Colin said.

"Robin doesn't get into their purpose, only their adverse effects on the body and how that can be ameliorated." Henrietta spoke briskly, no hesitation now that she had the green light from Jeremy Pearson. "His expertise includes sarin, VX, Novichok and a variety of boutique nerve agents."

Colin held back any reaction. "That's why Jeremy knows him?"

"I don't have that information, I'm afraid. Robin was a hopeless workaholic, and he and his daughter have never been particularly close."

"Georgina. Our chef."

Henrietta nodded, calm, as if she anticipated Colin's curtness. "Her mother—Valerie, Robin's wife—died when Georgina was small. He had an intense job and no idea how to raise a daughter on his own. She visited him last week in London. She left for Boston on Sunday. On Tuesday morning, Robin was found in a park near his flat. He was semiconscious and near death."

"What happened?" Emma asked. "Did he survive?"

"He's in intensive care in a London hospital." Henrietta stared at her teapot. "It's not a good prognosis."

Colin tapped the table with two fingers. "What made him sick, Henrietta?"

"Our first fear, obviously, was a nerve agent. We had the Novichok poisonings in the UK not long ago. It's only one of a number of substances that came to mind, but the cause of Robin's condition turns out to be much more mundane. He's an avid wild mushroom forager. Unfortunately, he consumed a toxic mushroom that grows in the park where he was found. Death cap, it's called."

"It's a deadly Amanita," Emma said.

Henrietta's eyes narrowed slightly. "Are you a forager yourself, Emma?"

She shook her head. "No. Please, go on."

"Apparently, Robin's daughter shares his interest in foraging. I assume you know that by now." Henrietta paused, glancing at Oliver, dutifully drinking his tea, letting her do the talking. "We don't know how or why he ingested the death caps. Given their delayed toxicity, there's quite a window of time in which it could have happened."

"What about Georgina?" Emma asked.

Henrietta shook her head. "They picked wild mushrooms on Sunday but didn't prepare any before she left. She knows about her father's condition. She's his next of kin. His doctor contacted her."

Colin frowned at Henrietta. "Jeremy left Robin fighting for his life and flew to Boston?"

"He says he didn't want Georgina to be alone." Henrietta gave a small shrug. "He's too sick for me to ask him many questions. He simply cleared me to speak with you and Emma. There's no indication Georgina was responsible for her father's illness. Robin could have made a mistake, or…" She stopped, fingered her teapot. "Attempted suicide is a real possibility."

Emma leaned back in her chair. "I'd like to hear about your trip to Dublin on Tuesday."

Oliver looked at Henrietta in surprise, but she smiled coolly at Emma. "You've been busy, I see. Your grandfather heard I was in town?"

"He saw you while he was at a party at Aoife O'Byrne's studio."

"She's a brilliant Irish artist. I thought I might pop in

to say hello and introduce myself, but I didn't once I saw she was having a party. I wasn't going to invite myself up. I flew to Dublin that morning. I met a friend for a bit of a shopping spree. We indulged ourselves at Brown Thomas and then had tea at the Shelbourne. I'd booked a room there, another indulgence. Didn't you and Colin stay at the Shelbourne in June on your honeymoon?"

"One night," Emma said. "It was a gift from my grandfather."

"I didn't contact him while I was in Dublin. I wasn't sure if he was still in Kerry on his walk, and I didn't get a chance to stop by his house."

"Who's the friend you saw?" Colin asked.

Henrietta didn't miss a beat. "A garden designer."

Not a bad tale, Colin thought—probably a mix of truth to it, should he or Emma decide to look into it. Henrietta didn't seem to care whether or not they believed her. Oliver looked on with admiration, although he'd seen her in action before.

"Robin Masterson was in Dublin on Monday," Emma said. "He bought a painting from Aoife O'Byrne."

"I see," Henrietta said.

It was about as noncommittal a response as there was. Colin said nothing, but Emma eyed the MI5 officer across from her. "I assume he flew back to London that evening, if he was found in the park on Tuesday morning."

"Easy to check, isn't it?" Oliver asked.

Emma nodded. "Are you aware of or do you suspect a connection between the painting Robin Masterson bought and his poisoning and then the yacht poisoning?"

"I haven't seen the painting, but what kind of connection could there be?"

Emma turned to Oliver. "What about you?"

He squirmed. Only word for it. Colin resisted the urge to jump down his throat. "Oliver, we're trying to help. Please tell us what you know."

Henrietta tilted her head back, eyeing Oliver suspiciously. "That's right, Oliver. Tell us."

He didn't quite meet her eye. Instead, he scooped a few grains of sugar off the table into his hand and dumped them into his tea, then shoved his cup aside. "I met Robin Masterson on Saturday at a gallery in London. Aoife's work was on display, and he was taken in by it. Transfixed, you might say."

Henrietta's blue-green eyes widened in obvious surprise. "You met with him? What does that mean?"

"He wanted to talk to me about the use of poisons in myths and folktales."

"You're joking," Henrietta said. "Why on earth—"

"I don't know why. I'm not on the why side of things. I'm on the *Oliver, I need you to do this, don't ask questions* side of things."

"And you didn't think to tell me about this meeting?"

"I had instructions not to tell anyone."

"Jeremy put Robin in touch with you. Bloody hell." Henrietta was close to sputtering. "He gave you the all clear to talk just now? When we visited—how? I was there the whole time. Did you two have a secret handshake?"

"He said we could tell everything we knew. He didn't just say everything *you* knew."

She slapped the table. "Well, there you have it, then. I didn't notice. I want to know everything about this meeting, Oliver. Every bloody word you and Robin said to each other. And Jeremy," she added. "Every word he said to you."

And it dinged with Colin. "Jeremy's off the grid."

Before Henrietta could respond, Georgina Masterson enter the cafeteria. She spotted them and stopped dead in her tracks. Then she bolted, charging to the exit to the meditation garden, not saying a word but pale, stiff, clearly on the verge of spinning out of control.

Henrietta started to her feet, but Emma shook her head. "I'll see to her."

12

Emma caught up with Georgina on a stone path that wound through tall, soothing grasses that did nothing to ease her obvious agitation. She was shaking, sobbing. "I didn't do anything to deliberately hurt anyone. I swear I didn't."

"Georgina, what's happened?"

She gulped in a breath. "Nothing, never mind."

"What are you doing at the hospital?"

"I wanted to check on Bill Hornsby. I rode up here with Nick and Melodie. They're seeing about Bryce. They're checking with his doctors now." She hugged her arms to her chest, shivering with emotion as much as the cool air. "I'm sorry I'm on edge. I'm not myself. I made a terrible mistake…" Her lower lip trembled. "Stupid, careless. Melodie was right about the tacos."

"Right about what, Georgina?" Emma asked.

"I went foraging yesterday morning at the local convent that provided us with fresh vegetables for the party. I picked a couple of dozen of chanterelles and slipped a few inedible mushrooms in with them. You're not supposed to mix different mushrooms together, but I did. I only had one bag, and I'd run out there…" She groaned in obvious frustration with herself. "*Russula emetica* is their Latin name. We know them as sickeners in the mushroom world."

Georgina lowered her arms to her sides. She wasn't in her crew uniform today and looked smaller, frailer, in leggings and a sweater, her short, fine hair wispy in the breeze. "I'm familiar with both mushrooms," Emma said. "They're quite distinct from each other and not easily confused, I would think."

"Not easily at all. Sickeners are red, for one thing. I didn't mix them together. I didn't serve the chanterelles. I grilled them thinking I might offer them to anyone who wanted to try them, knowing I'd picked them. I got cold feet and threw them out. I must have grabbed a few sickeners not thinking and added them to the mini tacos."

"You don't remember?"

She shook her head. "That's not typical of me. I was on autopilot. I'd forgotten I'd picked them, and it didn't occur to me I'd run into anything inedible in my galley. That's my usual practice. But I did, and it's my responsibility."

Emma ran her palm over the tops of tall, soothing ornamental grasses. "Sickeners have a strong bitter taste."

"Melodie noticed it. The tacos made her sick. She didn't think much of it at first since she doesn't usually go for spicy foods, anyway, and these were pretty hot. I can see others might not have noticed anything amiss, or just didn't want to say anything." Georgina gave a rueful laugh. "I did notice people didn't come back for seconds. Melodie's been very understanding. I'm an independent contractor. I work for the Fannings. Richie is sympathetic, but he'd fire me in a heartbeat if he could."

"Who else knows?"

"Nick, Richie, Melodie. She'll tell Bryce when he's well enough. And the doctors." She bit down on her lower lip, then exhaled slowly. "I can't make sense of much of anything right now. My father's very sick. I've been preoccupied with what to do—feeling guilty about not going to see him right away, trying to figure out when I should fly back to London. I've been in a haze of—I don't know what." She paused, staring at a hydrangea, its blossoms having turned a soft burgundy color for autumn. "Shock, I suppose."

"I'm sorry, Georgina."

"My mother died when I was little, and my father pawned me off on nannies and schools. We didn't have much to do with each other. Then I got into cooking and decided to sail the seven seas, as they say." Georgina picked up a few burgundy-colored hydrangea blossoms that had fallen onto the walk. She held them in the palm of her slender hand, staring at them as she continued. "I don't think he's going to make it, Agent Sharpe—Emma."

"Have you spoken with his doctors?"

Georgina nodded. She bit on her lower lip, then breathed out, as if trying to control her emotions. "My father accidentally ingested a lethal type of mushroom. He's an amateur forager, and he must have made a mistake. When I learned he was sick, I think part of me believed if I went about my life instead of running back to London, it meant he'd be okay. He'd rally."

"There aren't always clear ways forward," Emma said.

"The truth is, there's nothing I can do to help him, here or in London. He's in a coma. His liver and kidneys are failing. I doubt he'd know I was there, and he wouldn't expect it if he did know. It was to be a short, fun, beautiful cruise." She gave a mirthless laugh. "No one was supposed to get poisoned."

She dropped the hydrangea blossoms onto the walk. Emma remembered the first days after her father's death, and appreciated Georgina's sense of shock and uselessness. "How did you end up working for the Fannings?"

"Adventure. I'd been working as a chef for a couple of years for a charter business, and I ran into Richie and Nick—in Edinburgh, of all places. The Fannings were looking for a personal chef and I passed the test. Not a real test. I don't mean that. I cooked for them. They liked it, and they liked me."

"Were they in London when you were visiting your father?"

"Yes. Nick and Richie were there, too. We all looked at a yacht for sale and then went our separate ways. Bryce and Melodie had business in London. Nick and Richie visited friends and saw the sights." She brushed tears off her cheeks, red with the cold and her volatile emotions. "I'm sorry I screwed up."

Georgina sniffled, steadier as she and Emma rounded a curve, past a waist-high stone wall.

"It is a pleasant garden." Georgina nodded toward the cafeteria. "I recognize the man with you and

Agent Donovan. I don't recognize the woman. The man is Oliver York. I met him last Saturday at an art gallery in London. She was with him in Bill Hornsby's room a little while ago. How do you know them, Agent Sharpe?"

"Colin and I know Oliver through my and my family's work in art crimes. He's a highly regarded mythologist. We met Ms. Balfour—Henrietta—through him."

"They're seeing each other?"

Emma smiled. "Yes. They grew up together in the Cotswolds."

"And Bill Hornsby?"

"I don't know him well." It was an honest response, Emma thought, if not a complete one. "What about you?"

"He and my father have been friends for years, but I don't know him well, either. I imagine there's a lot I don't know about my father and his friends and colleagues, given the nature of his work. Much of it was classified, but he did teach and lecture on neurotoxicology. I wish I knew more about what he did."

They walk past more grasses, shrubs and mums in muted autumn colors. "How was your visit with your father?" Emma asked.

"It was great, actually. I realized I'm probably more like him temperamentally than I've wanted to admit. We don't go for deep, heart-to-heart chats. I'm about two notches more introspective than he is, but that's not saying much."

"Did you stay with him?"

She nodded. "For two nights—Friday and Saturday—and then I flew to Boston on Sunday to get ready for the foliage cruise. He was in good health when I left him. It's upsetting to think he's sick because of eating the wrong mushroom rather than due to a stroke or a heart attack."

"I'd like to hear more about the Aoife O'Byrne painting you mentioned," Emma said.

Georgina slowed her pace. "It wasn't at the gallery when I met Oliver, but three paintings in the same series were. I fell in love with them. The painting is a gift from my father. I don't know where he purchased it. Do you know Aoife O'Byrne's work?"

"She's a friend."

"Small world, but you must know a lot of people from your family's art recovery business and your FBI work. My father didn't steal the painting, in case that's on your mind. He's not that sort."

Emma smiled. "That wasn't on my mind. I'd like to see it. I'm not familiar with this new series."

"I'd love for you to see it, too," Georgina said, sounding genuine. "Right now I'm focused on making sure everyone recovers after yesterday and seeing to my father. I don't know what he was thinking buying me that painting. What am I going to do with an expensive painting? It shows how little he knows about my life. I suppose I wanted it that way, too. It suits us both. Now that he's sick…" She bit down on her lower lip again and winced with palpable regret. "I feel terrible for scorning his gift. Maybe it was crazy and extravagant, but it was also generous and kindly meant. That's what Bill Hornsby said, anyway."

"And spontaneous, from the sound of it," Emma said.

"Yes, I like that part. Bill Hornsby and Melodie wanted to see the Sharpe offices, but I understand no one's there? Everyone's in Ireland or someplace?"

Emma noticed the walkway was looping them back to the cafeteria entrance. "My grandfather and brother are in Ireland, and my mother's traveling."

"Aoife O'Byrne is Irish," Georgina said, matter-of-fact. "Buying one of her paintings for me was quite the grand gesture on my father's part." Her step faltered, but she stood straight, her eyes brimming with tears. "Then he goes and eats death caps. My poor, weird, impossible dad."

Her tone was filled with bemusement, pain and affection—the special kind of grief of an imminent loss. She was clearly uncomfortable with such strong emotions, as if she should be able to contain them. Tears spilled down her pale cheeks. She looked tiny, as if she could blow away as easily as a fallen leaf.

"Who else knows about the painting?" Emma asked.

"Only Hornsby."

"If it's missing, Georgina, we can help."

She shook her head, adamant. "I can't say anything to the Fannings or the crew. I'm on thin ice as it is. Can you imagine if I had the police search the yacht? No, it's fine. It's not a problem. I shouldn't have said anything to your husband. I wasn't thinking about him as an FBI agent. I was just thinking he'd been in Hornsby's cabin."

"Did you take the painting there?"

"No." Georgina pushed back strands of hair. "I'm glad death caps weren't involved yesterday. I can't see myself even accidentally bringing them into my galley. They can cause relatively mild symptoms at first. You can even start to feel better and think you're going to be okay. Meanwhile the toxin is spreading throughout your body and slowly killing you. All of a sudden you feel dramatically worse. At that point, it's often too late."

"I'm sorry about your father, Georgina," Emma said quietly.

"Thank you." Her shoulders relaxed slightly, and she seemed less tight and tense. "If he doesn't make it, I'm glad we had a good visit. We picked wild mushrooms in the same park where he was discovered on Tuesday morning. I wonder if he'd been out there all night, or if he'd gone for a walk early that morning. I like to think he'd just found a wonderful wild edible before he collapsed."

"Do you know who found him?"

"A passerby. Probably someone walking their dog." She sniffled, more under control. "He was a good man, Agent Sharpe, even if he was a crap father. *Is*," she corrected herself. "He's still with us."

They came to the soothing grasses at the cafeteria entrance. Georgina pointed at a mushroom poking up out of the mulch. "You see? Mushrooms are everywhere. It's a good year for them in England. I left my father happily playing in his kitchen with our haul of wild mushrooms and took the train to Heathrow." She paused, turning to Emma. "It didn't occur to me he'd eat death caps. Supposedly they're tasty, not like the sickeners."

"You're obviously conscientious and knowledgeable about what's involved with wild mushrooms," Emma said. "Are you sure it was your mistake yesterday?"

She hesitated for a split second. "It's the only sensible explanation." She scooped up a crab apple that had dropped onto the path and tossed it aside. "It's better than I turned my back and some well-intentioned idiot snipped inedible mushrooms into the tacos, or, worse, someone did it on purpose."

"Do you feel comfortable aboard the yacht?"

She spun around at Emma. "What? Yes, of course."

They came to the entrance. Melodie Fanning and Nick Lothian spotted Georgina and waved as they pulled open the glass door to the garden. Emma had met them briefly by the nurses' station outside Jeremy Pearson's room.

"There you are, Georgina," Melodie said. "Bryce is being discharged. Buck up, okay? I know you're upset you served the wrong mushrooms yesterday and made people sick, but it was just an unfortunate mistake. We can put it behind us. I told the doctors and that state police officer—the marine patrol one—that it wasn't in any way, shape or form deliberate."

Georgina nodded dully, the fight gone out of her.

Dressed in crisp black slacks and an orange knit top, with full makeup and jewelry, Melodie nonetheless looked tired. She stayed focused on Georgina, ignoring Emma. "Bryce and I want to get out of Heron's Cove and home to New York as soon as possible. He will need time to recover, but we should be able to leave tomorrow. It'll be a while before anyone trusts us to join us for dinner much less a cruise."

"Oh, it won't be that bad," Nick said cheerfully next to her. "Norovirus is a common scourge on big cruise ships, but people keep going on cruises. That's what most everyone will think happened here. What did happen was uncomfortable, but everyone's come out of it. I can't get too worked up about the wrong mushrooms ending up in the tacos. I don't like mushrooms myself. They taste like dirt and a bad walk in the woods to me."

Melodie laughed. "My first chuckle since this all happened, but you're right, Nick. All's well that ends well." She finally turned to Emma. "Georgina's been upset about her father, did she tell you?"

"We just were talking about their visit," Emma said, keeping her tone neutral.

"He sounds like a fascinating, brilliant man. I hope he pulls through." Melodie switched back to Nick. "Can you bring the car around to whatever exit we're supposed to use when Bryce is discharged?" She shuddered. "I hate hospitals, but everyone's been terrific here, I have to say. Georgina, will you be going back to Heron's Cove with us?"

"Yes, thank you," she said. "I'll meet you in the lobby."

Once Melodie and Nick were back in the cafeteria, Georgina spun around to Emma. "Thank you for your concern, and for your understanding." She motioned with one hand toward the glass door. "I'll go now. Apologies for the hysterics."

"Thank you for speaking with me," Emma said. "If you change your mind and would rather not stay on the yacht, for any reason—"

"I have Kevin Donovan's card, and Beth—the nurse. She offered to help. I'll be okay, though. Bill Hornsby won't be returning to the yacht, will he?"

"I don't think so."

"He delivered the painting to me, but he didn't bring any mushrooms, inedible or otherwise. The sickeners came from my foraging at the convent yesterday morning. I was preoccupied, and I made a mistake. The Fannings are private, wealthy people. I imagine they want to avoid unnecessary scrutiny. I can't blame them." Georgina smiled, clearly less stressed. "Your grandfather really is a private art detective?"

"He is," Emma said.

"That's excellent." She paused, staring at a cluster of mums. "I can't give up on my father yet. People have survived death cap poisoning."

"We'll stay in touch."

Georgina pulled her gaze from the mums and shifted to Emma. "Thank you for coming after me, and for being so decent. I'm enjoying Heron's Cove, believe it or not. Maybe one day I'll come back when my life isn't so chaotic. Give Bill Hornsby my best, won't you? In case I don't see him?"

She didn't wait for an answer and ran back into the cafeteria, presumably to hook up with Melodie and Nick to await Bryce's discharge.

Emma resisted the urge to walk in the meditation garden on her own. In her time with the sisters, she'd come to appreciate gardens designed for quieting the mind. Instead, she returned to the cafeteria.

Oliver was alone at the table. "Henrietta and Colin have gone to see about our art-consultant friend. I suspect they'll be discussing things to which I'm not privy, don't want to be and can't be, given my status as a mild-mannered mythologist and gentleman farmer. You, Emma, though—feel free to join them. I'll be fine here."

"I'll hang out here with you. We can talk."

He gave her a cheeky smile. "I was afraid you might say that."

Colin entered a small waiting room on Jeremy's floor. A handful of chairs were lined up against the wall, but Henrietta stood at the windows, looking out at the same view her MI5 superior had of the hospital's main entrance. She'd wanted to talk to Colin alone.

He eased next to her. "Just be sure whatever you tell me is the truth, Henrietta. No bullshit. No lies."

"Of course. I doubt I know anything you don't know or can't surmise. We're on your patch. Chances are you know more than I do, but I thought we should talk. Jeremy followed Georgina to Boston as William Hornsby and got himself invited on the cruise. She doesn't know his real identity, or mine. She met Oliver as himself." The faintest of smiles. "Although sometimes I wonder if anyone knows Oliver's real identity. He says I'm the only one who'd have him. The reverse is no doubt true, too."

Colin had worked under his share of false identities. "Does Robin Masterson know Jeremy's with UK intelligence?"

"Yes. William Hornsby is a cover story for public consumption."

"How long have they known each other?"

"I don't have specific dates. As an expert in neurotoxins, Robin helped in the dismantling of the Soviet Union's chemical weapon stockpiles starting in the nineties. I believe he and Jeremy met then, but I'm not positive. Before my time." Henrietta glanced sideways at Colin. "I don't know if Robin asked Jeremy to deliver the Aoife O'Byrne painting to Georgina, or if he took it upon himself to do so."

"Does he suspect someone deliberately fed Robin the poisonous mushrooms?" Colin asked.

"You mean tried to kill him, and likely will succeed in doing so? Everything points to suicide, but I don't know what Jeremy suspects." A hint of irritation in her voice. "I doubt at this point he has a clear grasp on what's going on, either—if anything *is* going on that concerns us in our official capacities. Poisonous mushrooms, a missing painting, a wealthy couple with God knows who for friends—not to mention church rummage sales and you lot."

"Don't forget bean-hole suppers."

There was a spark of humor in her eyes. "How could I ever?" She sighed. "Jeremy went his own way here, Colin. Your instincts are on target about that. Oliver and I are doing what we can to find out what he's up to, but we can only go so far."

"So Jeremy's AWOL," Colin said.

"I wouldn't go that far. All I know is I went to Dublin and when I returned, Robin Masterson was deathly ill. Next thing, Jeremy's here in Maine, vomiting off a yacht deck."

"Not quite so dramatic as that. He puked on his cabin floor."

"Well, then."

Colin expected there were multiple steps between "I went to Dublin" and "next thing," but he wanted to let Henrietta talk.

"I only got involved when I tried to reach Oliver on Saturday. I got that feeling one gets when I know Jeremy's asked him to do something. I called Jeremy, but he blew me off." Henrietta shrugged. "I decided to have a look at what he was up to these days and discovered Robin Masterson had called him on Friday."

"You found out Robin flew to Dublin on Monday and followed his trail."

"I *did* meet my friend for shopping and tea. I didn't expect to return to Robin near death. Of course my mind first went to contact with a nerve agent, but that's not the case. There were bits of these death cap mushrooms in his kitchen."

"Any other mushrooms in his place besides these death caps?" Colin asked.

"Loads, including chanterelles. They're a particular favorite of mine, or they were. I won't be in a rush to look at mushrooms after this mess, but I do love them. If Robin had been discovered an hour later, he'd have been dead."

Colin pictured the scene. "It wasn't a passerby who found him, was it, Henrietta?"

Her shoulders slumped slightly. "No, it wasn't."

"Did Jeremy tell you he found Robin, or did you have to find out on your own?"

"What do you think?" She left it at that. "I didn't know he'd asked Oliver to speak with Robin until just now in the cafeteria. Poisons in myths and folktales? An odd request, if you ask me. I understand Robin has a long-standing interest in art—hence, his friendship with 'William Hornsby'—and he's eccentric. I knew Oliver was holding back, but not about Thor or whatever. Or didn't Thor ever get poisoned?"

Colin smiled. "You're asking me?"

She managed a laugh. "I see Emma's knowledge hasn't rubbed off on you. How did we get mixed up with those two?" Her expression warmed. "But she's okay, isn't she?"

"She is. We are."

Henrietta spun around but didn't take a seat. Colin suspected her agitated mood had as much to do with Oliver and their relationship as it did with Jeremy's situation. She stared at a chart on congestive heart failure.

"So Robin Masterson meets Oliver at a London gallery on Saturday to talk poisons," Colin said. "Georgina falls in love with Aoife O'Byrne's paintings at the gallery. She and Dad go mushroom foraging on Sunday morning. He sees her off to Heathrow, flies to Dublin the next day and buys a painting for her—and then comes home, eats death caps and falls sick?"

"Those are the facts as I know them."

"When did Jeremy take possession of the painting?"

Henrietta didn't answer.

Colin studied her. "I see. *After* he finds his friend unconscious in the park."

"I don't know for certain. I didn't ask."

"Any chance Georgina poisoned her own father?"

"You are devious, Colin."

He shrugged. "Jeremy followed her for a reason."

Henrietta moved to a blood-pressure chart. "I think she's the daughter of a friend he's sorry to lose. Perhaps Jeremy feels he owes Robin, or that Georgina could shed light on her father's mental state when she left on Sunday. Something he said might make sense to Jeremy but not to her. You're an experienced agent, Colin. You get the drift."

"And Jeremy just ends up on the yacht?"

"He says he got caught up in events and didn't want to call attention to Georgina or to himself."

"You should have told me you were on your way to Heron's Cove."

"You had a good time at your brother's wedding, and you wouldn't have if Oliver or I had told you we were on our way. Also, you're assuming Oliver and I didn't announce our presence on US soil to someone on a need-to-know basis. I'm speaking hypothetically. That reminds me. How is Agent Yankowski? I apologize for not asking sooner."

"He's back to work. Rough recovery."

"Shot in the line of duty. One hears about it…knows people…"

"Feel free to call him," Colin said, cool.

"I sent him a get well card after he was shot. I'll cut to the chase, Colin. We have no reason to suspect any nerve agent is missing, stolen or was slipped into the US for any reason."

"Robin Masterson has the expertise to produce something very lethal."

"Yes, but he never has done. Why would he start now? He's retired, and he doesn't have the proper equipment in his flat." Henrietta gave up on the posters and turned to Colin. "To be perfectly frank, I rather suspect we've all been sucked into a difficult father-daughter relationship. Robin's been an eccentric, unavailable father with a critical job, and Georgina's had only him for most of her life. They have a passion for wild foraging in common and that's about it."

"You and Oliver are here on your own, unofficially," Colin said.

She pushed her hair back with both hands. "It's all knots and snarls with this seacoast wind."

End of discussion. Colin winked at her. "You should be here in January."

They left the waiting room and started past the nurses' station toward Jeremy's room. Melodie Fanning and Nick Lothian were outside Bryce's room farther down the hall. A passing, awkward wave from

Nick as they went in. The two women kept their eyes pinned straight ahead.

Henrietta smiled half-heartedly. "Pretending not to see the FBI agent. I know that move."

Colin did, too. He trusted Henrietta, to a point, but he wouldn't want to have his back to her if she needed something he didn't want to give her, or if he got between her and the success of an MI5 mission. Cynical, maybe, but also practical. She might not appreciate his attitude, but she'd understand it. Right now, though, she was a British intelligence officer stuck in Maine with a sick superior, needing information, cooperation and, very likely, the help of Oliver's two FBI contacts.

A nurse updated them. Jeremy would likely be released later that afternoon unless his condition deteriorated for some reason, but that wasn't expected to happen. Finian Bracken arrived at the hospital in his role as a local priest, visiting the sick, and repeated his offer of the rectory for the recovering MI5 agent.

"You are all very welcome to stay as long as you'd like," Finian said.

"You're a wonderful friend, Father Bracken," Henrietta said. "Thank you."

Colin figured Finian had a good idea Henrietta and Oliver's sick friend wasn't just an art consultant. He warned Finian about his remark about last rites. His Irish priest friend merely shook his head as he went in to see Jeremy.

Henrietta eased next to him. "Oliver and I will see to our Mr. Hornsby. We'll set him up in the rectory and stick to our story about how we all know each other."

Through the Sharpes, basically. "We'll get the rest of his things off the yacht."

"Thank you. I'll find Oliver—never mind. Here he is now."

With Emma, walking from the elevators.

Henrietta and Oliver ducked into Jeremy's room, passing Finian on the way out, off to visit other patients. "I ran into Kevin," Emma told Colin. "He's on the way to Heron's Cove."

"Great. I'll meet him there. Someone needs to clear out our friend's cabin, don't you think? What about you? Where are you off to?"

"I'll join you in Heron's Cove."

Colin ducked into the room and said goodbye to the three Brits. Jeremy lifted his fingers in what passed as a wave. He still looked pathetic, but Colin didn't know if he was putting on a bit—whether to keep his FBI friends or his MI5 colleague at bay was anyone's guess. He wouldn't want Henrietta on his case.

Oliver, for once, didn't say a word.

Colin met Emma at the elevators. He smiled, glad to be here, with her. "It's a beautiful day. We could be kayaking on the river."

"There's yet time before winter, if not before dark."

They hadn't had nearly enough time together in the weeks since her father's death, but he saw no resentment or bitterness or even regret in her green eyes. She was steady, analytical and centered, but she was also an optimist. And a good agent. As they headed to their vehicles, she asked him about his conversation with Henrietta. He told her. "Did you get anything else out of Oliver?" he asked when they reached her car.

"More complaints about the hospital tea."

"Figures." Colin kissed her on the cheek. "See you in Heron's Cove."

"Drive safe."

He grinned at her. "With Kevin out there mad at me? You bet."

13

Bryce's release was delayed—the doctors wanted to run a couple of precautionary tests—and Melodie decided to send Georgina and Nick back to the yacht so they could prepare for Bryce's release. Nick would then return to the hospital and pick them up. "Nick's cab service," he said cheerfully as he got behind the wheel of his rental car.

Georgina jumped into the passenger seat, marginally less embarrassed at having made a fool of herself in front of the FBI agents. "That's so cynical, Nick. The hospital's been great."

"Keeping our diners alive. Note I didn't say *your* diners."

She sputtered into laughter. "You're horrible."

He glanced at her with a grin, then made a face. "And you look terrible, Georgie. Damn."

"You have a great bedside manner, Mr. Lothian."

"Sometimes you have to cut through the lousy mood with irreverent humor." He started the engine and backed out of the parking space. "You're too hard on yourself."

"I poisoned people yesterday, Nick. I picked the inedible mushrooms. I allowed myself to get distracted and snipped them raw into a spicy hors d'oeuvres. I could have done a hundred other things with them and I probably wouldn't have made people sick, or people would have noticed their bad taste and spit them out like Melodie did. She just got lucky and noticed."

"I get it. You did the one thing that got a dozen people sick. Yuck. Ouch. Bad."

"I didn't want to believe it." She sighed out her window. She still *didn't* believe it, deep down, but what good would denying the obvious truth do? "It doesn't matter. I'm the chef. I'm responsible for the food served yesterday."

"We've all made mistakes, Georgina. Are you sure you're not falling on your sword because Melodie wants you to? Just because she didn't like the tacos doesn't mean it was the tacos, you know."

"She and Bryce want to get out of here as soon as he's medically cleared to travel. They don't need lingering questions about yesterday."

"With law enforcement, you mean."

She crossed her arms tightly on her chest. "It was an innocent mistake with mushrooms."

"Uh-uh." Nick turned onto the main road out of the hospital. "There's no reason to think the Fannings have anything to hide from law enforcement, but don't let Melodie pressure you into admitting to poisoning people unless you're sure you did, okay?"

She smiled at him. "Okay, Nick."

"Good. I wouldn't want the FBI sniffing around if I were Bryce and Melodie. It's like these doctors. They start looking for things, they're going to find something."

"You with the cynicism again."

"I'm just saying the Fannings can have nothing to hide while at the same time not want to invite scrutiny. Even if they do have something to hide, it doesn't mean it has anything to do with bad mushrooms ending up in the tacos."

"Inedible. They hadn't gone bad."

He grinned at her. "Okay, inedible mushrooms. And you're right. I am being cynical. The wrong mushrooms were served at an otherwise fun, uneventful party. End of story."

For you, maybe. But Georgina would accept blame for an unfortunate mistake in misidentifying mushrooms, and then they could be on their way out of Heron's Cove. She didn't know what would happen with Bill Hornsby, but he'd be okay—and he had friends here. He didn't need her to look after him.

She struggled to convince herself she'd added sickeners to the tacos and couldn't remember, but Melodie, Bryce, Richie and, if he were being honest, Nick wanted her to let it go. Cop to it and move on. Easier for everyone.

Her galley, her responsibility.

And the Aoife O'Byrne painting?

If someone had stolen it, misplaced it or destroyed it, what difference did it make to her?

None at all.

When they arrived at the marina and walked down

to the docks, Georgina saw Kevin Donovan alone out past the Sharpe offices. "I'll talk to him," she told Nick.

"You don't have to talk to him, Georgie. Let the skipper and the Fannings deal with the cops."

"I don't mind. He and a nurse gave me a lift back here last night. Anyway, I have nothing to hide. You can let Richie know if you want."

"No problem. Do your thing. I'll check in with Richie and head back to the hospital."

Nick trotted onto the yacht. Georgina hesitated, then approached Kevin and smiled at him. "I just got back from the hospital. I'm supposed to help get ready for Bryce Fanning to come back here. He's being discharged soon."

"Glad to know he's recovering," Kevin said.

"Is your brother joining you?"

"Two minutes out."

"The yacht's a lot more pleasant than when you two were here yesterday. You're welcome to check out the kitchen. The galley, as we say. It's my domain, and you have my permission to take a look. Open the drawers and cabinets, pull everything out of the fridge. Whatever you want."

Kevin frowned at her. "Are you all right?"

"Brilliant. It's been my kind of weekend." She heard her sarcasm—the catch in her voice—and looked up at the sky, a clear autumnal blue. She fought tears as she smiled again at the handsome marine patrol officer. "I'm now the mushroom poisoner extraordinaire. Don't mind me. I'm feeling sorry for myself. Give me a minute. I'll let Richie know I've invited you and your brother on board."

With that, she bolted, bursting into tears with no idea

what she'd do next. Calm down and let Richie handle the Donovans? Lock herself in her cabin? Jump into the river? She ran through a long list of options as she went up to the sundeck. By the time she found Richie on the bridge, she felt reasonably sane. Somehow articulating her options—from realistic to crazy—helped.

"Sure," Richie said when she told him about the Donovan brothers. "I'll look after them."

Georgina stifled a laugh of pure relief. See? A mountain out of a molehill. What she needed, she thought, was a good long run…and word from London that her father was improving. That would help most of all.

14

When Colin arrived in Heron's Cove, he found his youngest brother on the pebbled beach in front of the inn on the opposite side of the Sharpe offices from the marina. A few inn guests were sitting on the porch in the sun, reading books and watching the tidal river. "Hey, Kevin," Colin said. "You didn't bring Beth doughnuts this morning?"

"No."

"She made up an excuse to check on Hornsby and Bryce Fanning hoping to see you." But Kevin didn't answer, and Colin saw he was in no mood and gave it up. "What's up?"

"Georgina's gone on a run. We have permission to go on board the yacht. Check out her galley." He glanced sideways at Colin. "Have you pried the truth out of your British friends yet?"

"Working on it."

Kevin toed a river-polished stone loose. "Nick Lothian drove back to hospital to get Bryce and Melodie Fanning. Richie Hillier and the other crew members are on board."

"I'll collect the rest of Hornsby's things and then go up to the galley. Join me?"

Kevin scooped up the stone and stood up with it. "I'm good."

Colin felt his brother's coolness. "Kevin—"

"You don't need to explain to me, Colin. Do your thing."

"I know Bill Hornsby from my work. He's here because Georgina Masterson's father is deathly ill due to mushroom poisoning."

Kevin looked out at a dingy bobbing in the water on the opposite shore. "Who's the father?"

Colin told him what he could about the Mastersons, the Aoife O'Byrne painting and Henrietta's and Oliver's visit—without mentioning MI5.

Kevin got the picture. "Newly retired, just saw his daughter off after a satisfying visit—what, suicide?"

"That's what everyone seems to think," Colin said. "His final act was to buy Georgina the painting. She's having a rough time."

"Tough to lose your father, but to have him take his own life after you visit him…" Kevin rubbed his stone with his thumb. "That's bad."

Colin nodded and picked up a stone for himself. It was cool, wet; bits of sand stuck to it. He liked its solid feel in his hand as he and Kevin talked about death. "Georgina must wonder if she was the catalyst for her father poisoning himself. But we don't know that's what happened." He threw his stone but it was one lousy effort. Out of practice. "I called Matt Yankowski on my way down here."

"How'd that go?"

"He was just back from Sunday brunch with his wife and sitting in her knitting shop on Newbury Street."

"Knitting shop's doing well?"

"Yank says it is. Lucy's happy. That's what counts for him."

Colin hadn't seen Lucy Yankowski since Tim Sharpe's funeral. Yank had still been in the hospital. She'd given up her job as a clinical psychologist in Northern Virginia to move to Boston after he'd started HIT. It turned out she was ready for a career change, but she hadn't known that in those first tense, early months after he'd announced he was heading his own small team away from the crush of Washington and FBI Headquarters.

Kevin squinted at the sunlit river. "He's getting your team involved in this thing?"

"As needed."

"I won't ask you to elaborate." He grabbed another stone. "I don't need to give you room to maneuver. You'll take it."

"Kevin—"

His brother grinned. "Just stating the facts." He nodded toward the parking lot. "Emma's here. She'll want to join you packing up your buddy Hornsby's stuff."

"What are you going to do?"

"Head back to Rock Point." Kevin reared back and flung his stone into the water, beating Colin's by yards. "I'm meeting Beth for a drink at Hurley's after she gets off work."

"That beats doughnuts."

Kevin pretended not to hear him as he returned to his truck. Colin watched a seagull arc above the river and swoop past the channel out to sea. Part of him wished he could do the same, provided he had Emma with him.

He resisted another try with a stone and headed up to the docks to find Emma.

As far as Colin could tell, Jeremy's cabin was unchanged since yesterday morning—except for the cleaned rug. Emma sat at the end of the bed while he grabbed a battered soft-sided suitcase out of the closet.

Richie Hillier had followed them into the cabin. "We scrubbed down the entire yacht, but we only did the carpet in here. We didn't touch anything else. We decided to wait until we have Mr. Hornsby's permission or he leaves. He won't be returning here once he's out of the hospital?"

"He's staying with friends in the area while he recuperates," Emma said.

Colin placed the suitcase on the bed. "He's probably had this thing since I was in kindergarten. What was it like here yesterday before people started getting sick?"

Richie hovered in the doorway. "Georgina left early for her run to the convent. The nuns delivered the vegetable order about the same time she got back, and she went straight to work on the party. A few of the passengers walked up Ocean Avenue to see the summerhouses. Bryce didn't go out. He read on the sundeck. Melodie stayed to greet guests arriving for the day. It was a beautiful New England fall day, and everyone was enjoying it."

"And Georgina?" Emma asked. "How did she strike you?"

"About how you'd expect under the circumstances. It doesn't look good for her father, I'm afraid, but she's coping as best she can. She's been torn about what to do. They aren't close, but the Fannings have made clear she can leave anytime to be with him. We will do all we can to help. I have a daughter her age myself."

Colin collected an armful of clothes out of the closet and placed them in the suitcase. Everything was casual and understated but high quality, appropriate for a London art consultant. He hadn't paid much attention to what Jeremy had worn in their previous interactions.

Absolutely no sign of the Aoife O'Byrne painting. "Did Bill leave anything in another part of the yacht?" Colin asked.

"Not that I'm aware of," Richie said. "We'd have returned any of his things we found during cleaning—probably would have left them on the bed."

Emma stood up. "Were you surprised when Melodie Fanning invited him on board at the last minute?"

Richie shrugged. "She's done that sort of thing before. Bryce doesn't seem to mind. We'll leave as soon as he's well enough to travel. I doubt that'll be tomorrow, but maybe by Tuesday."

Colin walked over to the entertainment center. Not a bad place to spend a few days cruising the New England coast. He didn't notice anything that belonged to Jeremy. "Did you get a chance to interact with Bill Hornsby or any of the other passengers?"

Richie shook his head. "Not really. Hornsby chatted me up over Scotch Thursday night. I wasn't expecting that. It's not that it was unusual—people are interested in yachts, what I do—but it struck me as unusual for an art consultant. That could be my ignorance or prejudice. For the most part I don't interact much with passengers and guests. I'm too busy. I have a crew. It's not a problem for a short cruise, but I hope we'll have more people when the Fannings buy their new yacht—especially if they're going to have these spontaneous parties. I don't know what will happen with Georgina. I'm not sure she'll be back after she deals with her father's situation."

Colin looked at him. "Is she leaving for London?"

"Not yet that I'm aware of, but I don't think she has much longer if she wants to see him." Richie grimaced, awkward. "That's what Melodie said this morning. I don't have any information myself. Melodie's taking the mistake with the mushrooms well, but maybe she's just smoothing Georgina's way out of here. Let her go home to her father. Don't invite her back."

"She's passionate about wild edibles," Emma said.

"Loves foraging. She'll be happier with a job that allows for it. Working on yachts—not much opportunity to slip off to the woods to pick things. She sketches wild plants on her breaks. I've seen her. She'll have something simmering on the stove, and sit at the counter and sketch fiddleheads. She has some stored in the galley. I'll show you if you'd like."

Colin zipped up the bag. "That'd be great. I'm all set here."

He took the suitcase with him. Emma checked the cabin to make sure they had everything. Richie shut the door behind them and led them up to the galley. He went straight to a drawer by the refrigerator. He opened it up and pulled out a stack of sketches on thick white paper. "Here you go," he said.

He set the sketches on the peninsula in front of three

bar stools. Emma sat on one of the stools. Colin stood next to her. The top sketch was, in fact, of fiddleheads, a spring favorite with his father. It was precise and detailed, done with colored pencils.

Richie stayed on the other side of the counter. "Georgina says drawing her wild edibles, as she calls them, helps her memorize and recognize traits to make accurate identification easier."

Emma flipped through several more sketches, pausing at one of red-capped mushrooms. "These look like the ones Sister Cecilia pointed out this morning. Have you seen any mushrooms like this on the yacht?"

"No, ma'am," Richie said. "Are they what made people sick yesterday?"

"That's not for me to say."

She flipped to the next sketch, and Colin saw it was different from the first ones—dragons done in black pencil. Three of the dragons were in flight, and one was breathing fire from a cave. He glanced at Richie. "Dragons?"

"I haven't seen that one, but Georgina does enjoy her dragons. I think she's watched every dragon movie ever made. Look, is there anything else? I have work to do before Melodie and Nick get back with Bryce."

"Thanks for talking with us," Emma said.

"Right. No problem. Glad Mr. Hornsby will be okay. You'll see yourselves out?"

"Sure thing," Colin said.

With Richie gone, Emma took another turn through the sketches. "Dragons, fiddleheads, mushrooms, violets and dandelions." She eased off the stool and stood straight. "Drawing could be therapeutic for her, especially now with her father in such rough shape."

"Are you doing okay with this, given Tim?"

She smiled at him. "I am. Thank you for asking."

Melodie and Nick entered the galley. "Richie warned us you were here," Melodie said, beelining for the refrigerator. "We're just back with Bryce. He's resting. The drive from the hospital was taxing. He's worn out, poor guy."

"I imagine he is." Emma pointed at the sketches. "The captain showed us these."

"Oh, yes," Melodie said. "Georgina's work. A bit amateurish but she enjoys doing them."

Nick nodded. "She says having to think about whether to draw gills on a mushroom helps her remember identifying traits. I thought only fish had gills."

Melodie rolled her eyes but was clearly amused. She took a bottle of ginger ale out of the refrigerator. "Bryce is resting on the sundeck. He wants some fresh air, and he wants to talk to you, Agent Sharpe and Agent Donovan. You'll keep in mind he's ill, won't you? I'll put together a tray for him."

"Let me do up the tray," Nick said, edging her away from the refrigerator.

She set the ginger ale on the counter and thanked him. "Bryce will recover, but I've never seen him so sick. He's not angry with Georgina, either. We want her to go back to London and see her father. Get through that ordeal, and then we can figure out what's next."

Nick opened an upper cupboard and got a jar of applesauce and a box of saltines. "Georgie's a great chef. She's young. I hope this episode doesn't rock her confidence."

"I'm glad she's gone for a run," Melodie said. "She doesn't have to do any work for us before she leaves.

We can manage food without her. I didn't pressure her about admitting to using the wrong mushrooms, either."

"She's admitted to them, hasn't she?" Emma asked.

"Yes, but I think she suspected she didn't have much choice. I haven't told her, but I found the bag she took to the convent. It had bits and pieces of chanterelles and red mushrooms."

Nick microwaved a mug of water and pulled open a drawer for a tea bag. He seemed to be trying to focus on his work and stay out of the conversation.

Colin eyed Melodie. "Where was this bag?"

"In the galley pantry. The crew who cleaned in here wouldn't have noticed it. I'd seen her come back with it, so I knew what it was."

"Were you looking for it?" Emma asked.

"Half yes, half no." Melodie sighed, watching Nick. "I threw out the bag at the hospital. I was going to give it to Bryce's doctors, but I changed my mind. Everyone's on the mend. There's no way to prove any of the mushrooms Georgina picked were the actual ones that made people sick. It just doesn't matter at this point."

"I agree," Nick said.

Melodie shifted to Emma and Colin. "It was controlled chaos in here yesterday. Anyone could have grabbed the bag assuming any mushrooms inside were okay to eat. Given the state Georgina's in, I'm not surprised she did just that herself, no matter what kind of foraging expert she thinks she is."

Nick dug a tray out of a lower cupboard. "Anyone else want anything?"

"Nothing for me," Melodie said stiffly.

Emma shook her head. "We're fine, thanks."

"I'll bring Bryce a little of everything," Nick said,

opening up the ginger ale. "He can have what he wants, or nothing if that suits him."

"Thank you, Nick."

Colin could see she was tired and stressed. She watched Nick pour the ginger ale, as if she appreciated the touch of normalcy in her weekend. She led them to the sundeck. She took in a quick breath when she saw her husband tucked under a blanket on a cushioned lounge. "We had such a lovely few days planned," she said half to herself. "I know we're lucky it wasn't worse, but it's bad enough, thank you very much."

Bryce tried to sit up, but he winced and placed his arm across his midsection, the blanket falling to one side. He moaned, clearly in pain. "My muscles ache from vomiting," he said, his voice hoarse. "I'm never allowing mushrooms in one of my kitchens again."

"But you're doing so much better," Melodie said.

"I guess. Yesterday I'd have said get me a gun so I could shoot myself. Today I'm sitting in the sun. Progress." He shivered. "It's colder than I thought."

Nick arrived with the tray and set it on a low table in front of Bryce. He yawned, barely awake. Nick gave him a sympathetic look, but said nothing as he moved to the bar.

Melodie adjusted her husband's blanket. "Maybe we should get you to bed." When he didn't answer, she looked up at Colin. "He just wanted to say hello and thank you for your help. Best we let him sleep, I think."

Colin nodded. "Thanks for letting us collect Bill Hornsby's stuff, Mrs. Fanning. If you have any concerns, I gave your captain my card. Please don't hesitate to call."

He grabbed Jeremy-Bill's battered bag. Once they

were back out on the pier, Emma showed him a text from Oliver. We're at the rectory getting our friend settled.

As he read the text, Colin realized how much he hated this situation, an uneasy mix of personal and professional.

Emma pocketed her phone. "Meet you in Rock Point?"

He nodded. "Sounds good to me."

15

Oliver debated raking leaves behind the rectory. It was a glorious afternoon. Why not rake? He itched to do something productive. But not many leaves had yet fallen, and he had a distracted mind, dangerous with bean holes nearby. He didn't want to tumble into one and break a leg, but he'd discovered they were covered, presumably for safety purposes, until the pots went in them.

He'd about talked himself into searching for a rake—in the garage, perhaps?—when Henrietta banged out of the back door. She'd been getting her restless, irritable colleague settled in the rectory den. Oliver would have taken the sofa in the den, but the first item of contention between Henrietta and Jeremy had been over Jeremy's ability to get up the stairs. He said he could. Henrietta said it was foolish and would only delay his recovery, *and* she had no intention of scraping him off the steps if he should collapse. She'd finally argued it would be rude to their host. Jeremy hadn't agreed, he'd simply started to fall asleep.

"I wonder what his wife would do if she were here," Henrietta said. "Let him collapse and leave him where he landed, I expect. I've never met her. She must be— what's the word I'm looking for?"

"Intrepid."

"Long-suffering. I told him if he overdoes it, I'll phone for an ambulance and he'll be back in the hospital in a flash."

"He hates having you give him a hand," Oliver said.

"I told him better me than you."

Lame humor, Oliver thought. He'd offered to get Jeremy settled. Finian had, too, but Henrietta had seen it as her responsibility.

She glanced around the small lawn with its trees and shrubs. "Not many flowers." She smiled at Oliver. "I'm sorry if I shouted. Did I shout?"

"You didn't shout."

"In my head I was shouting." She sighed, stretching her arms above her and letting them fall to her sides. "If only we were here for a proper visit. Do you wish you'd stayed in England instead of letting me drag you to Maine?"

"I wish we were on a ramble at the farm. We could hold hands and listen to the baa of sheep, the moo of cows, the distant ring of church bells and the chirping of birds."

She sputtered into laughter. "I hope you've never aspired to write poetry."

He grinned at her. "Only to you."

"Oh, Oliver." She put her arms around him. "Why did we wait so long to fall in love?"

"There's a time for everything. Now is our time."

He kissed her softly, not caring who might turn up in the church driveway or out on the street. "I'm played out," she said, resting her head on his shoulder. "I don't know if I can do this anymore. The thought of that poor girl losing her father..." She didn't finish, stood straight and glanced around. "No rake?"

"There must be but I haven't looked."

"So you've been out here just contemplating raking?"

"And falling into bean holes."

"I was right to put out my shingle as a garden designer. I love it—I'd have found the rake and then contemplated while raking. We could do it, you know."

"Do what, Henrietta?" Her thoughts sometimes shot ahead of where he was in the conversation.

"I could design gardens, and we could do justice to the farm. Local sourcing is the rage. There are so many possibilities with vegetables and livestock." She tilted her head back, those incisive eyes on him. "Could you live a quiet life?"

"I do live a quiet life."

She snorted. "Compared to your days stealing art from alarmed buildings, I suppose you do, but our friend in the den keeps you busy. You won't be at his beck and call forever."

"Won't I?"

"Nor do you deserve to be," Henrietta added quietly.

"You're pining for more than investing in Dexter cattle and kale patches. What is it, love?"

"Babies," she said, then grinned. "And not cow babies and sheep babies. But, there. I've said it, and you can absorb it while we have whatever Father Bracken has in the oven."

Oliver wasn't exactly wobbly after her pronouncement, but he did feel a flutter in his knees as he followed her into the rectory kitchen. Leave it to Henrietta to drop something like that on him in the midst of a poison mushroom debacle. Why not on a ramble in the rolling Cotswolds hills or by the fire with a good Scotch?

But this was why he loved her. She could keep classified secrets as a trained, experienced intelligence agent, but in her personal life, once something gelled and needed to be said, out it popped. She wasn't one to stew.

He eyed a steaming casserole on hot pads. "It smells all right. What is it?"

"Franny Maroney brought it," Finian said, as if that provided insight into the casserole's contents. "She's the widowed grandmother of yesterday's bride. She referred to it as a noodle casserole."

"That leaves considerable room for interpretation and execution," Oliver said.

"Egg noodles, beef, cheese, tomato sauce, green olives. I've had it before. It's surprisingly delicious."

Oliver didn't want to come across as ungrateful. "Generous of her."

"Dropping it off also gave her an excuse to see what's going on here," Henrietta said.

Finian smiled. "I've learned never to underestimate my white-haired parishioners—which is most of them. They keep me on my toes."

Oliver pulled off his jacket and hung it on a peg by the door. "Given the sort of friends you keep, it's probably not a bad idea."

"No comment." Finian opened the refrigerator. "I'll make a salad. I doubt your sick friend should eat the casserole, even if he does decide he wants to give it a go. I can do toast and tea for him."

"I'll let him know and see if he wants anything else," Henrietta said. Oliver noticed she hadn't worn a jacket on her brief excursion outside. If anything, she'd needed a dose of the brisk coastal air.

Oliver waited until she withdrew. "I'm sorry, Finian. Henrietta and I never expected to put you in the middle of a drama."

"I'm delighted to help."

He didn't give any indication he wasn't sincere. Oliver supposed the events of the past twenty-four hours could have livened up Finian's life in the small fishing village. Rummage sales, bean-hole suppers, visiting the sick, hearing confessions, saying Mass, burying the dead. Not uneventful but not the same as getting mixed up with MI5 and FBI goings-on. Surely their Irish priest friend realized Henrietta wasn't simply a garden designer and William Hornsby wasn't simply an art consultant—not at all an art consultant, from what Oliver knew of his MI5 contact.

Finian was working on his salad when Colin and Emma arrived at the back door. Colin set a soft-sided bag on the floor. "Our friend's clothes and such from his cabin."

"Above and beyond the call of duty, surely," Oliver said.

Colin grinned. "Damn right."

"Any blackmail material?"

"Nothing that exciting. Boxers, Colgate, disposable razor. Pepcid."

"Pepcid must be a staple for him."

Henrietta returned from the den, smiling, less tired looking as she greeted Emma and Colin. She turned to Finian. "He's asleep. I wouldn't be surprised if he's out until morning. He's been through quite an ordeal. I told him we identified the probable mushroom in question. He has no recollection of eating anything that struck him as off. He questions his ability to taste. Too much Scotch, I told him. He scoffed. Even as a keen gardener, I would never trust myself with wild mushrooms."

Finian invited the two FBI agents to stay for dinner. They accepted, and Colin took the suitcase to the den, promising not to awaken his recuperating friend. Oliver struggled to call him by the name he was using with Georgina and the Fannings, but he did so, following Henrietta's lead. But when Colin returned to the kitchen, he looked at his priest friend. "We know William Hornsby as Jeremy. Keep it to yourself."

"Of course." Finian grabbed lettuce out of the refrigerator. "We'll eat in the dining room. I don't use it often enough."

"Here, I'll help," Henrietta said. "Breakfast, tea, lunch, dinner—I've lost track at this point but I'm famished."

Finian added a cucumber and tomato to the lettuce in the sink. "We need to bring cutlery from the kitchen. Everything else is in the dining room."

In another moment, Henrietta had cutlery heaped on a tray and Oliver was following her down the hall to the dining room. Emma and Colin were already there, setting out plates on a long rectangular table. The room had a faded, old-fashioned appeal with its simple furnishings and lace tablecloth. Henrietta set the tray on the table and chatted with Finian. Oliver knew what she was up to. She was pretending she was the garden designer friend visiting from England and had nothing to do with the recovering MI5 officer—art consultant in the den, the two glowering FBI agents or even him, the art thief. Finian wasn't involved, at least directly, in the current goings-on.

Finian opened a drawer and withdrew cloth napkins that looked as if they'd been in the rectory since the start of the Cold War. He set them in a stack on the table. "I'll get dinner," he said, retreating down the hall to the kitchen.

Oliver noticed an antique whiskey alcohol measurement device on the shelf of the cupboard. He was a whiskey enthusiast himself and knew its purpose. It was next to a nearly empty bottle of Bracken Distillers 15-year-old, a rare peated single malt Finian had put into casks himself, before tragedy had changed his life forever. Oliver could see Finian and Declan Bracken as lads, filled with hopes and dreams as they'd launched their whiskey business.

Colin grabbed several knives from Henrietta's tray.

Oliver distributed the napkins. "I've been thinking about my chat with Robin Masterson in London. I wonder if his questions might be relevant. There's no guarantee. I understand that."

"Best to err on the side of telling more rather than less," Colin said, almost amiable.

"I agree," Emma said. "We'd like to hear everything you can remember about your meeting."

Oliver glanced at Henrietta for confirmation. She nodded before he could speak. Reading his mind again.

She was good at that. He, on the other hand, was hope-less, ever the last to know what someone was thinking.

She lifted two long-stemmed goblets from the cabinet. "This was your first time meeting Robin?"

"Yes," Oliver said. "He was polite, grateful for my time and appreciative of my expertise. I did my best to point him in the right direction. Once Georgina was on her way, we walked to the pub and chatted about poisons over pints of lager."

"As one does," Henrietta said, setting the glasses on the table.

Oliver relaxed slightly, perhaps the intent behind her easy comment. "We covered a wide range of material. He wanted an overview rather than to drill down on any particular topic. As I said earlier, he was interested in the use of poisons in myths and folktales."

"That's a broad topic," Emma said.

"I didn't have a chance to prepare any materials." Thanks to Jeremy's short notice, Oliver thought. "I had to operate off the top of my head. We veered off-topic a few times. He mentioned he'd seen John Everett Millais's painting of the death scene in *Romeo and Juliet*."

Henrietta started putting forks on the napkins he'd placed. "Death by poison. Sadly. I wanted to change that ending as a teenager."

Oliver smiled, not surprised. Henrietta had a can-do attitude. He finished with the napkins and sat down as she, Colin and Emma continued laying the table. He needed to keep his wits about him with these three. "We started with monkshood, a highly toxic plant—in Greek mythology, Medea poisoned wine with it to try to kill Theseus—and went from there."

"Any discussion of Aoife O'Byrne's works?" Emma asked.

"Not in particular, no, but one of her new series of woodland paintings depicts a bed of bluebells. It's stunning, but according to an old Irish superstition, one can fall under a fairy spell and die if caught in a bed of bluebells. Their bulbs are toxic—it's theorized that could be the source of the superstition. Robin and I landed on that one, but we didn't spend much time there."

Colin placed the last of his knives. "Was there any tale of particular interest to him?"

"Loki. He's a compelling figure in Norse mythology."

"I persuaded Oliver to watch the Thor movies with me," Henrietta said with a wry smile.

"They're fun. Liberties are taken, of course. Robin had seen the movies, too. I told him a version of the tale of Loki getting poisoned by snake venom, as punishment by the gods for his misdeeds. He's chained in a cave and a serpent is placed above him, dripping his venom into a bowl. When it overflows, a few drops land on Loki. He's left to suffer in agony, but Loki being Loki, he does eventually escape." Oliver paused, picturing Robin Masterson, an eager listener who three days later was himself poisoned. "As we finished our chat, I realized Robin was particularly drawn to fictional world-building. He was a fan of *The Lord of the Rings*, *Game of Thrones* and the Marvel franchises. Books, comics, movies."

"Was he building a world of his own?" Colin asked.

Oliver shrugged. "We didn't get that far. He did say snakes weren't his thing. He'd have poisoned Loki a different way."

Finian arrived with the casserole. He placed it on the table on hot pads and removed the lid, just as someone pounded on the front door. He started toward the entry, but Colin swept past him.

A breathless Georgina Masterson burst into the entry. She was in running clothes, panting, perspiring and angry. "You are all spooks, and my father is a spook, and now he's dying." She barely managed to choke out the words. She held up a folded sheet of white paper. "And this." She gulped in air. "My father didn't make a mistake with death caps, did he? It's one of his bloody nerve agents that's killing him."

Colin shut the door behind her. "You'd better come in."

16

Emma got Georgina seated between her and Henrietta at the table. Finian hurried out of the dining room to fetch a towel and a glass of water from the kitchen. The sheet of paper she'd brought with her clutched in one hand, Georgina flicked sweat off her brow with the fingertips of her free hand and then grabbed a napkin. She was still breathing hard, from both her long run from Heron's Cove, Emma thought, and from spilling her pent-up emotions.

Colin sat across from her, studying her. "How did you know to find us here?"

Georgina looked stricken at his stern tone "I knew Bill Hornsby was staying with the Rock Point priest. I googled the church's address. It's about a mile farther than I needed to run today, but it felt good. Bill Hornsby is here, isn't he? I want to speak with him."

"He's not well," Henrietta said. "He's asleep."

"I don't care. Wake him." She wiped more sweat off her upper lip. Her fine hair was matted and her running shirt drenched with sweat. "I took the coastal route. It was gorgeous with the waves crashing on the rocks. It'll get dark soon but I'll manage. I've run in the dark lots of times. Running clears my head."

Oliver sat at the far end of the table, next to a bay window overlooking the side yard and church. Emma could tell he was itching as much as she was to get a look at Georgina's paper.

"Georgina," Henrietta said, "Oliver tells us he met you and your father in London last Saturday. Bill Hornsby recommended him. He's a friend of ours. I'm Henrietta Balfour, by the way. I'm a garden designer."

"I deserve answers," Georgina said, holding her ground.

Emma nodded to the paper. "What's that, can you tell us?"

Georgina placed the sheet on the table. It was crookedly folded, but she opened it and smoothed out the thick sketch paper. It was wrinkled and sweat-stained given her run, but the pencil drawing was clearly visible. Openmouthed snakes, horned devils, a winged dragon, something that looked like a goblin. A mishmash of images, as if to experiment without wasting paper.

"I found it in my cabin," Georgina said, calmer. "I was gathering up some packing materials to drop off at the marina's dumpster. It was in between some of the brown paper and plastic wrap, like it'd gotten stuck there."

"These are the packing materials for the painting Bill Hornsby brought you?" Colin asked.

She nodded. "Yeah." She raised her eyes to him. "The sketch isn't my work. I don't draw that well, and it's creepy. I don't do creepy."

Emma peered at the images. "What about the dragon sketch in the galley?"

Georgina looked blank. "What dragon sketch?"

"It's not your work?"

"No. I have no idea what you're talking about. I only draw wild edibles. I love dragons but I don't draw them."

"When did you last touch the sketches in the drawer?" Emma asked.

"What difference does it make if—"

"When, Georgina?"

"I worked on them in England and put them in the drawer when I got back. I didn't look at them."

"Did you show them to anyone?"

Her lower lip quivered.

"Georgina," Colin said quietly.

"My father." It was a barely coherent mumble. "On Friday. Then I put them in my suitcase and didn't think about them until I boarded the yacht in Boston and unpacked. I put them in the drawer in the galley."

"And this sketch?" Emma asked, pointing at the sweat-stained sheet Georgina had brought with her. "Did your father—"

"I never saw this sketch until just before I went on my run. I didn't say anything then. I needed to think. I don't know if it was there when I unpacked the painting. I was focused on the painting itself. I could easily have missed it and binned it with the packing materials." She bit her lip, holding back tears. She raised her chin defiantly at Henrietta and Oliver. "Did MI5 find anything like it when they searched my father's flat? Because if you're not MI5, you're in touch with them."

"Let's not leap ahead," Colin said. "Could your father have done these drawings?"

Georgina's eyes teared up. "I don't know. My first impulse is to say no, but what do I know anymore? He loves art and talks about taking up drawing now that he's retired, but he hasn't that I'm aware of. He was pleased that I was drawing plants as a way to learn to identify them. He said he thought that was great." She spun around to Oliver. "Could the sketch be Aoife O'Byrne's work?"

Oliver didn't hesitate. "No." He took a closer look at the drawing. "We talked about some of the images here, but not all of them. Dragons and devils didn't come up."

"It's so bloody weird it could be my father." Georgina pushed back her chair hard, as if she wanted to jump out of it, but she stayed put. "I never saw anything like this when I visited him. It's pathological, isn't it? He has something wrong with him, and that's why he's in a coma." She narrowed her eyes on Oliver. "Do *you* think he did the sketch?"

"He didn't mention sketches to me," Oliver said. "We had a general conversation about poisons in mythology. He didn't seem overly concerned about anything."

"And Bill Hornsby recommended you. And you're here in Maine with him and two FBI agents who happen to be mutual friends." Georgina stopped, her breathing less shallow and rapid as she seemed to take a moment to process her thoughts, think before blurting something that would later haunt her—like mentioning the Aoife O'Byrne painting in the first place. "How interesting given my father's expertise in chemical weapons."

"We know each other through the Sharpes," Henrietta said.

Oliver gave Colin a cheeky smile. "Even FBI agents have friends. Right, Colin?"

For a split second, Georgina smiled, and Emma thought she might break out of her dark mood. But it was only for that fleeting moment. "Here's what I think." Georgina cleared her throat. "I think Bill Hornsby is a lying spook who's kept an eye on my father and used him for years. What's the word nowadays? Counterintelligence? You're all worried my father has gone mad in his retirement and he was trying to sell his knowledge about chemical weapons to the black market and ended up poisoning himself. Well, he's weird, but he..." Tears spilled out of her eyes. "Oh, damn. Damn, damn. I hate this. The hospital called while I was on my run. If I want to see my father, I need to get to London, fast. There's nothing I can do to stop this from happening. He's going to die and I won't see him..."

Finian returned with the water and towel. She took them and gulped down most of the water in one go. She set the glass on the table, away from the sketch and thanked Finian, her eyes widening as Jeremy Pearson— Bill Hornsby to her—staggered into the dining room.

He raised a hand. "Georgina."

She balled her hands into tight fists and leaped up, charging toward him. Emma started to her feet, but Colin had better position and swooped between her and Jeremy. He swung an arm around her. "Easy, Georgina. Just take a deep breath and get hold of yourself."

"I'm sorry," she sobbed. "I ran too fast. I probably should eat something. I obsessed for—what is it, five miles? Six? I obsessed about the sketch and my father and you people. He can't die because of me. Because I visited him and we had two great days together and it gave him a chance to say goodbye. That's why he bought me that painting. It was a farewell gift. If he did this to himself, let it be because of his work, not me."

Jeremy edged toward her, his bloodshot eyes filled with compassion, but he wobbled, then collapsed to his knees. Colin went to him, but he waved him off. He took Georgina's hand instead, steadying himself as he got back to his feet. "I wish I could make everything better for you, Georgina. I'm so sorry."

She seemed taken aback by his kindness as well as his weak condition. Emma stood next to her with the towel and the rest of the water. "You might not want to dive into a casserole right now, but we can find you something to eat."

"That's okay." She patted her running belt. "I have an energy bar with me."

"Great," Emma said. "There's a bathroom down the hall if you need one. We'll get you back to Heron's Cove. You don't have to run."

Mention of such practical matters had an impact. "Thanks. I'm okay. I'm sorry. I'm not usually one for big emotional displays. My dad taught me well on that score."

Jeremy held on to the back of a chair. "Who else knows about the sketch?"

"No one. I'm leaving it here. You can burn it for all I care. I never want to see you again."

"I want you off that yacht, Georgina," Jeremy said, unsteady, hoarse. "Stay here. You can have the couch, or you can stay with Colin and Emma. We'll put you up at an inn."

She looked less tight, angry and emotional. "I'm fine, I promise. I don't need anyone to take care of me. I want to pack and get myself to London. Thank you for understanding my state of mind. Please know that my father would never tell me or anyone else anything he shouldn't about his work. He's eccentric but he's incorruptible."

Jeremy started to protest, but he lost hold on the chair. Colin was there, steadying him. Jeremy cursed, but he didn't have much strength behind it.

"Come, my friend," Finian said. "Let's get you back to the den."

"Don't argue," Colin said. "Otherwise I'm the one who helps you."

"Been there, done that," his friend and colleague muttered.

Georgina shivered. Now that she'd stopped running and the sweat was drying on her, she was getting chilled. Her hands trembled as she held the glass. "I usually bring water and an anorak with me."

Henrietta pointed at the window. "Your ride?"

Emma saw Nick Lothian making his way up the front walk. Georgina almost managed a laugh. "He texted me. I told him where I was going, and he said it was too damn far to run to Rock Point and back before dark. He looks after everyone. The Fannings are lucky to have him on the crew."

Emma walked with her into the entry. "If you change your mind, we will help you find a place you're comfortable staying."

"I appreciate that. I feel perfectly safe with the Fannings and the crew. And for the record? I didn't poison my father."

"And the mushrooms yesterday?"

Her lower lip quivered. "I'm sorry people got sick," she said as Nick came to the door. "Sorry, again, and thank you. Please tell Bill I hope he feels better soon."

Nick said a quick hello and took her water and towel. He held them up to Emma. "They won't be missed for now?"

"Take them," Emma said.

He turned to Georgina. "You all set or do you want to run back to Heron's Cove? Me, I'm driving." He grinned at her. "Always thinking ahead."

His infectious cheerfulness had Georgina smiling as they shut the door.

Oliver sank back in his chair. "I don't know about anyone else, but I'm ready to put the drama aside for a bit and enjoy Franny Maroney's noodle casserole."

"For once we agree," Colin said as he returned to his seat.

Emma set the sketch aside. It raised questions, but they'd keep for now. Colin had those incredible ocean blue-gray eyes on her, and she smiled as he served the casserole and Finian returned with a bottle of wine.

"No good deed goes unpunished, Colin."

Jeremy's voice was raspy but stronger than it had been that morning. Colin considered that a good sign. His MI5 colleague was stretched out on the sofa, propped up with pillows. "Thought we'd have to call another ambulance for you."

"So do I. I should have let Robin ship the painting to Georgina. Instead, I had to volunteer to take it to her."

"Nah. You wanted to spy on her and her friends."

"I didn't do a good job of it, did I? Carted off the

yacht in an ambulance. A night in hospital. Now here with you. I should have said I'd recuperate on the yacht."

Colin shook his head. "That makes no sense."

Jeremy sighed. "I'm more worried about Georgina's mental state than anything else. She doesn't know those people. She's alone and her father's dying."

"She wouldn't be alone if you hadn't eaten those mushrooms."

"Go to hell."

Colin grinned at him. "Glad to see you're getting your spine back." He placed the sketch on the coffee table. "What do you think?"

Jeremy eyed the images. "I didn't get a good look when Georgina was going for my throat. Someone's been having fun with a sketchpad, I see."

"Thought you might have seen it before you passed out."

"I didn't pass out."

"Recognize it?"

"No."

"Is this sketch or one like it why you set up the meeting between Robin Masterson and Oliver?"

"I've never seen this sketch or one like it."

"Not what I asked."

"No," Jeremy said, sinking into his pillows. "It's not why Robin got in touch with me. He had—he has a long-standing interest in art. He said he'd taken a course on how to read paintings and understand various biblical and mythological themes. He wanted to talk to someone who could answer questions he had about mythology and folktales."

"Nothing to do with his daughter?"

"Georgina was visiting. He was worried about her—

that he didn't know enough about the Fannings and she would be exploited by them and people in their world. I didn't take that to mean anything to do with his work."

"Until he turned up near death on a park bench," Colin said.

Jeremy looked drained, gray. "Yes."

"Was he losing it, do you think? Mentally ill?"

"Eccentric but clear-eyed. He's one of the smartest people I've ever known. His ability, or whatever you want to call it, to hyperfocus on his work has been an asset for us—and for the world, I would argue—but not for his daughter."

"Did she do this sketch?"

"Is she playing us? No, Colin. She's a twenty-three-year-old chef. I'd have liked to talk to her properly, but best I wait until I'm more in my head."

He flopped against his pillows and shut his eyes—or his eyes shut on him. Colin waited a moment, not knowing if his friend was done for now or could continue. "Can I get you anything? One of Fin's parishioners made us a noodle casserole."

"I don't know what that is, but I smelled it and almost hurled."

Jeremy hadn't opened his eyes. Colin figured that he was talking was a good sign. "It's the best. You're missing out."

"I'm sure I am, but no, thank you, I'll stick to tea and toast for now."

"I'll let you recuperate, but you and this sick neurotoxicologist. What else do I need to know?"

"Nothing."

"What's this about, Jeremy? Is Georgina the daughter you never had? Is that it?"

"Just as well I never had kids. I wouldn't have been a good father. You would be."

"So it's Henrietta," Colin said. "*She's* the daughter you never had?"

Jeremy opened his eyes. "You shouldn't taunt a sick man."

"Henrietta's a little old to be your daughter."

"Damn right. Her parents neglected her emotionally, but she had Posey—and she remembers Freddy, her grandfather who died when she was five."

"Freddy Balfour, MI5 legend."

"She has Oliver now, but he's always been there. He and Henrietta bonded as children, even before his parents were murdered and he was kidnapped."

"They still have time for children," Colin said. "They can make you the honorary grandfather."

Jeremy grunted. "You just said I was too old to be her father. How could I be her kids' grandfather?"

"I said honorary."

"Oliver's redeemed himself. She's done her bit. Time for a new chapter in their lives."

Colin sensed as tired and spent as he was, Jeremy appreciated having a chance to talk and think about something other than whether he was going to upchuck again. "Thought you roped Henrietta into staying with the service."

"She could have a quiet job with us, or do her garden design for real. Oliver can do more with the farm, and he set up a small foundation in memory of his parents. I don't think he'll go back to Hollywood to consult."

"He could do something useful with his stone-carving skills."

Jeremy grinned. "You're an unforgiving bastard, Donovan."

"As if you aren't."

He coughed, moaned, swore. "You and Emma are young. What are your plans for the future?"

"Figure out who poisoned Robin Masterson, who poisoned you, what happened to the Aoife O'Byrne painting, who drew that sketch and why Georgina is lying about the mushrooms and who knows what else."

A wry smile from Jeremy. "I meant after all that."

"I know you did. I notice you didn't argue with me."

"What's the point?"

"The Fannings?"

Jeremy leveled his gaze on him. "You are avoiding the topic of your future."

"Noted."

"I didn't get a chance to do a background check on the Fannings and their guests."

"Dived in headfirst," Colin said. "What about the passengers, guests and crew?"

"Nothing jumped out at me before I ate those bloody mushrooms."

"You really didn't notice the bad taste?"

"I wasn't alone in that."

"Or people were too polite to say anything. When your hosts are Bryce and Melodie Fanning, I guess they get the benefit of the doubt."

Jeremy's eyes shut and his head drooped to one side.

"You're done in, my friend. Get some rest. Stay put. Call me if you decide to tell me more."

Jeremy lifted two fingers but said nothing as Colin left him and went to the kitchen. Finian was alone, cleaning up a few dishes while his guests had tea in the dining room. "I'm sorry about all this, Fin."

"I'm happy to help." He shut the dishwasher. "Is Aoife involved, Colin? Is she safe?"

"Georgina's father bought a painting from her. As far as I know, that's the extent of her involvement."

Finian rinsed out the sink, turned off the faucet and arranged a dish towel on a hook. "Sean and Kitty are delighted to have Aoife in Declan's Cross. I hope she'll be happy there."

Colin saw the strain in Finian's expression.

"It's your second autumn in Maine. Is the novelty wearing off?"

"I'm not here about novelty, Colin."

"Here to hide from your life in Ireland?"

"I'm not hiding from life."

They'd been down this road before. Colin didn't know why he was bringing it up again. "I know. You're embracing your call to the priesthood. Visiting the sick, burying the dead, hearing confessions. Weddings, baptisms, First Communions, confirmations. Mass." He smiled, trying to take some of the edge off his mood. "Drinking whiskey with me."

"That's high on the list of my priestly duties."

"It's not a bad life. Father Callaghan was a jolly sort. You're friendly and people like you, but I wouldn't call you jolly."

Finian gave a mock shudder. "Lord, I hope not."

"Need some help digging a few more bean holes?"

"A couple of lads from the church are stopping by on Tuesday. They're in their eighties but in good shape."

"I'll tell my father. He's still in his sixties. Maybe he'll get competitive with the old guys and come help."

Colin wiped a few stray cookie crumbs off the counter into his palm and dumped them in the trash. "I can stay here overnight, Fin. I'll camp out in the living room."

"Imagine the gossip if your family and friends discover you're sleeping here and Emma's at home. Go, Colin. We'll be fine."

Of that, Colin had no doubt. Henrietta was an experienced intelligence officer, and Oliver had spent a decade eluding law enforcement, private security and Wendell Sharpe. They were on Jeremy's side.

Henrietta entered the kitchen with a tray of tea dishes. "Oliver and Emma are going on about the use of poison in Norse mythology. I didn't stay. I'll bring tea to our friend in the den."

Finian grabbed the kettle and stuck it under the faucet for fresh water. "And Jeremy is his real name?"

"I think it is." She gave him a brazen smile. "We spooks, you know. We have our secrets."

Finian said nothing, and Henrietta elbowed him aside and insisted on making tea.

When Colin and Emma said goodbye, Finian followed them out through the front door. "I won't ask questions of my guests. It's early yet but enjoy your evening."

"You, too."

He smiled faintly but said nothing as he went back inside.

Colin felt mildly uneasy leaving Finian with the two MI5 officers and art thief, but he climbed into his truck. He'd parked behind Emma's car. She pulled out ahead of him, and he pushed back a surge of regret their first weekend together in a month had turned out the way it had. Except for Andy and Julianne's wedding. He smiled at the thought of the two of them enjoying their own Irish honeymoon.

He parked on the street in front of the house and when he went inside, Emma was wrapping up a call in the kitchen. She tossed her phone onto the counter. "That was Sam. He's run into a brick wall on information on Robin Masterson. So far, no red flags on the Fannings—legit business in London and they are in the market for a yacht."

"Jeremy sure as hell went to a lot of trouble to get on board that yacht."

"Maybe it's for the reasons he says it is—to bring a sick friend's daughter a painting and to check on her life as a personal chef on a luxurious yacht. Never mind that the friend is a chemical weapons expert and he's your MI5 buddy."

"Jeremy's not himself. Something's off with him besides mushroom poisoning. My guess is he wouldn't be here unless he thought Robin was deliberately poisoned."

"Think that's what the daughter believes, too?"

"Maybe it's easier than accepting he did it to himself. We have a nerve-agent expert in a coma due to mushroom poisoning, and we have a senior British intelligence officer recovering from mushroom poisoning. Hell, Emma, tell me we're not wasting a beautiful Sunday chasing down a case of overzealous mushroom foragers."

She smiled. "At the moment, I'm grateful Granddad and Lucas are in Ireland and my mother is in Paris. What do you think Sean Murphy knows about Henrietta's trip to Dublin?"

"It's hard to say what Sean knows."

"He'll keep an eye on Aoife—and on Granddad and Lucas if they step out of line."

"What do you think, any chance she and Lucas could get together?"

"On paper, yes. He's focused on the business right now, and grieving. And Aoife…"

"She has her eye on our good Father Bracken," Colin said.

Emma nodded. "Her heart, at least."

Colin took her hand. "A walk before pouring whiskey?"

They ended up at Hurley's. Kevin and their folks were at the bar. No Beth Trahan, Colin noted, but she could have an early shift, laundry to do—he decided not to bring her up. He was good at compartmentalizing, and wanted to appreciate the company and enjoy his family and friends. Mike and Naomi would be heading back up to the Bold Coast soon, but they were thinking about settling back in Rock Point. Getting their security work out of their system, or deeper into their system— Colin looked forward to a deep conversation with his older brother. He had his own future to sort out. He suspected that Emma, intuitive as well as analytical, knew he had that on his mind. They'd talk about it when the time was right. But he'd completed his last undercover mission. He knew that much.

The director herself had approved. He'd met Mina Van Buren in her office in DC before returning home. *We need you elsewhere, Colin, and you need to be elsewhere.*

Home in Rock Point raising kids and teaching them how to catch lobster and kayak?

He could do that and his FBI work.

And Emma?

He smiled. Whatever she chose to do, she'd have his support.

By the time they walked back home, the stars were out and the wind had picked up. He had whiskey in the front room while Emma took a bath upstairs. "You've got that look, Colin," she said as she started up the stairs.

"Which look is that?"

"It's the one that says you're going through your mental files for any connections to the Fannings and Mastersons that you might have missed or might not remember."

He raised his glass. "A few sips of whiskey will help focus the mind."

He settled by the unlit fireplace and went back through his five-year history with Jeremy Pearson. There was serious black market potential for chemical weapons, but he and Jeremy knew each other through trafficking in illegal arms. Guns, bullets, missiles and explosives. They'd dismantled an international arms trafficking network over the past few years. The people involved might have toyed with trafficking in chemical weapons, but nothing more than that.

Which didn't mean the bastards wouldn't kill him or Jeremy first chance they got.

"Just not with mushrooms," Colin muttered and got to his feet.

He headed to the kitchen and washed his whiskey glass.

No, he hadn't missed or forgotten anything.

When he went upstairs, he found Emma snuggled

under the quilts in their bed, asleep. She stirred as he slipped under the covers next to her. The windows were open, the night air cool as he slid close to her, feeling her warm skin against him.

He heard an owl, and the wind.

This life, he thought as he placed a hand on Emma's hip and kissed her softly, glad to be home…uneasy about his future, and the friend recuperating in the local rectory. He was alive because of Jeremy. He owed him. It was the unspoken bond between them, and no one knew, not Yank, not Mina Van Buren—not Emma.

17

Georgina looked out at the stars above the Atlantic, past the river channel, the wind in her face as she fought an explosion of tears and shivering that threatened to surge out of control. She'd made a fool of herself, again, with the FBI agents, and with their friends and her father's friend—and the kindly Irish priest. But she was right. She knew it.

Spooks.

She was leaving Maine tomorrow. She'd checked the drawer in the galley and tossed all the sketches in the compactor without looking at them. She'd start fresh after she saw her father. She didn't want to see the dragon sketch. It would only upset her.

She also didn't want to say anything to the crew or the Fannings about the Aoife O'Byrne painting. It would only draw attention to herself, stir up more drama around her. Someone must have stuck it somewhere having no idea it belonged to her. It'd turn up, and they all could claim she'd been so preoccupied with her father, she'd forgotten all about it.

She loved the smell of the sea, the feel of the wind in her hair. She swore wind had a different quality near the ocean. Yet as much as she tried to focus on her surroundings, her mind filled with snapshots of her past, walking as a young child with her parents on either side of her, holding her hand…sitting on her mother's lap reading *Madeleine* while her father cooked dinner…waiting at school for her father to pick her up for the Christmas holiday, laughingly telling everyone he was absentminded and always late…foraging with him, because it was one thing, the only thing, they had in common…

What they'd had up until now was all they would ever have.

The creepy sketch, the gorgeous, expensive painting—had her dad started to lose his mind before he ate the death caps? Was that *why* he'd done it? She had vague memories of her mother in her last days. Herself but not herself, the brain tumor eating its way at her life and spirit.

She was grateful when Nick brought her a drink, interrupting her thoughts. "Just wine. I'm not good at mixing drinks, and I know you don't like your liquor straight."

"I might tonight." Georgina smiled and raised her glass. "Thank you."

"No problem."

"Where's yours?"

"Nothing for me in case the Fannings need anything overnight."

"How is Bryce?"

"Sleeping comfortably last I checked—which was ten minutes ago."

They retreated to a seating area under the awning. Richie joined them. He had a drink in his hand, but he was in a serious mood. "Georgina, if yesterday wasn't a simple culinary mistake on your part—if you're not a hundred percent certain you added those mushrooms to the tacos—you need to speak up. Don't let anyone pressure you, directly or indirectly. It's not worth it. Tell the truth."

"I'm with Richie," Nick said. "If you're not positive it was your mistake, say so."

"I appreciate the pep talk. I just want to get to Boston and onto a flight to London to see my father."

"It's not a pep talk," Richie said. "We live and work on this boat."

"The Fannings haven't mentioned getting food tasters," Nick said. "That's a joke, by the way."

Richie, Georgina observed, didn't laugh. He settled into a chair across from where she sprawled onto a couch. She loved being on yachts. Every inch of space was put to use, often in clever ways. No waste and, even on a luxury yacht like this one, no excess, at least not the kind she'd seen in the homes of some of the people she'd cooked for during her adventures at sea. She drank some of the wine, recognized it was from an open bottle from yesterday's party, barely used given the onslaught of sickness.

"Georgie?"

She heard the concern in Nick's voice. "I was thinking about how nice this yacht is. The one Melodie and Bryce will buy will be just as nice, probably nicer."

She glanced out toward the sea again, noticing lights here and there onshore. "They don't want to risk giving the police a reason to crawl through the yacht. I'm not suggesting they have anything to hide, either. But who would want that kind of scrutiny?"

"Don't lie for them, Georgina," Richie said. "Seriously. Don't."

She smiled. "And here I was thinking you'd fire me in a heartbeat."

He winked at her. "That's different."

She appreciated his light tone, but his overall mood remained serious. "As mushrooms go, *russula emetica* is a poor choice as a murder weapon." She grinned at the two men. "Just saying." But her attempt at gallows humor fell flat, not just with them but with herself. "Melodie says I don't need to cook again before I leave tomorrow."

"Unfortunately," Nick said. "She's happy with sandwiches and frozen pizza until we get back to Boston, and Bryce is sticking to mild foods."

"You two stocked up nicely on recovery foods," Georgina said.

Richie got to his feet. "I told the guys not to leave anything in the galley except unopened packaged goods and tins. Regretting that now, I think."

Georgina set her wine on a table. "Really, I don't mind preparing food for the crew before I leave. I'll have time."

"Focus on your well-being," Richie said. "We can fend for ourselves."

They said good-night and left her alone with her wine and starlit view. She debated calling them back, asking them about the painting…the sketch… William Hornsby and his FBI friends, his English friends…but she didn't. Nick and Richie would have said something if they'd run across the painting. Melodie and Bryce could easily have assumed one or the other had brought it on board and tucked it aside, intending to get to ask about it at some point. They were enthusiastic art collectors who'd only been married for a year. They loved to surprise each other with expensive, original gifts.

Georgina took her wine to the bar and dumped it in the sink, ran the water. She felt her emotions rising up inside her as if they were a force of their own. Her throat tightened, and tears spilled down her cheeks with sudden, overwhelming grief. Her knees buckled as she bit into her hand, trying to smother the sound of her sobs.

"Oh, Dad… Dad…"

She heard the distress in her voice. She wouldn't get to London in time. She knew it, and it was her own doing, because she hadn't acted on the news of his sickness.

I'll be an orphan now. I'll be alone.

Will you greet him, Mum? Did you love him in the end?

Georgina splashed water on her face. She felt the two long runs in her thighs and lower back, but they'd steadied her, centered her—which made her sputter into laughter. How much worse would she be if she *hadn't* gone for those runs? Or maybe she, too, was losing her mind…

Finian Bracken had whiskey in the rectory kitchen since the den was occupied by the recuperating British agent. At least he was clear on that point, although it didn't matter. Jeremy, Oliver and Henrietta were here, and that was that.

Still on UK time, Henrietta and Oliver had gone upstairs.

Not a peep out of the man in the den.

Finian had opened a bottle of Redbreast he had on a shelf in the kitchen rather than slipping into the den for the Bracken he'd served. The Redbreast was as good an Irish whiskey as there was.

He checked his email for the first time in hours and saw he had one from Andy Donovan. *We're at the cottage. It's beautiful. We're doing a tour of Bracken Distillers tomorrow (Monday). Thank you. Love, Andy and Julianne.*

Attached to the email was a photograph, a selfie of the happy couple in front of the stone cottage, its door still painted the same blue Sally had chosen. It was late in Ireland, but Finian wrote back, assuming Andy and Julianne would pick up his message sometime tomorrow—perhaps after they'd toured the distillery.

Thank you for getting in touch. We'll chat when you're back in Rock Point. Enjoy Bracken Distillers. My sister Mary is in charge of the whiskey tours and the whiskey school. She'll take good care of you.

He hit Send and then, on a whim, texted Sean Murphy: *I have a house full of people.*

He didn't expect an answer but Sean texted him right away: *I know.*

Finian smiled. He supposed he wasn't surprised Sean knew, given his position with the Garda, his affection for the O'Byrne sisters, his natural concern for his friend in Maine—and his knowledge of the Sharpes and the Donovans. Are you in Declan's Cross?

Yes. Wendell and Lucas are here, too.

Finian started to reply, but he received another text from Sean.

And Aoife.

She was with family and friends, then. Are you at the farm?

Having whiskey in the kitchen. Wish you were here to join me.

Finian had engaged in many long chats with Sean in the kitchen of the old Murphy farmhouse. To be there now. To listen to the sheep in the fields, and the waves washing on the rocks at the base of the cliffs. Was it a clear night, with stars sparkling, feeling so close he could think he could touch them?

Sentimental nonsense, perhaps, but he did have a house full. He typed his response to his friend: I'm raising my glass to you. Sláinte.

Whatever is going on, stay out of it. Sláinte.

That didn't call for a response. Finian put away his phone. He looked again at the photo Andy and Julianne had sent. He could see his girls running outside to catch a rainbow arcing over the bay, Sally laughing, appreciating their excitement. It might have been yesterday, and yet…he knew it wasn't yesterday. It was years ago. His wife and daughters had gone to God far too soon, but he felt no pain, no rawness, no bitterness remembering them—seeing them, hearing them, feeling their presence. Gratitude surged within him for the time they'd had together and the love they'd shared. Their loss had changed him, but their lives had blessed him.

I love our quiet life here, Fin.

Ah, Sally. Was there such a thing as a quiet life?

Finian finished his whiskey and got up from the table. Given his British guests, and his FBI friends a few blocks away, and poisonings and an unsettling sketch and dear God only knew what else, quiet moments would have to do for now.

18

Declan's Cross, South Irish Coast

Of all the rooms in her uncle's house that Kitty O'Byrne had revamped and transformed, the one most unchanged from her uncle's day was the drawing room—now the boutique hotel's reading room, located at the top of the sweeping stairs up from the small lobby. Lucas slipped into it after breakfast. He noted an Aoife O'Byrne seascape above the fireplace, moody, richly atmospheric, unmistakably hers. But he found himself standing at the two Jack Butler Yeats paintings, stolen a decade ago, returned last fall. John O'Byrne, not poor but not wealthy, had purchased the landscapes of west Ireland before Yeats's stratospheric rise in popularity and price.

Seeing the two paintings—not just photographs of them—made everything real, didn't it?

Lucas could visualize Oliver York brazenly walking into the rambling old house on a classic dark and stormy Irish night. John O'Byrne had been on vacation in Portugal, only Sean Murphy's elderly uncle on the premises—dead asleep, he hadn't heard a thing. Although this was his first heist, Oliver was good. Later, he'd broken into more challenging locations.

"What the hell were you thinking, Oliver?" Lucas asked in a whisper.

But the wealthy young Englishman hadn't been thinking—he'd been coping with searing trauma, grief, isolation and shreds of memory that only years—decades—later would make sense to him.

Wendell Sharpe hadn't gotten involved in the Declan's Cross heist until six months later, after Oliver had helped himself to a landscape painting in a small Amsterdam museum. He'd sent Wendell, living in Dublin by then, a small, polished stone engraved with a stripped-down version of the Celtic cross he'd lifted from the O'Byrne house.

I like the guy, Lucas.

His grandfather at breakfast. But why not like Oliver and allow him to make amends—return the art, put his skills to use for the so-called greater good—since it was impossible to prosecute him, anyway? It didn't mean he was excused for what he'd done, despite the mitigating factors, absence of violence and whatever else went to his side of the ledger.

Discovering the identity of their elusive art thief had been one of the bigger changes in Lucas's work and personal life in the past year, and perhaps more than any other, illustrated the challenges he faced taking full control of Sharpe Fine Art Recovery from his aging grandfather. He'd started his business in his early twenties. It'd been just him for years. Decades. He had his ways, as he was fond of saying.

Sometimes Lucas wondered what secrets his grandfather hadn't told him.

Other times, he didn't want to know.

And yet he knew Wendell Sharpe was a man of integrity, and he followed the law.

"Still doesn't mean he's without secrets."

Lucas had counted on his father as a buffer between them. Tim Sharpe had been born with a milder temperament than either his father or son, and years of chronic pain had only made him more contemplative, analytical and observant. And now he was gone. Wendell had been ambivalent about full retirement and kept sticking his fingers in the business—for the most part helpful—but losing his only son had taken a lot out of him.

Lucas accepted he and his grandfather both had things to figure out. Maybe Emma would quit the FBI and come back to the family business. Colin could join her. Lucas laughed to himself. That'd be something, wouldn't it? Utter madness, no doubt.

A ray of sunshine took him to the windows in the attractive room. The morning light was spreading across the sea and the hotel gardens. Despite his promises to himself after yesterday's brunch, he'd indulged in the O'Byrne House Hotel bread basket at breakfast. So much for low-carb.

He saw grandfather pacing on the terrace below the windows.

Lucas sighed. *You promised.*

No way out of it.

Time for his granddad's banshees.

* * *

By the time Lucas trotted down the stairs and out the French doors to the terrace, his grandfather was in an aggrieved mood. "You don't have to go with me. I don't need you to babysit me." He waved a hand in the general direction of the headland. "I want to walk up there. You can go for a run."

"Not with a pound of bread in me. I'll go with you." Lucas grinned at the old man. "We can take it slow. I'll kick back and enjoy the scenery."

"It's a good thing your grandmother liked you. I never did." But his grandfather grinned and put his foot up on a metal chair to tie the laces. "Beautiful Irish morning. We'll have fun."

"It'll be a bonding experience," Lucas said, not too sarcastically.

"What the hell is a bonding experience? Never mind. Aoife O'Byrne's cottage and Sean Murphy's farm are up there."

"And a lot of sheep," Lucas said. "Want to take the car up onto the headland, at least? It flattens out—"

"Nope. Walk."

They set off, maintaining a steady pace through the pretty village of Declan's Cross with its simple buildings painted in a variety of bright colors. A few overflowing flower baskets hung on black-painted lampposts, even now in October. Brushed by the Gulf Stream, Declan's Cross didn't get as cold as Maine in fall and winter.

When they came to a cute bookshop and turned up the hill onto the headland, Lucas noticed his grandfather growing more pensive—not his style. Banshees, his son's death, his own sunset years. Whatever was on Wendell's mind, Lucas figured talking meant neither of them was overstraining. "Aoife's in love with Finian Bracken, you know," he said casually.

"Genuinely, or as a convenience? He's the classic forbidden love. Telling herself she's in love with him allows her to focus on her work without having to bother with the distractions. Finding a man, raising a family."

"An excuse to be self-absorbed?"

Wendell shrugged, zipped up his jacket. "Maybe so."

"We've seen that type in our work," Lucas said. "They tell themselves they're focusing on their art when they're indulging their narcissism. They'd be narcissists if they did something else."

"Voice of experience?"

Lucas had dated his share of that type, ever to his regret, but he toned down the edge in his voice. This was supposed to be a pleasant walk. He didn't need to go deep with his grandfather on his love life, such as it was. "I don't know Aoife well enough to say what her motives are, but there are plenty of brilliant artists who manage relationships successfully. A discussion for another day."

"Do you see Father Bracken often?"

"Not often."

"Emma said he did a great job at your dad's funeral. You're not angry with me for staying here?"

"Not in the least," Lucas said without hesitation. "It didn't occur to me to be upset. It would have been tough on you to make that trip, Granddad. Fortunately you'd just seen each other, and you had him and Mom close by in London for the past year."

"And your mother—she mad at me?"

"She told Emma and me to beg you to stay in Ireland, and not because she thinks you're a pain in the ass."

Wendell grinned. "I think I'd rather have that than the age thing again. One can do what one can do, whatever the age. Tim felt as if he was living on borrowed time since that fall on the ice. He lived each day to its fullest. A good example for us, Lucas, no matter how many days we have left—since we don't know."

The lane wound close to the cliffs and sea. With the tide coming in, crashing onto the rocks, Lucas could taste the salt spray on the breeze. "Well, I expect we'll have today, don't you?"

"So far, so good, but it's not yet ten o'clock."

They continued up the hill at a slower pace, Lucas commenting on the fencing, the sheep, the hazards and temptations of Irish country roads—until he just gave up and walked in silence. They passed the yellow-painted bungalow Aoife had rented for the past few months. Lucas didn't know if she'd chosen a place to purchase now that she'd decided to live in Declan's Cross full-time. Her car was parked in the driveway, a few articles of clothing on the line in the side yard and a window cracked open, but no sign of the artist herself.

"You don't fancy Aoife yourself, do you?" Wendell asked.

Lucas shook his head. "She's a beautiful, fascinating woman, but no, I don't."

"That new assistant at the Heron's Cove offices?"

"Granddad."

"Were you invited to that Donovan wedding on Saturday?"

"I was."

"Maybe the bride has a sister."

"She doesn't."

"Glad I moved to Dublin?" They paused at a hedgerow, topped with barbed-wire fencing and, on the other side, sheep grazing in a lush, green field. "You remind me of your father right now. You're more forthcoming by nature than he was. He was private even as a little tyke. He never told his mother and me he was serious about Faye until he'd proposed to her."

"I still miss Grandma."

"She was something." Wendell watched as two sheep waddled to him. "Tim handled his heart condition in a way that suited him. Your mother supported his choice. It had to do with who he was, not who we are."

Lucas noticed the splotches of blue paint on the sheep's wool that served as a brand. He assumed the sheep belonged to Sean Murphy, who owned a farm on the headland but worked as a detective in Dublin. Wendell had lived in the same town house in Dublin, where he'd been born, for sixteen years now. He'd never expected to be widowed so soon, but he'd made a good life for himself in Ireland—away from the memories in every step he took in Heron's Cove.

"I carved out a studio apartment for you in the new offices," Lucas said. "You're welcome to move in anytime."

"Always good to have a bolt-hole." His grandfather started along the lane again. It leveled off, and the rest of their route would be easier going, if not entirely flat. "How is Emma, Lucas?"

"I haven't seen much of her since she got back from Ireland. She says she's been buried in work."

"And Colin's been away."

They both knew why. Colin was an undercover agent. Lucas suspected it was dangerous work, and isolating— for him and for his family, and especially for Emma, now his wife. But she was an FBI agent herself, and she'd had her time with the Sisters of the Joyful Heart to help her know herself, center herself.

The lane narrowed further and became a dirt track before dead-ending at the stone ruins of what once had been a church. Lucas followed his grandfather over a hedgerow and through a scatter of crooked, lichen-covered gravestones to a grassy hillside—part of the Murphy farm—and finally up to three large Celtic stone crosses. It was here, in August, Wendell was convinced he'd heard a banshee keening shortly before his only son's death.

Lucas shuddered when the wind gusted, whistling among the crosses and ruins. "I told Emma if I hear a banshee, I'm turning tail and running back to the hotel."

"I'll be right behind you."

"Technically, I don't believe in that stuff, Granddad."

"My mother did. Your great-grandmother."

They stared at the sea, churning under a clear sky. It wouldn't last. Clouds were due to move in by early afternoon.

"I heard what I heard, and what happened, happened," Wendell said. "That's all I know."

"It's a beautiful place."

"It is. I know that, too."

Aoife waved to them in her cottage door on the way back to the village, but she wasn't alone. She stood aside, and Sean Murphy took her place. Dark-haired, blue-eyed and handsome, he had a grim look. "Wendell, Lucas. Come in, both of you. Please."

But it wasn't a request.

They joined Aoife and Sean in her kitchen. She had

something simmering on the stove that smelled wonderful—apple compote, she explained. "I'm feeling very domestic these days. Nesting, I suppose, now that I'm settling in Declan's Cross. Sean walked up from his farmhouse."

"I saw you two pass by," Sean said. "You went out to the ruin at the tip of the headland?"

"Beautiful morning for a walk," Wendell said. Lucas took his vague, pleasant remark as a clue not to mention banshees to the Irish detective.

Sean pointed at a watercolor painting set on a wood chair pushed against the wall at the entrance to the adjoining sitting room, now Aoife's studio. "This is a new installment in a series Aoife is doing set in a woodland not far from here. The one she sold last weekend in Dublin is part of the same series."

Aoife moved to the stove and her bubbling compote. "The man who bought it was delighted and went away happy."

"Robin Masterson," Lucas said.

Sean got out his phone. "Aoife describes him as a man in his late forties, dark, gray eyes, scars on his hands."

"The scars were disconcerting," she said. "They came from a fight not a cooking accident. I'm sure of it. He had a rough air about him."

Sean passed his phone to Lucas, who'd sat next to Wendell at the pine table. "Take a look at this man. What do you think?"

Lucas expected a man as Aoife described, but the one in the photo was older, early sixties, maybe. Balding. Glasses. Definitely not a "rough air" about him. He showed the phone to his grandfather, who peered at the photo and shook his head, obviously with the same reaction Lucas had. He handed the phone back to Sean. "Who is this?"

Sean pocketed the phone. "Do you recognize him?"

"I don't," Lucas said. "Granddad?"

He shook his head. "No. Who is this man, Sean?"

"He's Robin Masterson. The real Robin Masterson."

Aoife placed her stirring spoon on the stove. "But the paperwork—it was all in his name."

"I know, Aoife," Sean said. "You didn't do anything wrong."

But there was more. Lucas could see it in Sean's narrowed eyes, his intensity. "What else, Sean?" Wendell asked.

"Robin Masterson died in a London hospital early this morning."

19

Emma studied the photo Lucas had texted. It was of an Aoife O'Byrne painting in the same series as the one Georgina said her father had bought for her. Her brother was still on the phone with her. He'd called early, but she was up, making coffee, thinking. Colin was awake, too, taking a shower. Fog had settled in on their stretch of the Maine coast, as if to lure them to Hurley's in sweatshirts and jeans for coffee and pancakes. They'd wait for the sun to burn through the fog and the harbor to glisten with the promise of another beautiful autumn day.

She put the phone back to her ear. "I know this spot, Lucas. It's one of the few woodlands on Lamb's Head in Declan's Cross. Are you still up there?"

"Granddad and I just left Aoife's cottage. Sean Murphy is one unhappy detective, Emma."

"We'll expect him to be in touch, then."

"Do you know who posed as Robin Masterson?"

"I have an idea, yes. How's Granddad?"

"He perked up having a mystery to solve." Lucas paused, and Emma could picture the two of them on the headland lane, the sea to their right as they walked back to the village. "We went out to the ruins where he heard the banshee before Dad died."

"How was it out there?" Emma asked.

"No banshees. It was peaceful. You could feel it, Emma. Just…peaceful."

"What will you and Granddad do now?"

"Stick around here until we know how this plays out. This guy who bought the painting—he's why Henrietta Balfour was in Dublin?"

"I don't know, Lucas. Did Sean mention Henrietta?"

"No," her brother said. "Granddad didn't bring her up. Since I didn't see her myself, I kept my mouth shut. Want us to go back and tell Sean?"

"We'll deal with Sean. I suggest you and Granddad resume your plans for the day."

"If you need us, get in touch. We were supposed to head back to Dublin today, but I think we'll book another night here. Granddad's worn himself out walking. He'll need a nap."

Emma smiled when she heard her grandfather muttering in the background. She said goodbye, uneasy but also confident the two Sharpes could handle themselves. Her confidence was bolstered by knowing Jeremy Pearson—the man Aoife had described—was across the Atlantic in Rock Point, down the street from her at St. Patrick's rectory. He was Colin's friend. She didn't know the details, but they had a history that had formed a bond between them.

Colin came into the kitchen, freshly showered. He poured coffee and she showed him the photo from Lucas. "I recognize this spot," she said of the woodland scene, transformed with Aoife's artistic eye and skill.

Colin pointed at the ground. "Mushrooms?"

Emma nodded. "Chanterelles."

"Same mushrooms Georgina picked with her father last Sunday in England and then at the convent on Saturday. Doesn't mean anything by itself, but let's go see who's up at the rectory. Good plan?"

"Excellent plan."

They grabbed jackets and headed out. As tempting as it was to walk, they decided to take separate vehicles the few blocks to the rectory, given the uncertainty about what the next steps were.

When they arrived, Henrietta was raking leaves in the front yard. "Oliver and I were up on London time. We've already been to Hurley's for doughnuts." She sighed happily, standing the rake upright next to her. "It's premature to rake, I suppose, given the number of leaves yet to fall, but it can't hurt to get a jump on the work."

"We're not here about raking," Colin said.

She narrowed her eyes on him. "I know. Oliver's in the kitchen with Finian, preparing tea and toast for Jeremy. He's awake. We spoke briefly after I got back from breakfast." She paused, plucked a few leaves that had stuck to the rake tines. "He knows Robin Masterson died earlier today."

She dropped the leaves she'd plucked into the small pile she'd managed to assemble. "Jeremy spoke with the hospital. They've been in touch with Georgina, so she knows about her father."

Colin toed a few of the leaves in Henrietta's pile. "Has Jeremy spoken with her?"

"I don't believe so, no."

"With Thames House?"

Henrietta tossed her head back. "The fog's quite mysterious and lovely, isn't it? A different quality to it here on the coast. I can feel the sun wanting to break through the gray." She studied a red spot on her right index finger. "I suppose I should stop before a proper blister comes up. I don't do nearly enough raking at home. Oliver and Martin get the farm workers to do the heavier work there, and I've let Aunt Posey's garden go to ruin, I'm afraid."

"Busy days chasing after a boss who's gone rogue," Colin said.

"He's not gone rogue," she snapped back, then shrugged. "Not quite."

"A matter of opinion?"

"He hasn't broken any laws in America. The rest is none of your concern. And he's not my boss. He didn't take Robin's death well, but it wasn't a surprise." She squinted up at the changing leaves on the maple tree. "It's a fantastic old hardwood, isn't it? Imagine what it's seen in this spot since it was a sapling."

"Henrietta," Emma said. "We need to know what's going on here between the Mastersons and Jeremy, and between you and Oliver and Jeremy."

"It's my belief we're intruding into what amounts to a personal situation. Jeremy tried to help patch up things between Robin and his daughter. Robin ingested death cap mushrooms, and here we are."

"Why did you go to Dublin?" Colin asked.

She lowered the rake and stabbed at a scatter of freshly fallen red-orange leaves.

Emma felt chilled in the fog but noticed Henrietta was sweating from her raking. "Robin isn't the one who went to Dublin to buy the painting for his daughter. You know that, don't you, Henrietta?"

"He did. He just did it through Jeremy." She stopped abruptly, stood up the rake again. "He and Robin were more friends than anything else. I didn't know that. So I flew to Dublin to sniff around—and to see a friend and do a bit of shopping."

Colin gave her a skeptical look.

"I told you, Colin. That wasn't a lie." Henrietta rubbed a thumb along her reddened finger. "Don't assume I know everything about what's going on because it's not what I'm assuming."

"We try not to make assumptions," Emma said.

Henrietta softened slightly. "The likeliest scenario is that Robin was depressed about retiring and killed himself after he had a good visit with his daughter. It's not the only scenario, but perhaps their visit crystalized what he'd sacrificed for his work. He knew there was no going back and putting things right. I'm speculating. I didn't know him."

"He was already beyond hope when Jeremy arrived in Boston," Colin said.

"Robin was beyond hope when Jeremy found him in the park. Jeremy delivered the painting to Georgina as a friend, without telling anyone. It was wrong of him to do things the way he did, but human. Some would be surprised he has a human side never mind let one get the better of his judgment."

Colin put out a hand and she gave the rake to him.

"Any chance Robin taught Georgina how to whip up a batch of nerve agent?"

"It's a good thing you have my rake or I'd knock you on the head with it. Honestly, Colin. No. It's completely outrageous and ridiculous to think she has any interest in chemical weapons or knowledge of their production, distribution or use."

He shrugged. "And you never asked that question yourself, huh?"

She ignored him. "It sounds as if Robin regretted giving up so much for his work, but it seems to me it was his way. If he'd become an art professor instead of a scientist, he'd still have hyperfocused and short-changed his personal relationships. I'm not close with my parents, but it's not because they were overly absorbed in their work. They were dedicated to having fun without me."

Colin set the rake against the tree trunk. "My parents are trying to rope me into helping clean out the cellar and attic at the inn. They shoved stuff in them when they renovated, figuring they'd get to it eventually."

"And now 'eventually' has arrived. I suppose I should be careful what I wish for," Henrietta said with a quick smile. But it didn't last. "I'm truly sorry about Robin. It must be awful for Georgina."

"When did you realize something was up with Jeremy and the Mastersons?" Colin asked.

"Oliver didn't tell me. He kept his word to Jeremy." She picked up a pair of pink-flowered garden gloves next to her pile of leaves. "I found them in drop-offs for the rummage sale. They don't do any good if I don't wear them, but they're too small. They're unused. I'm sure they'll sell."

"Henrietta," Colin said.

She walked over to the steps and placed the gloves next to the rake. "Martin Hambly told me Oliver had to go to London unexpectedly, and I took it upon myself to find out why. Jeremy avoided me. I don't like to be avoided." She pushed her tangled hair behind her ears. "When I got back to London from Dublin, Robin was fighting for his life. Georgina was in Boston by then. Jeremy had returned from Dublin on Monday night with the Aoife O'Byrne painting and discovered Robin the next morning. He took measures to keep himself out of any investigation, but he got Robin immediate medical attention. As we now know, there wasn't much to be done."

"And then Jeremy took the painting to Georgina himself," Emma said. "That's quite a gesture."

"Yes, it is. He told her he hadn't seen the painting himself, but that was only because he didn't want her to know his role. It was a gift from her father. In Jeremy's view, that's all she needed to know." Henrietta waved a hand. "He's better today. Best you speak with him."

They went into the rectory through the front door. Oliver was alone in the kitchen, at the table with a mug of tea. "Finian had work to do at the church. I offered to sort rummage. I don't think he believed I was serious. Tea, anyone?"

Henrietta said she wanted some, but Emma left her and Oliver to it and followed Colin to the den. The door was ajar, and he rapped on it as he pushed it open. "Look at you. Shaved, in clean clothes and sitting up."

The senior MI5 officer was tucked under an Irish wool blanket, reasonably awake and alert, his color improved since last night. "I won't be upright for long. I'm done in. I need a nap."

Colin sat on Finian's lounger, close to Jeremy. "You can take a nap after you talk to us."

"What if I don't want to talk to you?"

"We can turn you over to Maine law enforcement for questioning about a report of a missing painting. My brother would be glad to get involved. He's a nice, easygoing guy, but don't let that fool you."

"I shouldn't forget he's a Donovan, too." Jeremy winced, placed a palm on his abdomen. "I'm still a sick man. What do you want?"

"Tell me about you and Robin Masterson."

"I told you—"

"What you told me isn't good enough, Jeremy."

He shifted to Emma as she sat on a chair near his feet. "I've known Colin since his first undercover assignment, did he tell you? Green as a frog."

"Compared to a grizzled old spook like you, yeah," Colin said. "Emma doesn't distract easily. Trust me."

Jeremy sank back against his pillows. "I met Robin when I was a young SAS officer, a few months before I joined the intelligence services. Robin was helping dismantle the Soviet Union's massive stockpiles of chemical weapons. He and his wife were good to me."

"This was in England?"

"Mostly. Valerie Masterson was a research chemist. She was studying antidotes to various nerve agents when she developed a brain tumor. She died within weeks of diagnosis. It was sudden, brutal and tragic. Georgina was seven. Robin went to pieces. He was already a workaholic, but to cope with Valerie's death, he buried himself even deeper in his work."

Emma could see the pain in Jeremy's face—not from his mushroom poisoning, but remembering that long-ago loss. "Did you stay in touch with him?"

"On and off. I had my own work. Georgina isn't wrong or exaggerating when she says he was a crap father. He was. He'd tell you so himself. She took it a step or two outside the lines by convincing herself doctors would have caught her mother's tumor sooner if he hadn't been so absorbed in his work. I don't think she still believes that, but she did through her teen years, at least."

"She felt abandoned," Colin said.

"Robin would say he did abandon her. It wasn't what he wanted to do, but it's what he did." Jeremy licked his raw-looking lips. "She was a sweet little kid."

"Did someone miss something with the mother?" Colin asked. "The brain tumor—did she come into contact with a toxic substance in her or Robin's work that caused the cancer, and you feel you owe her husband, her daughter?"

"Your mind, Colin," Jeremy said. "No. It was just one of those things. Bad luck, genes, I don't know. It had nothing to do with neurotoxins or anything similar. We were friends. It happens even in our line of work."

Colin shook his head in that stubborn, confident manner Emma knew well. "Nope. There's more to it. You posed as Robin, flew to Dublin the day after he and Georgina admired Aoife O'Byrne's paintings and bought an expensive one so your friend could give it to his daughter."

"It was a favor."

"Why didn't he go to Dublin himself?"

"Because I was at a loose end and offered."

"Why pose as him?"

"It kept things straightforward. I didn't want to get into the middle of his relationship with his daughter, but I wanted to help."

"You went to a lot of trouble to help. Why the urgency?"

Emma expected the quick back-and-forth to tire Jeremy, but he paused only for a half beat. "Robin rarely had a clue what to do for Georgina. He'd missed most of her birthdays. He wanted to get her the painting after seeing how she'd reacted to Aoife O'Byrne's work. He was going to ship it to her, but when he fell sick—I went. The painting was still in my possession. It was simpler just to fly to Boston and give it to Georgina myself."

"Was Robin worried about her and this foliage cruise?" Colin asked.

"He was worried about her in general. I think he saw her visit as a chance to mend their relationship, and it didn't work out quite the way he'd hoped. He thought they could have a few meals together, she could sleep in her old room, they could forage for wild mushrooms— and after two or three days, all would be well." Jeremy reached for his water glass. "Robin realized it was going to be harder work than that."

"No magic wand to make things better," Emma said. "But progress?"

"When I left for Dublin to buy the painting, I'd have said yes."

Jeremy took a sip of water but lost his grip on the glass. Colin grabbed it before any water spilled and set the glass back on the table. "Did you speak with him after you left?"

"No."

"Did he know you were going to Dublin to buy the painting?"

Jeremy didn't answer at once. "Not specifically, no."

"But he okayed it—he knew you were buying an expensive painting for his daughter, on his behalf."

"There you have it," Jeremy said, his voice hoarse now. "It's my personal business, Colin. It has nothing to do with my work, his work or your work."

Colin folded his hands on his middle, a gesture Emma knew to be deceptively casual. Probably so did Jeremy Pearson. "Quite a bond between you and Robin to go to the trouble of sneaking to Ireland, buying a painting and personally taking it to Boston. What name did you use to go to Ireland?"

"Doesn't matter."

"You used William Hornsby to sneak into the US without telling me."

"I didn't sneak anywhere."

"Eye of the beholder," Colin said.

"I approached Aoife O'Byrne as Robin. Otherwise…"

"You were William Hornsby, a man who doesn't exist."

"He exists. I'm right here."

"Why didn't you stay at Robin Masterson's bedside, if he was seriously ill and you two were such good friends?"

"Did I say we were good friends? Don't take advantage of a sick man, Colin."

Colin scratched the side of his mouth. He glanced at Emma. He was used to men like Jeremy Pearson. In many ways, she knew, he was one himself. But he hadn't been doing this work as long, and she wondered if he worried one day he'd go too far—sacrifice too much.

He shifted back to the senior intelligence agent. "You aren't convinced Robin committed suicide. A neuro-toxicologist with his experience in wild mushroom foraging doesn't accidentally ingest a deadly poisonous mushroom."

"No."

It was all Jeremy said. Emma knew Colin could wait a week and his British friend wouldn't say more. "That leaves homicide. Murder, Jeremy."

"It does, doesn't it?"

"What direction does the evidence point, then?"

"It points to suicide or accident."

"Round and round," Colin said. "Henrietta found out you went to Dublin and followed your trail. Then you're off to Boston, and she grabs Oliver and follows you. Either you're directing her or leading her on, or you went AWOL on her and she's trying to save your skin."

"I don't need anyone to save my skin. Does Georgina know about her father? You're going to see her? I'll go with you." Jeremy threw his blanket to the floor and staggered to his feet. He teetered unsteadily and grabbed the arm of the sofa. "I'm bloody useless."

"You need time to recover," Emma said, touching his arm. "Can I get you anything?"

He shook his head. "When people first started getting sick, I thought it might be the same thing that made Robin sick. These death cap mushrooms."

"Onset of symptoms was too fast for death caps," Colin said.

A thin smile from his friend. "The things we've learned about mushrooms, eh?"

"You're not going anywhere, my friend," Colin said, helping him back to the sofa. "Rest up. I'm sorry about Robin's death."

"He died alone. For a long time I thought I would, too. I might yet if my wife disowns me."

"Just one more question before I scoot. Why did you put Robin in touch with Oliver? Did you know they were going to talk about poison art?"

"He said he wanted to talk to someone familiar with mythology and art. He didn't mention poisons to me, just to Oliver. He was retired and curious, he said. I didn't believe that was all there was to it, but I wasn't alarmed. I assumed his interest had something to do with Georgina and her visit. I still do." Jeremy sank against the sofa cushions. "Anything else? Thumb-screws next?"

"We'll talk later."

"Georgina…"

"I'll give her your best."

"She knows me only as Hornsby."

"But she has good instincts," Colin said. "Spooks, she called us last night."

"She might be slightly built and emotional right now, but she has a spine of steel. No one should underestimate her, including me." Jeremy raised his bloodshot eyes to Colin and Emma. "But we know some bad actors, the three of us. Henrietta and Oliver, too. See to it she's okay, won't you?"

"We will," Colin said.

"Rest," Emma said. "Get well."

They returned to the kitchen. Oliver was looking out the back-door window, contemplating bean holes, he said. "I can try my hand at a pie, too. I discovered recipes in a folder. Apparently, the menu for the supper hasn't changed in decades."

Henrietta was at the sink, up to her elbows in water and suds. "Is Heron's Cove next on your agenda?"

Emma nodded. She knew it would be on Henrietta's agenda, if their situations were reversed. Colin thrust a finger at Oliver. "You, go with Emma. I'll meet you there. Henrietta, stay here with Jeremy. I don't want to leave him alone, and I don't want to leave Fin Bracken alone with him. He's not Fin's responsibility."

Oliver turned to her. "Henrietta?"

"Go," she said. "I'll be fine here."

Colin leveled his gaze on her. "Don't leave church property. We'll be back."

She pulled her wet, heat-reddened hands out of the dishpan and took a towel off a hook. "As you wish."

Oliver raised his eyebrows, obviously surprised by her acquiescence, but he didn't comment. He grabbed his jacket from a row of pegs and kissed her goodbye. Colin pulled open the back door, letting Oliver and Emma go ahead of him.

When they reached Emma's car, Oliver paused. "Why do you want me in Heron's Cove?"

"Because you're an art thief," Colin said. "We need someone who thinks like an art thief to help us figure out what happened to that painting."

Emma unlocked the car doors while Colin headed for his truck. "We'd appreciate your help and cooperation, Oliver."

He smiled as he got into the car. "Happy to do what I can to help the FBI."

* * *

Richie Hillier was smoking a cigarette on the pier by the yacht when Colin, Emma and Oliver arrived. "Agent Donovan, Agent Sharpe. I can't say I'm glad to see you. It's been another terrible morning with news of the death of Georgina's father." The captain tossed his cigarette into the river. "Sorry, a bad habit—smoking and tossing the butts into the water. I hope you won't fine me. To be honest, I can't wait to get out of here."

He brought them up to the sundeck, where Bryce Fanning occupied a lounge, a blanket over his out-stretched legs, a glass of ice and an open bottle of an upscale local ginger ale at his side. And Nick Lothian, in khakis and navy polo shirt. "Is there anything else I can get you?" But Bryce dismissed him with a curt shake of the head. "Rough morning," Nick said in a half whisper as he passed Colin and headed across the sundeck to the bar.

Melodie came out from behind the bar with a plate of saltine crackers and applesauce. "Bryce had a good night," she said, placing the plate next to the ginger ale. "Progress is progress. He needs to keep his fluids up and get his electrolytes back in balance. This whole ordeal has been a stress on his body."

Bryce grinned. "It's Melodie's polite way of saying I'm overweight and out of shape." He adjusted his position, clearly weak. "I'm hoping we can head home tomorrow morning. It'll take at least a week for me to get back to normal. Then I've promised my lovely wife I'll make an appointment with my doctor, a trainer and a nutritionist—one who doesn't recommend mushrooms."

"I read a while back that mushrooms might help with brain health," Melodie said.

Emma wasn't sure if she was serious or joking, but Bryce obviously thought the latter. "Too soon," he said with grunt. But his eyes sparked with amusement, suggesting he appreciated his wife's sense of humor, and her company. He looked up at his guests. "Now, what can I do for you?"

"This is Oliver York," Emma said. "He's a friend. He's visiting in the area and planned to meet up with Bill Hornsby."

"Oh, right. You're the mythologist Melodie mentioned," Bryce said. "Excuse me for not standing up. I understand you know Georgina, our unlucky chef?"

Oliver nodded. "We met briefly in London last week."

"Please, take a seat, all of you. Nick can get you coffee, tea. Help yourself to saltines. I only eat them when I'm sick to my stomach, but I don't know why." He took a moment to catch his breath. "Just talking gets my heartbeat up. Imagine if I got on a treadmill. Georgina is on another of her runs. Third day in a row."

"Is she alone?" Colin asked.

"Nick offered to accompany her," Melodie said. "She wanted to go alone. It was foggy when she left, but it's burned off—it'll be beautiful along the water. I hope running helps her come to terms with what's happened. We're putting her in a car to the airport in Boston as soon as she gets back and takes a shower. She's already packed. We have her booked on a flight this evening. She'll arrive in London early tomorrow morning."

Bryce picked up his ginger ale. "We're sorry it'll be too late to see her father alive, but he never regained consciousness. It's been eating her up. She never should have come on this cruise. Melodie and I could have done the cooking. We're not helpless."

Melodie tucked herself on the lounge next to her husband's feet. "She says running helps clear her head, but it's hard not to worry about her with such awful news. She's so young to have lost both parents. My father died seven years ago, and I still think about him nearly every day. We had a good relationship. I still have my mother."

"God love her," Bryce muttered.

She grinned at him. "Don't you dare start on my poor dear mother." She shifted back to her company. "Sometimes it's harder to lose a parent when you didn't have a good relationship, and now you know you never will. The fantasy can die hard."

Bryce drank some of his ginger ale. "That's going down well. For a while there, I thought Melodie would be collecting my life insurance. Now…damn, I like this sea air." He took in a breath. "I like Georgina, but she has a lot on her plate. It's just as well she's leaving us. I want to be on our way. I'm used to boats. I don't have to worry about getting seasick, and I won't need a doctor."

"If you do, Richie and Nick will handle it," Melodie said. "Georgina can get her father's affairs settled and figure out what's next for her. If he'd fallen ill before she left London, she'd never have made this trip. We wouldn't have allowed it, even if she'd wanted to. In hindsight, I wish we'd sent her to London as soon as we found out ourselves."

Bryce nodded in agreement. "She's been distraught and distracted, understandably. Ripe for mistakes." He paused, his eyelids heavy. "Is there anything else we can do for you? I'm going to sleep. I feel like a sick old dog. Nick can fix you up with drinks and a snack, if you'd like."

As Emma got to her feet, she noticed the sky was a clear, cloudless blue. "Does either of you draw or paint?"

Melodie seemed surprised at the question. "No, I don't. Bryce took a few art classes in college, or so he tells me."

"She was in diapers then," he said.

She smiled. "Kindergarten."

"I was never any good at drawing or painting," he added. "Melodie and I collect art as an investment, but it has to be something we like. We appreciate art, but we're not artists and we have no desire to become artists. Why do you ask?"

Oliver had wandered off to the rail and was looking out at the Sharpe offices, situated between the marina and an inn and parking lot. Emma knew he was listening to the conversation with the Fannings. "Do you have any particular interest in art with mythological themes?" she asked them.

Bryce frowned. "You mean like Zeus and Athena?"

Melodie chuckled, amused. "I suspect Bryce's knowledge of mythology begins and ends with the Greek and Roman gods and goddesses."

"I read Edith Hamilton in high school," he said, grinning back at her. He yawned, wincing. "Muscles in my face and abdomen are still sore. Even a damn yawn hurts. To answer your question, no, no particular interest in mythology but I wouldn't rule it out."

"Provided it's not gruesome art," Melodie said. "Not my thing, even as an investment."

Nick came forward with a mimosa for Melodie.

"Georgie and I planned to binge-watch the *Lord of the Rings* trilogy on our off hours on the cruise. That doesn't count, does it? Dragons, fairies, wizards. Anyway, we're not going to get to it, obviously. Georgie's the only one I know on board who draws, and she sticks to plants."

"Her wild edibles," Melodie said, taking the mimosa. "Is Bill Hornsby involved in all this? It was my idea to invite him to join us. Bryce tells me I'm too trusting, but I thought he was interesting."

"Did you meet him in London?" Colin asked.

"Hornsby? No, we didn't, nor did we meet Georgina's father. Now…" Melodie raised her mimosa. "I'd like to put my feet up for a few minutes and not think about sickness and death."

Colin stood. "Thanks for your time. I left my card with the captain. Please don't hesitate to get in touch if you think of anything else."

"I hope Georgina enjoys her run," Emma said. "Please give her our best."

"Of course," Melodie said. "She'll appreciate that."

"I understand you wanted to visit the Sharpe offices. Someone will be there today."

"I'll keep that in mind, but it was Bill Hornsby's idea to visit. I thought it'd be fun to stop in if we had time. I've heard of them, of course. You're family, I understand. Must be interesting."

Bryce yawned again, sinking under his blanket. "If there's nothing else…"

"Nick will walk you out," Melodie said.

Emma could see the stress of the past few days was getting to Melodie. Even Nick didn't say anything until they reached the docks. "Do you think one of us should go after Georgina, make sure she's okay? She was upset when she left, understandably. She has her phone with her, at least. Richie insisted she take it with her."

"Maybe give her a call," Colin said.

"I'll do that."

He returned to the yacht. A stiff breeze caught the ends of Oliver's tawny, curly hair as he squinted at the yacht and then back at the docks. "I'd keep it simple if I were to remove a painting from the yacht," he said. "I'd time it when there were a lot of people around. In this case, during Saturday's party—the prep, when guests were arriving or when people were getting sick. It doesn't mean I would need to be the one responsible for making people sick. I could seize on the moment."

"Wouldn't you plan ahead?" Colin asked.

"If possible. I'd be ready to jump on the right moment. There's no need to risk slipping it off the yacht during the night, but it's an option. Either way, key, I would think, is what's next? Where would I hide the painting? How much time would I have to hide it? If I'm a passenger or crew member, I might have different options than one of the guests who arrived just for the day."

"A passenger or crew member wouldn't have a car," Emma said. "But someone on board could have been working with a guest."

"Feels like a solo operation to me," Oliver said. "This assumes the painting was removed from the yacht by someone other than its owner, of course. Georgina is upset. It's a gift from her father."

"What," Colin said, "she threw it overboard and is in denial?"

Oliver shrugged. "I have no idea. She could be right and it's misplaced on the yacht somewhere."

Emma noticed Kevin Donovan walking toward them. She turned to Colin, saw he'd spotted his brother, too. "No one was at the offices this weekend," she said. "They're right here, and Melodie and our British art consultant were interested in them. Why don't Oliver and I go over there and have a look?"

"Okay. I'll see what's up with Kevin." Colin paused, glanced at Oliver. "Be good."

But Oliver had his gaze narrowed on the Sharpe offices, the small backyard, the marina next door, bordering shrubs, slips and boats. He drew in a breath and turned to Colin. "I'm sorry, what did you say?"

"Nothing. You're in art thief mode with no art to steal." Colin touched Emma's hand. "Stay in touch."

20

Emma took Oliver through the small backyard of the Sharpe Fine Art Recovery offices—her grandparents' former home—and up the steps to the porch. She rang the doorbell, but needn't have bothered since Ginny Bosko, Lucas's assistant, was at the table in the kitchen off the back door. She jumped up and pulled open the door. In her early twenties, ambitious and smart, she had made herself indispensable in her first few months on the job. "Emma, great to see you. I just got in. No one else is here. Quite a weekend at the marina with the food poisoning on the yacht. I can't say I'm sorry to have missed that."

"Fortunately, everyone will make a full recovery," Emma said.

Ginny peered at at Oliver, standing off to Emma's side. "Is this—aren't you—"

"Oliver York," he said with one of his charming smiles.

"Ah. That's what I thought. Pleased to meet you, Mr. York."

Until that moment, Emma hadn't been sure if Ginny knew about Oliver. "Did anyone from the yacht get in touch with the office over the weekend?"

"Not that I'm aware of. Lucas already asked the same question. I double-checked, and we didn't get any voice mails or emails from anyone who said they were on the yacht. No requests for tours of the offices, appointments, coffee. Lucas went through the names involved. Let me see—Hornsby, Fanning, Hillier, Lothian, Masterson and Balfour. And York," she added, blushing slightly. "People know Lucas is in Ireland with your grandfather, so it's been quiet."

"Thanks, Ginny," Emma said. "Did anyone drop off a package?"

"I didn't see any when I got in." She gestured behind her. "I came in through the front door. I didn't see any sign of a break-in, if that's your next question. If I had, I'd have called 911, but we have an alarm system. It's basic. We don't keep valuable art in here. Take a look around if you'd like."

"Out here first, if you will, Emma," Oliver said next to her.

"I'll leave you to it, then," Ginny said. "I'll be in the front room if you need me."

She stepped back into the kitchen, shutting the door behind her. Emma turned and faced the water and the docks. She didn't see Colin or Kevin. She shifted to Oliver. "What do you think? I know you could sneak inside despite the alarms, but since you weren't involved with taking the painting—"

"I wasn't," he said calmly.

"I know. The past few days would have gone down differently if you had."

He moved away from the door, toward a table shoved up against the back wall. When her brother had launched the extensive renovations of the old house, Emma had lobbied him to keep the porch instead of converting it into more offices, a study, a library—it didn't matter. The porch was the one spot she'd wanted to leave unchanged, or at least as little changed as possible. When he'd finally tuned in and given it some thought, Lucas had agreed.

In August, she'd last seen her father out here. He'd been in a great mood after picking wild blueberries that morning. She still had a quart of them in the freezer, awaiting a Thanksgiving pie. Lucas had been there that warm, beautiful morning, too, but he lived in Heron's Cove and worked in the family business, and he'd therefore had more contact with their parents since they'd moved back to Maine from London in the spring.

Oliver pushed past the table to a gas grill in the corner, a new addition Ginny had bought on sale in September, with plans for taking advantage of the offices appealing location for client and staff get-togethers. Lucas had reluctantly admitted they could do more socializing on the premises. He and Emma had exchanged texts about the grill. She remembered how baffled and amused he was, and how much they'd both needed that distraction in the early days after their father's death.

But Oliver stood back, pointing at the grill, covered in black tarp. "Emma."

"Hold on, Oliver." She raced to him and pulled his

hand away from the tarp. "Let's make sure they're not booby-trapped or doused with poison."

"My, how you think. They're not rigged with anything dire."

"Still, you're a guest, and I'm…"

"You're a Sharpe and an FBI agent." He gestured with one hand. "Have at it, Special Agent Sharpe."

He stood back, and she saw he hadn't pointed to the grill itself, with the prospect of something hidden under the tarp. Instead, he'd pointed to a slender plastic-wrapped package tucked between the grill and the porch wall.

"It's Aoife's painting," Emma said as she rolled the grill back a few inches.

The Irish woodland scene was visible through a thick, milky plastic wrap that encased the painting. It was small, maybe eighteen-by-twelve inches. The plastic was crooked, loosely taped, as if someone had grabbed it out of the rest of the painting's packaging materials and covered it in a hurry.

"Looks as if it was put here in haste," Oliver said behind her. "I'd say the choice of the Sharpe offices wasn't simply opportunistic but, rather, deliberate. Our thief didn't run up the porch steps with the painting thinking it was a random summer home on the water."

"Could be designed to look like a theft," Emma said half to herself.

"Yes."

She noticed a white sheet of sketch paper to the right of the painting, pressed against the porch wall. She shoved the grill back a few more inches to get a better look. The sheet fell faceup to the floor. Another pencil drawing. Oliver peered at the sketch over her shoulder. "More images like those on the sketch Georgina had last night," he said.

Emma nodded. "I see them."

She leaned forward and saw what appeared to be a small plastic bag peeking out from behind the sketch. With one finger, she touched the edge of the sketch paper and pulled it back, revealing the rest of the bag. Inside were pieces of what she took to be mushrooms.

"I'll guess we wouldn't want those grilled up for breakfast," Oliver said.

Emma left everything where it was and stood up. "Do you know who put these things here, Oliver?"

"I have no idea what's going on."

"Oliver—"

"No, I don't know. May I take a closer look at the sketch?"

"Just don't touch anything."

She stepped back, allowing him a clearer view behind the grill. "This is an actual scene rather than the random images in either of the similar sketches from the galley or last night. It's as if the artist had been experimenting with those and with this one, tried his or her hand at telling a story."

"One you and Robin discussed?" Emma asked.

"Not in particular, no. It's trying to be an original creation, I'd say, rather than a depiction of any one myth or folktale." He stood back, looked out at the tidal river, a seagull perched on a post. "It's well done, carefully done—not thrown together as the images were last night. It's not signed. Neither was the sketch last night. Why not, I wonder? They're good, if twisted."

"I think twisted is the point, don't you? The artist is going for an effect."

"The chaos, efficacy and death that can come with poison. There are countless myths, legends and folktales in which poisons are used as a means of attaining or exerting power and control, revenge, self-defense. Robin didn't mention sketches when he talked to me, but what if drawing was one of his new hobbies? He did spend decades studying various types of poison."

Emma went to the rail and waved to Kevin, alone on the dock. She didn't see Colin. "Kevin," she called to him. "Need you up here." She shifted back to Oliver. "If there's anything you haven't told me, Oliver, now's the time."

He shook his head. "There's nothing, Emma. I've racked my brain in case I forgot or overlooked anything. Jeremy, the Mastersons. Henrietta. Aoife O'Byrne. Any mention of your family, or you, Colin, Finian Bracken. If there's anything else, I've missed it."

Kevin crossed the lawn at a fast clip and trotted up the steps. "Colin left for Rock Point. I'll meet him there. What's going on?"

She told him. He gritted his teeth in a way that reminded her of Colin. Kevin would secure the painting—and the sketch and mushrooms bits—and contact the Heron's Cove police. "Georgina could have put this stuff here herself," Emma said. "She'll have some explaining to do, but if it's just trespassing—"

"Good outcome." His eyes narrowed on her. "You and Oliver heading out?"

She nodded. "We need to find Georgina, Kevin."

"Nick Lothian and Richie Hillier have gone to find

her. Different directions. The Fannings want to make sure she's back in time to meet her car."

"They're starting to see her as trouble," Emma said.

Kevin glanced at the painting in its plastic. "Not without reason."

Ginny came onto the porch. Emma left Kevin to explain the situation and went with Oliver through the kitchen and out to the front offices, so different from when young Wendell Sharpe had set up his art detective business in the front room. He'd been married then, and he and his wife had raised their son here. Emma noticed a framed picture of them on the front wall where her grandfather had his desk. The place was changed—modern, state-of-the-art, even the upstairs bedrooms given over to office space—and yet, in many ways, it was the same.

Oliver frowned at her from the front steps. "Emma?"

"On my way."

Emma took the scenic coastal route to Rock Point, past large summer homes and classic rockbound Maine coast. Oliver stared out the passenger window. "It's a beautiful day for a run. I'd go this way if I were Georgina."

"Do you run?"

"Only when I have to get away from something or someone." But his cheekiness fell flat, and he added, "I'll keep an eye out for her, don't worry."

"Did you know you were following Jeremy when you headed to Boston, or did you really think you'd be enjoying fall foliage with Henrietta?"

"I knew it wasn't an ordinary visit with friends."

He glanced sideways at her. "Then nothing is ordinary with you and Colin, is it? Or with our Father Bracken, for that matter."

Emma made no comment. She didn't point out he'd played a role in complicating their lives the past year.

He turned to the window again. "I'd like to take you through everything. Something that seems trivial to me might not to you. And I want the timeline clear in my head. I want to be sure Jeremy isn't playing us—not just Henrietta and me. You and Colin, too." He paused. "Maybe especially Colin."

"Because of their friendship," Emma said, not making it a question. "Okay. Talk to me."

"I hadn't spoken with Jeremy in several weeks when he found me at Claridge's a week ago Saturday. He had an agenda, but he always does—and he doesn't share it with me, ever. I understand he can't. But this was different."

"How so?"

"From the start, it felt personal. He sat across from me while I was having breakfast and asked me to speak with Robin Masterson." Oliver watched as they passed a jogger, a rail-thin middle-aged man in shorts and a tank. "He asked. That should have been my first clue. Jeremy doesn't ask."

"When had you arrived in London?"

"The night before. I stayed at my apartment. I'm selling it, did I tell you? It's the right time. I'm not the little boy who saw his parents killed there. I can let it go. It needs to take on the energy of a new family. With its posh Mayfair address, I'll do well. Henrietta says I can do what I want with the profits, but she has farm improvements in mind." He waved a hand. "No matter."

"If selling the apartment is right for you, that's what counts, I think," Emma said.

He looked at her, his green eyes soft with emotion. Thirty years ago, he'd witnessed his parents' murder in the apartment's library. "Thank you."

"Does Jeremy know you're putting it on the market?"

"Jeremy knows everything. He stayed perhaps five minutes at breakfast. He didn't have so much as a cup of tea. He was his curt, no-nonsense self." Oliver kept his gaze on the sea, not a hint of fog even out on the horizon. "He asked me not to discuss his request with Henrietta."

"Where was she?" Emma asked.

"At her aunt's old house in the Cotswolds, digging dahlias and sorting through Freddy Balfour's opera collection. When Jeremy left Claridge's, I knew I was to meet with Robin Masterson, a retired scientist interested in mythology, and I wasn't to tell Henrietta."

Emma slowed to cross a narrow stone bridge. "Did Jeremy tell you Robin was interested in poisons?"

"No. He remained vague. Maintaining plausible deniability, perhaps."

Or he hadn't known. "Did he tell you Robin was a chemical weapons expert?"

"He did not. Again, he kept it vague. 'Retired scientist.' He did tell me Robin knew him as an art consultant named William Hornsby. I got the impression Robin was aware Jeremy is with MI5, but we didn't go there. The Voldemort approach."

Emma smiled. Oliver and his MI5 handler did have

an interesting relationship. "Did you walk to the gallery straight from your breakfast?"

"I took a long walk in St. James's Park first. Then I walked over. I got there about fifteen minutes ahead of Robin Masterson."

"Did you have a description of him, or did he have your name?"

"Jeremy—Hornsby, so-called—had given him my name. He told me Robin's daughter might arrive with him."

"Who else was at the gallery?" Emma asked.

"The owners. It was early, quiet. Georgina only stayed a few minutes, but I got the impression it was longer than either she or her father expected."

"Because of the Aoife O'Byrne paintings," Emma said.

"It was love at first sight for Georgina." Oliver stared out his window, watching the crashing waves as he spoke. "Her father seemed utterly delighted. If she's responsible for these unpleasant sketches, one can see why he'd be pleased she was struck by Aoife's Irish landscapes. I can see a father wanting to encourage an interest in paintings of woodlands, rainbows and the sea—not trite in Aoife's hand, mind you—instead of death art."

"We don't know she did those sketches, Oliver."

"No, I suppose not. In any event, I said hello to her but that was the extent of our contact."

"Did you mention you know Aoife?"

"No, we didn't discuss her work. It never occurred to me her father would buy one of her paintings, and certainly not go all the way to Dublin for it. Georgina left, and Robin and I had our chat over pints. He didn't strike me as suicidal, but then again we now know he kept lethal mushrooms in his fridge. But he was a neurotoxicologist and an experienced forager, so maybe it wasn't a big deal to him."

"Compared to sarin, I suppose."

He turned and again stared out the window. "After Robin left, Jeremy stopped at the pub but only for a few minutes, not long enough to stop dripping. I didn't give it much thought. It felt like he'd done a good turn for an eccentric friend."

"Did you see Robin or Georgina after that?" Emma asked.

"No. I left London and drove to the farm the following afternoon. Henrietta wasn't there. I took Alfred for a good walk, and Martin and I had dinner at the village pub and whiskey by the fire." Oliver was silent a moment. "I've come to trust and admire Jeremy, Emma. I appreciate the enormous burden he has in his work, and the sacrifices and contributions he's made to keep people safe from the worst imaginable threats."

The coastal road ended, and Emma turned onto the main road into Rock Point. "But?"

"But Colin and I have a better chance of becoming friends than Jeremy and I do. I wouldn't be surprised if he's had the goods on me for years and was waiting for the right moment to pounce so I would do his bidding."

"That's the closest you've come to admitting to being our art thief."

"Your what?" He glanced at her long enough to give her a sly smile. "I didn't say what goods. I could have slept with his wife for all you know. Have you ever met her?"

"I've only just met Jeremy."

"He and Colin are friends as well as colleagues. Interesting, isn't it? A taste of what it's like to appreciate someone and yet…" He sighed, thoughtful. "I don't know if Jeremy's crossed any lines he shouldn't, but his connection to Robin Masterson and his daughter transcends his MI5 work. I'm sure of it. Now Robin's dead of mushroom poisoning and Jeremy's recovering from mushroom poisoning, and we have a painting depicting mushrooms—if delightful ones—and these strange sketches. Given his background, if Robin wanted to kill himself, why use deadly mushrooms?"

At first Emma didn't realize Oliver had paused because he was waiting for her to respond, not just collecting his thoughts. "I don't know, Oliver."

"Would you tell me if you did know?"

"If I could. But I don't know." Emma picked up her speed now that they were on a less twisty road. "What about Henrietta's behavior this past week?"

"She disappeared. No details. She finally turned up at the farm on Thursday and told me to pack for Maine. We left on Friday. We spent the night in Boston and drove up here on Saturday."

"Were you two in touch before Thursday?"

"No. I knew she was doing MI5 work."

"When did you find out Robin was sick?"

"Yesterday at the hospital with Henrietta and the dreadful tea. The same time you did."

Emma realized her grip had tightened on the wheel and deliberately loosened it. "I see."

"I think she suspected Jeremy had posed as Robin to buy the painting from Aoife and had gone a bit off the grid. I knew she was chewing on something. Everything runs through her head. It's her nature. She considers every possibility, no matter how barmy, and does it at lightning speed, so it doesn't impede her. She's not the type to get bogged down."

"She didn't speak with Aoife in Dublin," Emma pointed out.

Oliver cracked his window, letting in a bit of autumn air. "She didn't need to, did she? She confirmed somehow it *had* been Jeremy in Dublin, not Robin, and she decided to find him. Your grandfather wasn't involved, was he?"

"He says he wasn't."

Oliver snorted. "Well, that convinced me."

Emma couldn't always tell when Oliver was being dramatic, sincere or deflecting and redirecting. "If the yacht mushroom poisoning was intentional—and that's a huge leap at this point—it doesn't appear intended to maim or kill anyone, just cause sickness, chaos, perhaps a tarnishing of Georgina's reputation as a chef."

"Unless the perpetrator got the wrong mushrooms."

"We don't know there is a perpetrator, Oliver. That's why it's dangerous to jump too far ahead of the facts."

She didn't know if he'd heard her. "I tell you, Emma, there was nothing in my conversation with Robin that led me to suspect anything terrible was about to happen. It was an intellectual discussion, prompted by his fascination with wild plants, his profession and his newfound freedom as a pensioner. He didn't strike me as a man about to kill himself or worried he was about to be killed."

"It's easy to go down that road," Emma said. "I urge you to resist, Oliver."

He heaved a sigh and sank back against his car seat. "I assumed Jeremy chose the gallery for Robin and me to meet because it was convenient for me. Now that I think about it, that's absurd on my part. Jeremy's never done anything simply because it was convenient for me. What if he chose the gallery because he wanted Georgina to see Aoife's work?"

"Was it new to Robin as well as to her?"

"If it wasn't, he did a good job faking it." Oliver considered a moment. "How does Henrietta strike you?"

"I don't know her well enough to say."

"She's been unusually pensive lately," he said, answering his own question. "She says her grandfather's opera records have her thinking about the past. Freddy Balfour died when she was five. She's considering writing a book about him, did she tell you? Posey's house and garden are on her mind, too. Maybe she's thinking of dumping me. I'm not the usual sort of bloke, you know?"

"I'm sure you'll figure it out."

He smiled. "Staying out of it, are you? Now you sound like Colin. Do you two ever think about quitting the FBI and living in Rock Point full-time? I suppose it's not necessarily quieter. There's a poison victim in the rectory and a missing painting, an unsettling sketch and likely toxic mushrooms at your family's place of business."

They came to Rock Point. Emma turned onto a side street that would take them to the rectory.

"Henrietta and I have known each other since childhood," Oliver said. "We're sharing a wonderful life together at the moment. But she's a part of Jeremy's world, Emma. I'm not suggesting he's out to cause harm, but she trusts him in a way I don't and never will."

"Maybe because they have a professional history and she knows things you don't."

He grinned unexpectedly. "Isn't that what I just said?"

"I appreciate your taking me through this past week from your perspective. If you think of anything else—"

"Do you suppose Jeremy is the one who's been worried about what Georgina is up to?"

"He and her father have known each other a long time," Emma said.

"He has enemies. Robin must have had enemies. What if that's what this week's been about? Enemies who want to exploit Georgina, use her..." He moaned, half to himself. "My head's spinning. Henrietta wouldn't be fazed. She'd be ten steps ahead of me." He paused. "Maybe Jeremy just wanted to give Georgina that painting to make her father look good to her."

Emma slowed for an intersection, not far from St. Patrick's rectory. "You see now why speculating is dangerous."

"One rabbit trail leads to another and another."

"What's your gut say, Oliver?"

"It stopped talking to me when you and Colin discovered Oliver Fairbairn is my pseudonym for my Hol-

lywood consulting work. If not for that, I wouldn't be
here right now."

"I don't know about that. You and Henrietta grew up
together. She was MI5 before Colin and I ever met you.
How far back does she go with Jeremy? Do you know?"

"Far enough."

Emma didn't push him for further explanation as
she navigated the quiet residential roads to the rectory,
and, she hoped, some answers.

21

Finian was at the kitchen table with his laptop when Colin entered the rectory through the back door. Henrietta hovered by the sink, arms crossed on her chest, impatient, frustrated. "He's chatting with Ireland," she said, nodding to Finian.

Colin stood behind Finian, saw that Aoife O'Byrne was on the screen, with Wendell and Lucas Sharpe on either side of her. Colin recognized the bar lounge at the O'Byrne House Hotel. Aoife had her hair pulled back, and her vivid blue eyes focused on Finian. "Do you have a photo of the man you believe posed as Robin Masterson?"

"I don't, I'm afraid," Finian said.

Henrietta glanced at Colin. He could see she was tempted to drag Jeremy out of his sickbed so Aoife could take a good look at him, but Colin didn't think she'd actually do it. Henrietta already knew Jeremy had gone to Dublin and bought the painting. But Aoife wanted to be certain she hadn't got it wrong. Sean Murphy, no doubt lurking off camera, would, too. The two Sharpes—hard to say.

Colin produced a headshot of Jeremy on his phone and held it up to the screen. One couldn't be too careful in making assumptions with his MI5 colleagues.

Aoife nodded. "Yes. That's the man who bought the painting. I'm positive."

Colin didn't lower the photo. "Wendell? Lucas? Have you seen this man?"

Aoife stood back, allowing them a closer view of the image on the screen. Both men shook their heads. "I've never seen him before," Lucas said. "Granddad?"

"No. Never. I'd remember a face like that."

It wasn't the best photo. Jeremy could, when it suited him, meld into a crowd, and even pass himself off as an art consultant. Aoife, Lucas and Wendell explained they hadn't recognized Robin Masterson, the man in the photo Sean had shown them.

Finian sat still in his seat, dressed in his clerical garb. He looked drawn and tired, as if he couldn't believe he'd dragged his friends in Declan's Cross into another mess. He hadn't, of course. Jeremy had posed as Robin Masterson in Dublin before he'd shown up in Rock Point, and Aoife hadn't known Henrietta had walked past her studio. Wendell had, and maybe if his son hadn't just died he'd have wondered if something was up and notified Emma, at least—but he hadn't.

Colin decided he needed to throttle back the intensity in the room. "You're looking good, Wendell," he said.

"Nothing like walking the Irish hills to nourish the soul."

The old man sometimes talked like that, Colin had learned. But Wendell did look good, a relief given the tragic loss of his only son. Colin wanted to get to Ireland and see him, but he was glad Emma had gotten out there…that she and Wendell had walked those Irish hills.

Aoife smiled pleasantly. "Lucas tells me it's bean-hole-supper season there, Finian."

"We're getting ready for one this weekend. It's a busy time with the foliage at its peak. Then things quiet down a bit before the holidays."

"You do have a knack for staying busy. Maybe I'll get to one of those bean-hole suppers one day."

"You'd love it," Finian said.

Colin winced at his friend's awkwardness. Finian was usually amiable and quick-witted, but he looked as if he'd rather be anywhere than on a video chat with his friends in Ireland. It had to be his relationship with Aoife. Unfinished business there, Colin thought.

Sean Murphy appeared on the screen. "Colin? Anything you can tell me?"

"I wish. Thanks for your help, Sean. How's the farm? Still have that Bracken fifteen-year-old on top of your refrigerator?"

"Saving the last of it for Fin's next visit. Fin? When are you coming home?"

"You'll be the first to know if you have some of the fifteen-year-old left."

"I have enough to toast your return."

Finian's expression didn't change. "Send Kitty my love, Sean."

"I will, and you stay safe, my friend."

Sean might as well have told Finian to get new

friends. Colin didn't blame him. They said goodbye to
Aoife, Wendell and Lucas, but no one seemed satisfied
by the conversation. It had obviously stirred up questions beyond those that had to do with the tragic death
of the British neurotoxicologist. When the screen went
blank, Colin found himself feeling strangely apart from
his brother-in-law and grandfather-in-law in Declan's
Cross, as if they were unprotected, alone, in danger.
For once, he didn't trust his gut. Lucas and Wendell
were fine, in good hands with Sean breathing down
their necks. Colin's uneasiness arose, he knew, from
his own unresolved feelings about Tim Sharpe's death
and his undercover work these past weeks.

And he had his own unfinished business.

Henrietta dropped her arms to her sides and stood
straight. "Sean Murphy isn't one to underestimate, is he?"

Finian smiled at her, looking more relaxed now that
he didn't have Aoife on his laptop screen. "One would
be wise not to. I've seen Sean in action."

"And Aoife," Henrietta said. "Add gorgeous to in-
sanely talented."

To that, Finian had no comment.

Colin broke through his own emotions and pulled
Henrietta aside. "I need to speak with our friend in the
den. Is he awake?"

"He was a little while ago. I told him I'd get him out
for some air when he was up to it. As you can imagine, he doesn't take well to being cooped up. He's a
man of action."

"But he told you to go to hell, he'd get himself out
for air?"

"That's a good summary." She moved away from the
sink. "I'll go with you."

They headed down the short hall to the den. Colin held off updating her on what was happening in Rock Point. Kevin had called him. He had secured the painting and sketch until they had a chance to talk with Georgina Masterson. A local police officer was keeping watch on the yacht. Kevin would join Colin in Rock Point as soon as he could. Emma was on the way with Oliver.

The door to the den stood open, held in place by a sheep doorstop, a present from a Bracken sister and another tangible reminder of Finian's home in Ireland. "Company, Jeremy," Henrietta said. But as she stepped into the cozy den, she swore under her breath.

The sofa was empty, a blanket crumpled on the floor. "Is he in the bathroom?" Colin asked.

"His shoes and jacket are gone, but I'll check."

Henrietta disappeared down the hall to the half bath. Colin went into the den. Jeremy didn't appear to have left in a hurry, with a fresh bout of stomach upset, for instance, but he hadn't packed and tidied up, either. Wherever he was, he planned on returning.

Colin saw a note on the table by Finian's chair, held in place by the Bracken pot-still bottle. He could read it without moving it:

Henrietta:
You're right. Fresh air is in order. I'm off for a bit. Didn't tell you because I knew you'd try to stop me. Not to worry.

The note wasn't signed, maybe because he couldn't decide on Jeremy, Bill, William or some other alias he'd used, or a last name.

"He's not here," Henrietta said from the doorway.

"I know. He left a note."

She fumed as she snatched it from under the whiskey bottle and read it. She slapped it back on the small table. "I wouldn't have tried to stop him. I'd have done it. Bloody fool."

"Is the note legit?"

"It's his handwriting. I recognize that scrawl. I should have planted myself at the door, but it wouldn't have made a difference once he decided to leave."

"If someone took him?"

"Even sick, only if he wanted to go."

"Georgina's on a run."

Henrietta nodded without comment.

"Is he protecting her, Henrietta?"

"From what?"

"Herself."

"I trust him, but his behavior this past week hasn't been easy to decipher." She pushed a hand over her curls, fiddled with the clip that held them back and finally stopped. "He's weak, Colin, and he's not himself. We need to find him."

"I'll go look for him. Stay here with Finian. Emma and Oliver will be here soon."

"I don't need anyone to look after me. Oliver doesn't, either. I don't know the area, but I can help—"

"You can help by not arguing with me."

A quick smile. "That's what they all say." But her eyes darkened as she looked at the empty sofa. "I checked on him fifteen minutes ago. Given his physical state, that's not much of a head start." She dug her phone out of a pocket or something in her voluminous skirt and hit a number. Waited. "He's not answering."

She clicked off, palmed the phone. "Don't let me hold you up."

Colin tried Jeremy on his phone, in case his friend was avoiding Henrietta, but he didn't get an answer, either. He left a message. "Call me." His tone said what it needed to: *don't push the bonds of our friendship*.

"We need to find Georgina, too," Henrietta said.

Colin nodded. "Agreed."

Finian came down the hall and quickly assessed the situation. "I'll check the church."

"Not alone, Fin," Colin said.

Henrietta grabbed her jacket off a peg. "I'll go with him. You'll stay in touch, Colin?"

He didn't like the worry in her face. He nodded, then headed out through the front, texting Emma as he ran down the front steps. He'd hoped he'd find Jeremy crumpled up in the shrubs, lesson learned about overdoing it against doctor's orders. He spotted Franny Maroney's notorious cat prowling at the base of a spruce tree. That was it.

He got in his truck and reminded himself to breathe. He'd met Jeremy the first week of his first undercover assignment. Before Emma. He'd been totally green if not out of his element, untrained, or particularly afraid. In Jeremy, Colin had sensed a kindred soul—the kind of independent thinker needed for deep-cover work but also the kind that sometimes had trouble with the bureaucracy and hierarchy of an MI5 or FBI.

Colin had never dealt with anyone more focused or more dedicated to his work than Jeremy Pearson—and to this life. The importance of the work, the dangers, the bonds, the lives he could save.

And had saved, including Colin's own.

But there could be a fine line between dedication and confidence—knowing a job had to be done and you could do a job—and arrogance and addiction. Always, Colin thought, he had to know he could walk away. Let someone else take his place. Never think he was so damn good he was indispensable.

In the five years he'd known Jeremy Pearson, Colin had sensed crustiness, a touch of burnout, regret at some of the sacrifices he'd made—the unnecessary ones, the ones it was easy to tell yourself you needed to make to do the job—but he'd never sensed anything that sounded any alarms. Jeremy Pearson had always been a professional, a man who knew himself and his limitations.

Until now, with this neurotoxicologist and his chef daughter.

Was there something between Jeremy and the Mastersons that had him breaking rules, pulling out the stops? Fraying friendships and professional relationships?

Colin turned toward the harbor. Georgina was on a run. Yesterday her route had taken her along the water. Ten to one she was meeting Jeremy somewhere. As Henrietta had suggested, a fifteen-minute head start would be a lot if Jeremy hadn't crawled out of his sickbed. If Colin hadn't seen the guy's barf and IV himself, he'd question whether his friend and colleague had eaten any of the offending mushrooms at Saturday's party.

He checked sidewalks and yards in case Jeremy had collapsed.

Franny Maroney was out walking, or snooping on what was up in the neighborhood. Colin pulled in next to her and rolled down his window. "Have you seen anyone out here—"

"That man who's recuperating at the rectory. I stopped by to pick up my casserole dish. I didn't get a good look at him, but I'm sure it's the same man I saw a little while ago. He said he was getting some air. Doctor's orders." She pointed down the street, in the same direction Colin was headed. "He was going to look at lobster boats."

"Thanks, Franny."

"Anytime. Should I have called Father Bracken to get him back to the rectory?"

"No, you did fine."

"Julianne and Andy emailed me to let me know they got to Ireland okay. They love Father Bracken's cottage. Can you believe we're family now, Colin?" She leaned in closer to him. "They told me not to expect to hear from them again. That's good. I want great-grandchildren."

Colin thanked her and got out of there.

22

Staying as still as she could manage, Georgina focused on the stunningly bright red leaves on a tree in front of a small house not far from the rectory where she'd run last night. She tried to control her breathing. She had slowed her pace to a walk a mile ago, when she'd noticed the first ripples of nausea.

Don't move...don't think...

The leaves are more magenta than true red...

If she moved, she'd throw up. She'd taken the coastal route on her run but made a wrong turn on the residential streets. She didn't want to risk taking her phone out of her running belt to check Google Maps.

It has to be nerves. Stress.

Grief.

Oh, Dad... Dad, Dad...

The leaves fluttered in the wind. Georgina lowered her eyes to the ground in front of her. One step, she thought. She could take one step…and then another step. It couldn't be far to the rectory and her father's friend.

Your father passed away early this morning. I'm so sorry, Georgina.

The doctor who'd treated him had been to the point but gentle. Most of what he'd said was a blur. She'd mumbled an incoherent thank-you and told him she would be in London in the morning and see about making arrangements. Who else was there, after all? Her father had never remarried, and he hadn't been in a relationship. He had friends, didn't he? Other than this art consultant, William Hornsby—this secret agent.

What if her father *didn't* have real friends? What if he'd only had her?

A fierce cramp gripped her, doubling her over with such abruptness she tripped on her own feet. She clutched her lower abdomen with both arms and moaned. The cramp eased, but she kept one arm across her middle as she tried to walk a few more steps.

She'd had it out with her father on Sunday in the park, foraging for wild mushrooms. Grievances she hadn't even realized she had caught her by surprise, and bubbled to the surface. She couldn't stop herself.

Not bubbled, she thought. Surged.

I love you, Dad, but you abandoned Mum and me. Your work always came first.

That's not true. Georgina, what's this about?

It is true. At least admit it.

I have—I had a demanding job. I don't deny that. I'm aware I haven't been the best father. It's not too late for me to do better. You're the most important person in my life.

Mum...

Gone too soon. Would that it weren't so.

She'd thought...a starting point. Even now, she could see the rivulets of sweat on his brow as he'd ducked under trees, searching for chanterelles. It must have taken a lot for him to get out those words. She'd met some of his more gregarious colleagues, but he'd always struggled articulating how he felt. Then again, so had she, and their natural reserve and lack of introspection had allowed them to carry on instead of becoming estranged. She'd never been hostile to him.

But their awkward, painful, short chat had turned out to be the start and the end of any kind of closer father-daughter relationship. She'd left for Boston, and not forty-eight hours later, he'd been found near death, only steps from where they'd picked mushrooms and she'd poured out her heart to him, for the first time ever.

If he'd killed himself, she'd driven him to it.

Wouldn't an expert in toxins choose a quicker, easier demise for himself than death cap mushrooms? She couldn't get that thought out of her mind. She'd thrashed all night, barely sleeping, wondering if he'd wanted her to know he'd suffered. Was there something poetic to him about dying of mushroom poisoning? Maybe it felt more natural than dosing himself with one of his synthetic nerve agents. Maybe he didn't have access to them, couldn't just produce one in his kitchen at home.

Georgina felt an acidic taste rise up in her throat.

No...

Another cramp seized her. She stopped, doubled over, staring at the ground.

The Aoife O'Byrne painting...her father's goodbye, his way of telling her how much he loved her, how sorry

he was for what might have been. That had been her reaction to the depiction of the Irish woodlands—somehow, she'd found herself longing for the impossible, the
hopeless, the things that might have been in her life.
Had that been the artist's intention?

More likely giving her the painting had been her
father's ineptness at work, thinking an extravagant
gift was how to show she mattered to him. She hadn't
wanted to do that to him—to make him think he'd failed
her. Because he hadn't. Spending that time with her
showed her he cared. Talking to her about how he felt
about retirement showed her. Cooking with her. Having him give a damn—ask her about her life, her ideas,
her dreams, her goals. *It's not prying, Dad. It's caring.
If you're being intrusive, I'll say.*

For years, she'd told herself it was okay, she didn't
need that from him, or even want it. But last weekend,
for once she'd just wanted him to dig himself out of his
world of neurotoxins and tune the hell in.

The cramp passed, and she pushed back the urge to
vomit and continued to a quiet intersection. Could she
ever live in a place like Rock Point? Her life had always
been different, abnormal.

She'd talk to William Hornsby. *Insist* he tell her the
truth. Demand it.

Or what?

She'd figure something out. She'd get Hornsby away
from the rectory and appeal first to his friendship with
her father. She didn't think it was entirely fake, part of
his job. She'd sensed something genuine there. Whatever his real name was, William Hornsby had seemed
to care about her and her relationship with her father.

He wants to be a good father to you, Georgina. It's never too late.

He is a good father in his own weird way...

She dropped to her knees, vomiting in the grass like a bloody dog. She tried to get to her phone but couldn't. She couldn't deny what was happening any longer.

What did I eat?

The gooey meatball sandwich at lunch. Richie had picked up a variety of sandwiches at a local shop, in what he called an antihealthy mood—his standard operating procedure, he said, whenever any kind of illness worked its way through a crowded vessel.

Easy to conceal sickeners...

Georgina swore she could taste them now.

Her head spun, and she collapsed, writhing in pain even as consciousness slipped away.

23

Oliver leaped out of the car almost before Emma had a chance to come to a full stop in front of the rectory. Henrietta and Finian were searching the yard between the rectory and the church. "We haven't seen Jeremy or Georgina," Henrietta said. "I don't know why Jeremy slipped out, but I promise you he did it on his own—we didn't help him. We were on a video chat with Aoife and your grandfather and brother."

Franny Maroney bolted up the street, panting as she waved a hand. "Hurry. Come quickly. There's a young woman. She's terribly sick. I don't have my phone. She needs an ambulance."

Finian rushed to her. "Where, Franny?" he asked.

"I'll show you."

"No," Emma said. "Just tell us."

Franny breathed in deeply, gripping her shirt at her chest. "On the corner, under the oak. I'm okay. I won't have a heart attack. Just take care of that poor girl. I'll sit on the front steps and catch my breath."

"I'll stay with Franny," Finian said. "I'll call an ambulance."

Emma ran up the street, in the opposite direction of where she and Oliver had wound their way to the church and rectory. He and Henrietta fell in behind her, and in thirty yards, they came to Georgina Masterson, sprawled facedown in the grass under an oak tree. No one appeared to be home at the house on the small, tidy corner lot.

Emma knelt beside Georgina and noticed the strong smell of vomit, then a splatter of it trailing to a pool closer to the sidewalk. "Georgina," Emma said. "We're going to help you. An ambulance is on the way. Can you speak?"

She stirred, clutching her lower abdomen. "I want to talk to Bill Hornsby. Where is he? He needs to tell me what's going on. Who poisoned my father." She grunted in pain. "And me."

Henrietta stared down at her. "It must be more mushrooms."

"Sickeners," Georgina mumbled. "Not an amatoxin."

Emma hoped she was right. As sick as she was, best it was due to *russula emetica* mushrooms. "Did you get in touch with Hornsby?"

"No. I was going to surprise him."

"Did you tell anyone else your plans?"

"Everyone knew I was going for a run." She moaned, tucking her knees up toward her chest. "Please tell me my father didn't get this sick…"

"I'm sorry, Georgina, but if you can help us understand what happened. Do you have any idea what's made you sick?"

"I don't know for sure. Meatballs…"

"We found the painting and another sketch at the Sharpe offices," Emma said. "Did you put them there?"

"No… I don't know who…oh, God, I feel awful…"

She started to sit up, and Henrietta eased in next to her and got her by the right arm. "Let's sit still, shall we? The ambulance will be here soon. Are those sketches your work, Georgina?"

"No…no…or my dad's."

Her face twisted in pain and she lurched to one side, away from Henrietta, and vomited, finally sinking back into the grass, not unconscious but unable to communicate.

"I need to go," Emma said. "Can you—"

"Father Bracken and I will see to Georgina." Henrietta looked up. "Find Jeremy. Take Oliver with you. He knows the poison mythology lingo if you need it."

"If Hornsby returns, Henrietta, don't confront him until we have more information about what's going on here."

"Don't worry," Henrietta said "I can handle him."

Emma looked at Oliver. He gave a curt nod, and started for her car. Finian Bracken and Franny Maroney were walking toward them. Franny looked fine. "Go, Emma," she said.

Kevin pulled up in his truck. "Hurley's is being evacuated. There's a fire. Arson. I'm on my way. A witness at the marina saw your guy Hornsby at the Sharpe offices on Saturday morning. He walked down the porch steps and across the yard to the docks." He paused. "Thought you'd want to know."

"He left the rectory. We don't know where he is."

"Where's Colin?"

Emma gave a tight shake of the head. "I don't know."

"We'll stay in touch," Kevin said, and rolled off.

Emma got out her phone and saw Sam Padgett had texted both her and Colin: Call me. Now.

Oliver was already at her car. He climbed behind the wheel. "Do your thing, Emma. I know the way."

"The harbor—"

He nodded. "I see the smoke."

The fire at Hurley's started with a small explosion under the floorboards at the far side of the building, opposite the parking lot. Colin had spotted Jeremy on the docks and was a few yards away when he heard the blast. It wasn't powerful enough to cause any serious damage—to him or to Hurley's—but it caught that part of the building on fire.

Not an accident.

A distraction charge, Colin thought. Noisy but not meant to blow up the building or target anyone. It was an old place, and the fire would spread quickly. With the busy foliage season, the popular restaurant was crowded for a Monday. Colin spotted his brother Mike, Beth Trahan and a couple of volunteer firefighters in the process of evacuating the building. The local police and fire trucks were on the way.

They didn't need him. He could focus on finding the person who'd set the charge, probably some kind of black powder mixture. His weapon drawn, Colin approached Jeremy, sprawled among lobster traps on the dock. A small Boston Whaler was tied up next to him.

Nick stood over him, breathing hard.

"Hands where I can see them, Nick," Colin said.

"I caught him. Hornsby. He set the fire. He was trying to distract everyone while he escaped on the boat."

"Hands up, Nick. Now."

He raised both hands, a butcher knife in his left hand and a small bottle in his right hand, poised between his thumb and forefinger as if it was something special. "I'm not pointing the knife at anyone. I took it from your buddy here."

"Put down the knife and then give me the bottle. Then we'll sort out the rest. I'll handle Hornsby from here, Nick."

"Oh, no. No, no, no. Do you think I trust you? This bastard is your buddy. He's trying to frame me. I'm getting out of here. With him. In this beat-up Boston Whaler. Whoever owns it practically left the engine running. Handy."

"You won't get out of the harbor."

"I'm trying to help, Agent Donovan. You need to take care of the situation at the restaurant. All those people. Don't think this asshole will settle for setting off one explosion when he could set off more."

Jeremy looked terrible, sunk against the lobster pots. "Where's Georgina?"

Nick glared at him. "You tell us, you sick son of a bitch. Did you kill her? Is she dead? You saw her last night. Did you feed her a slow-acting poison then? Or did you leave some nasty brew in her cabin?"

"She was going to meet me here…"

Colin stepped onto the dock. "Let me deal with him, Nick. Put down the knife."

"You can't shoot me. I'm not threatening anyone. I'm the victim here. Hornsby or whatever his name is—he fed Georgie's dad poison mushrooms. He killed him. He poisoned everyone on Saturday, including himself. Classic misdirection. He's slippery. He's MI5. But you know that, don't you? You'll let me take the fall to protect him. I haven't done anything wrong."

"Nick," Colin said, "I know about your past. I spoke to a colleague. His name's Sam Padgett. Emma spoke to him, too. We get it. Let us help. A ton of cops are on the way. You can turn Hornsby over to any of them. Put down the knife. Give me the bottle. We'll wait together."

"I'm not threatening anyone. He'll kill me if I put down the knife. He planted a vial of nerve agent somewhere in the restaurant or on the docks. He'll tell me where it is if I get him out of here. If not, people will die."

"What's in the bottle, Nick?"

He held it up higher. "I took it from him. I need to get him into this boat and get out of here and let him tell me where he planted the other one. Then you can chase him to hell and back if you want to—if you aren't as corrupt as he is. Georgina's dad knew how to make a lot of scary shit."

"I know that," Colin said. "You interned for him as a young chemistry student. We want to talk to you about what happened. Hear your story."

"Robin Masterson smuggled nerve agent out of his lab, Agent Donovan. This bastard stole it. That's what's in the bottles. Ask him. Even the small amount in this bottle is enough to kill hundreds of people."

Nick was in overdrive but Colin was confident whatever was in the bottle, it wasn't a viable, lethal nerve agent. "No one's going to hurt you, Nick, but I need you to drop that knife."

"Robin found out Hornsby stole the nerve agent and was using Georgina and her contacts through the Fannings to sell it on the black market." Nick remained steady, intense, not the easygoing, good-humored yacht guy Colin had met on Saturday. "Robin kept two small, old-fashioned perfume bottles in velvet boxes in his apartment. Georgina told me. They'd belonged to her grandmother—her mother's mother—and she wanted them. They reminded her of good times with her mother. I told her to take them while she had the chance. And she did. I had no idea…" Nick glanced at Jeremy at his feet. "This bastard found out and took advantage. That's why he brought Georgina the painting. I thought it was all her. I really did. But it's him."

Jeremy tried to sit up. "Nick…for God's sake. Do as Colin says and put down the knife before he shoots you dead. He's not going to aim for your kneecap, and he's not going to let you kill me. It's done."

"If he shoots me, the bottle breaks, and you die, anyway."

"Most of what he just told you is bullshit, Colin," Jeremy said.

Nick fastened his gaze on Colin. "Trust me. We're dealing with a dangerous operative who has planted a powerful chemical weapon. Your family and friends are in profound danger."

"This is all unraveling, Nick," Jeremy said, hoarse, leaning on one arm. "Georgina didn't tell you about the perfume bottles. You already knew about them. You knew twenty years ago. You helped Valerie Masterson steal them from Robin's lab."

Nick's grip on the knife faltered slightly. Colin moved toward him, confident in his aim, in the timing. And in Jeremy, he thought. "Come on, Nick. Let's talk. It's time you told your story. It's time everyone knows the truth."

"I'm getting into this boat. I'm leaving. You can have him. He can't hurt me. I have the nerve agent."

"It's perfume, Nick," Jeremy mumbled.

Out of the corner of his eye, Colin saw Kevin eased in next to him, his weapon drawn. "Beth spotted Nick in the area of the fire before your friend got here," Kevin said. "Marine patrol's got the harbor covered. He's not getting out of here."

"I'm one of the good guys," Nick said. "I'm telling you. You'll see. This man is corrupt, and he's a killer. He's been messing with Georgina's head, using her, making it look as if she's crazy and obsessed with poisons and drove her father to suicide."

Without warning, Jeremy rolled, as if he'd summoned his last shreds of energy, and surprised Nick, knocking him off balance. He hit a stack of lobster pots, and the knife flew out of his hand. Colin leaped to him, grabbed the bottle and hurled Nick onto his stomach. Kevin swooped in and cuffed him.

Jeremy collapsed onto his back and breathed out at the sky. "Sorry about that. I was starting to shiver. It's cold on the water."

Colin held up the bottle. "What's actually in here?"

"As I recall, Chanel N° 5."

Kevin recited Nick's Miranda rights, but he was spewing his story. He shouted obscenities at Emma and Oliver when they arrived, and then focused his tirade on Jeremy. "You're finished. You know it and I know it."

"Giving up on framing me, eh? Good idea."

"You were a chemistry student, Nick," Emma said.

"You dropped out after your second year. What happened?"

"Robin Masterson ruined my life. That's what happened. I was this kid, this eager young intern who wanted to cure diseases. A beautiful woman, a brilliant woman, decided to steal vials of a powerful chemical agent from her husband's lab. He screwed up in letting her near them. She was dying of a brain tumor and having an affair with a handsome, young SAS soldier. The classic dangerous man." Nick's eyes narrowed on Jeremy. "That was you."

Jeremy grimaced. "And you're that cracked intern. We forgot about you. You were an incompetent kid who lost your internship because you couldn't cut it."

"Liar. I was expendable. The truth would have destroyed not just Valerie but her husband, and you. I got kicked to the curb. Dismissed. My career was destroyed, but I quietly went away and worked on yachts."

"Valerie Masterson was sick but she didn't have an affair," Jeremy said. "And she didn't steal nerve agent. You did, my friend."

Nick snorted. "See? The lies continue. I never forgot the injustice I suffered. Never. Finally, I hear Robin's daughter is a personal chef. I get her hooked up with the Fannings."

"You saw your chance to get revenge against those who hurt you," Emma said. "Why Georgina? She was seven when you were an intern. You drew those sketches and planted them to implicate her, make her look like she had an unhealthy fascination with poisons."

"Why should I suffer and Robin and Valerie Masterson's daughter not suffer?"

Colin shook his head. "You wanted Georgina to suffer because you got kicked out of an internship? Okay. You also used her to frame Hornsby, and you could have framed her if he didn't work out."

Nick turned away. "No matter what I did, I'd win."

Oliver stared at him. "Who's in cuffs, mate?"

"Who's dead, mate?" Nick countered.

"Revenge won't feel so sweet in time," Oliver said. "Trust me."

Nick looked uncomfortable, but a local officer arrived, one of John Hurley's nieces Colin had known in high school. Kevin got Nick to his feet. "Come on. Let's go."

Once they left the dock, Jeremy flopped onto his back and moaned. "I'm dead this time, Colin. For sure. Bloody hell."

"No, you're not, but you do need medical attention."

Jeremy shook his head, his eyes shut. "A good whiskey. I like the fresh air even if it does smell like dead fish out here. I'm glad the bottle didn't break. God, I hate perfume."

Beth pushed her way past the knot of law enforcement officers to check her patient, an exhausted Jeremy Pearson. Emma suspected Beth had a good idea he wasn't an art consultant. "You need to see a doctor," she told him. She looked up at Kevin, who'd returned after handing off Nick to the locals and the state detectives. "Anyone else injured?"

"Nope. We're good."

"Leaping on boats, tackling a man with a knife."

"He dropped the knife."

"Oh, well, there's *that*. Seriously, everyone's okay?" Kevin nodded. "Seriously."

Emma liked her already. Jeremy refused an ambulance. Whiskey and ice were all he needed.

Hurley's was taped off as a crime scene. No other devices and no nerve agent had been found, and the fire damage was confined to the storage room. "A miracle it didn't burn down," Kevin said.

Mike Donovan joined them. "I must have threatened to torch this place a hundred times as a teenager."

"Imagine if you hadn't gone into the army," Colin said.

"I'd be getting out of prison about now."

Mike's humor. Emma was used to it now. Kevin just shook his head. He watched Beth as she stood up, Jeremy prone on the dock, hugging a blanket to him and cursing the earth for spinning too fast when it was his head. "You heard him refuse further treatment. He's British, I know, but he fits in with you Donovans."

"This 'you Donovans,' Beth," Kevin said. "What's that about?"

She gaped at him. "Are you serious? Hurley's blows up and who's here? A man takes a sick man hostage and threatens to kill him, and who's here?"

"We live in town."

"Oh, so it's a coincidence. No cause and effect at work."

"I kind of get her point," Mike said. "So, our villain turns out to be a guy with a butcher knife and a bottle of perfume? Lucky."

Colin grinned at him. "Yeah. Lucky." He squatted next to Jeremy. "Sorry your first visit to my hometown involved poison, explosions and a chemical agent threat. It's pretty, though, isn't it? The changing foliage against the sea."

"I smell dead fish."

"Better than barf," Colin said. "Can you get up on your own and walk or do you need us Donovans to carry you?"

"Go to hell, Colin. I'd call you Donovan, but I don't want your brothers to think I mean them. They look like good lads."

"The knife, Jeremy. Nick could have killed you."

"But he didn't. Getting sick on those bloody mushrooms threw me. I didn't think Georgina was in danger. I didn't see it. Just was worried about her with her father sick, his state of mind given that visit with Oliver. And the painting. I wanted to give it to her in person after her father got sick."

"Nick played the easygoing yacht guy well. He wasn't looking to kill you on Saturday. He could have— he had the expertise, and he knew where to find a few even nastier mushrooms if he'd wanted to. He was out and about before the party. Slipped the painting and sketch onto the Sharpe back porch and sneaked a few of Georgina's so-called sickeners."

"She probably told him about them," Jeremy said. "She and Robin both could go on about their mushrooms."

"Good for them. It's not their fault Nick did what he did."

"He hid the painting and planted the sketches. He was after revenge—against Robin, against me, even Georgina. I had no idea. Didn't register who he was."

"It was a long time ago. How much can you tell Kevin?"

"I'm a mild-mannered art consultant who was nearly killed by a raging psychopath obsessed with revenge for something I didn't do. But it doesn't matter. Kevin knows the score."

"Kevin's like that."

"Tell him whatever you want. The feisty nurse?"

"His match, I think."

A small smile from Jeremy. "Something happy this dark day. Robin was a decent sort, Colin. You just had to get past your own ideas about what he should be like. Georgina?"

"She got a dose of *russula emetica* mushrooms. She'll recover."

"Poor kid."

Colin helped Jeremy to his feet while Mike joined the firefighters coming out of Hurley's. The place would need a few repairs but all in all, it was in decent shape. "We're stuck with Hurley's for another forty years," Kevin said.

Oliver stayed close to Jeremy as he rallied. Too late, Jeremy admitted he shouldn't have left the rectory. "I thought I was meeting Georgina. I should have had her come to the rectory. Robin told me how much she loved the Aoife O'Byrne paintings at the gallery, the woodland series in particular. He wanted to encourage her interest."

"He'd seen Nick's sketches and thought they were hers?" Oliver asked.

"At first, yes. I see now that's why he wanted to talk to you. Nick messed with Robin's head. He must have gone to see him on Sunday after Georgina left for Boston. Robin muttered something when I found him about a student. I thought he was delusional. But he meant Nick." His eyes sunken, his skin ashen, Jeremy managed to look up at Colin. "Nick used both Robin's and

Georgina's vulnerabilities and interests in foraging, sketching and certain books and movies to cover up his misdeeds and exact his revenge. He wanted her to suffer, too. Robin wanted to get her a painting, but he knew he never would. So I told him I would."

"That's when he realized you had loved his wife?"

"I think deep down he always knew. She was a lovely woman, Colin. I was a young SAS officer doing my bit, ripe for a grand romance. She was older, lonely. She knew how I felt and treated me kindly, but she never… we never…" He stopped, looked out at the harbor. "The painting was a beautiful gift Robin gave to Georgina, and I was happy to help make it happen. I'd have given her a one-way ticket back to London away from these people and set her up with a cooking job."

"Nick was a chemist," Emma said.

"Robin remembered him in the end. A lot of interns didn't cut it. It wasn't a big deal. You always hope they go on to better things, but I wasn't involved. Nick got wrapped up in his hatred and self-pity. He never had a nerve agent in his possession."

"Nick had knowledge, and he had motive," Colin said. "That's a dangerous combination when you're dealing with something as lethal as a boutique nerve agent. Is there a chance he had ampoules tucked away no one's ever known about?"

"No. But you'll search the yacht in full hazmat gear?"

"Already happening. What were his plans for the nerve agent?"

"Profit. Chaos. Revenge. Toss it into the sea once he was free of the hold Robin and I had on him. Doesn't matter because he didn't have any, and he's not good enough to produce more. He's obsessed with revenge, and he likes to let the world burn and sit back and watch. Profit was secondary to his desire for revenge, but I'd take a good hard look at what he's been up to the past seventeen years. He strikes the match telling himself the kindling and tinder are there and not his doing. He benefits. Why shouldn't he? He liked the drama of vengeance. It wasn't about justice."

They got in Colin's truck. Jeremy sank against the seat and didn't bother with a seat belt. "Have I ever told you I hate boats? It's one thing your boss and I have in common."

"You know Matt Yankowski?"

Jeremy shut his eyes and smiled. Colin started the truck. Well, hell. Of course Jeremy and Yank knew each other. How else had he sneaked into the country?

24

Finian returned from the hospital and lined up whiskey glasses on the dining room table. He would check in with Franny Maroney later, and the regulars at Hurley's. He was one himself, he thought. But Rock Point locals being who they were, volunteer work crews were already forming to help tackle the damage once the building was released as a crime scene. There was insurance but it wouldn't be enough, and they wanted to get started. They already planned to be open for breakfast with a reduced menu. There were lobstermen to serve at 4:00 a.m., and doughnuts to make, eggs to cook, batches of clam and haddock chowder to make. Finian had messages from parishioners who wanted to use the church kitchen to prepare food for the crews. Whatever the damage at the popular restaurant, Hurley's would be back at full steam sooner rather than later.

He opened the cupboard and got out bottles of

Bracken, Yellow Spot, Redbreast, all good Irish whiskeys, and, for Oliver, Scotch—Auchentoshan, Talisker, Glenfiddich. Two by two he set them on the table, remembering when he'd toured each of the distilleries back when he was a whiskey man.

"You miss it, don't you?" Henrietta asked as she entered the room.

He shut the cupboard glass door. "Miss what?"

She smiled. "The life." She picked up the Bracken Distillers pot-still. "Home."

"I'm where I'm needed."

"You're where you need to be, at least for now. You're a man apart in Rock Point, but I suppose to a degree any priest would be." She set the bottle back on the table. "It has its attraction."

Finian studied her as she touched the Auchentoshan label. He saw the dark circles under her eyes. "Are we talking about me, Henrietta, or about you?"

She angled a look at him. "Me?"

"The work you do. The secrets you must keep."

"Maybe so. Once Nick realized Jeremy was part of something that happened to him in the past, there was no turning back for him. He needed to kill him. Simple as that. And I didn't see it."

"Did Jeremy?" Finian asked.

She hesitated and then shook her head. "He says he walked right into it. At one time, I thought hearing those words would be music to my ears. They're not." She squared her shoulders, tossed back her rich curls. "I don't have all the details, and you don't need to be burdened by them. Thank you for helping with Georgina."

Finian took the bottle of Redbreast and opened it, splashed some into a glass and handed it to Henrietta.

"I'll look in on Georgina in the morning. She pushed herself hard the past few days with her running, and she's dealing with the shock of her father's illness and death."

"His murder," Henrietta said, swirling her whiskey. "Nick did a decent job of making it appear to be a suicide. I'm sure watching Georgina suffer gave him a great deal of satisfaction."

"His secret knowledge gave him a sense of power."

"Yes. Bloody bastard." Henrietta took a gulped of the Redbreast. "I will get Georgina home—assuming the FBI hasn't already escorted Oliver and me onto a flight to London."

Finian replaced the cork on the Redbreast bottle. "Expect them to barrel through the front door at any moment, do you?"

He welcomed the spark in her eyes. "I'd be considering it in their place." But she, serious again, took a more modest sip of her whiskey. "She's alone, our Georgina. Oliver and I are only children, but I have my parents and other family in England, my colleagues, my work, my gardens. Oliver. I have him, although some days…" She didn't finish. "He's solitary, and he suffered a terrible trauma as a boy when his parents were murdered in front of him. But he's not alone. Do you think he realizes that?"

"I think he does."

"He has Martin, and Alfred. And me. And we have our twee Cotswolds village." She sniffled back sudden tears. "I want a family, Father Bracken."

He couldn't stop himself from glancing at the photo of himself and his wife and daughters at their cottage.

His heart ached but not as much for the past, he realized. For the future.

"You'll make a wonderful mother, Henrietta."

"And Oliver?"

"He'll make a wonderful father."

"You didn't hesitate," she said.

"No, I didn't."

"Well, we'd never lack for tales by the fire."

Finian saw himself with his young family in front of the fire in his Kerry cottage. A good memory. He picked up the Glenfiddich. "Oliver likes a good Scotch."

Henrietta set her glass on the table, walked over to him, kissed him on the cheek. "When the time is right, Finian, you'll know what to do, just as you knew when you needed to enter the priesthood. Trust that you'll know."

He opened the Glenfiddich. Out the front window, he could see Oliver coming to the door. The light shone on the brightly colored leaves on the maple tree. Finian had come to love this place, no matter that he'd never be a part of it the way he'd been a part of things with Bracken Distillers, his brother and sisters and Sally and the girls.

"It was all bloody-minded revenge and fantasy on Nick's part," Oliver said, angry and disgusted as he burst into the dining room. "He didn't have to kill Robin. That poor man. Nick couldn't accept he'd bollixed up his own life. And what was wrong with the life he had? Working on yachts and…" He stopped midsentence. "Am I interrupting?"

"As if that would stop you," Henrietta snorted affectionately. "Father Bracken and I were just processing the day."

Oliver glanced at Finian. "Glenfiddich will help."

Finian grinned and handed him a glass, and then poured a *taoscán* of Redbreast for himself, triple distilled, matured in oak casks—a taste of home.

Henrietta swept up her glass. Finian held up his glass, noting how Oliver eased next to his love, the way she brushed her fingertips across his hand. Finian smiled. "*Sláinte*, my friends."

"*Sláinte*," Oliver said.

Henrietta hesitated. "To knowing when the time is right." She raised her glass. "*Sláinte*."

Emma wasn't surprised the Fannings didn't take news of Nick's actions well. She and Colin met with them on the sundeck as a team finished searching the yacht. Shocked and angry, Melodie couldn't stand still, or temper her language. "How dare you come here like this, with Bryce weak from his ordeal. We didn't know what was happening. It was terrifying. We had no idea Nick was…that he's…my God."

"We want to be sure the yacht's safe," Colin said. "Nick knew he wasn't coming back here, and he set off a crude explosive device at a restaurant in Rock Point."

Melodie paled. "You mean he could have left a bomb here?"

"We just needed to be certain."

Nick hadn't left anything, but the search team found his tablet in his cabin. It was where he'd done the bulk of his drawing before copying his sketches onto paper in order to implicate Georgina and upset her father. A scientist by training, he'd documented his activities, fueled by his arrogance, narcissism and sense of grievance.

A lot to talk to him about in his jail cell, Emma thought

The Fannings were cooperating with the FBI and local and state police detectives, but they were free to go home.

"We lead quiet, uneventful lives," Melodie said.

Bryce nodded next to her and took her hand. "We'll buy that yacht and sail the Caribbean for the winter."

Emma thanked them and headed out with Colin. "Their idea of a quiet, uneventful life and mine are two different things," he said.

"You'll take an afternoon kayaking out of Rock Point harbor?"

"With you."

When they arrived back in Rock Point, Sam Padgett called, already on the case in Boston. Emma took his call on the rectory front steps while Colin went inside. "Yank's even dragged himself into the office," Sam said. "Nick Lothian was a busy guy. Revenge might have been his driving motive, but he was collecting some interesting materials on various people he'd encountered in his yachting life the past few years. The Fannings look to be clean, but that doesn't mean all their friends are."

"Blackmail potential?"

"Uh-huh. We're not interested in the salacious stuff, but there some real issues to dig into."

"And Yank?"

"Says you two did okay with poisons, considering Colin's an arms trafficking undercover agent and you're an art crimes analyst."

"He knew our three British friends were in country?"

"Yank knows everything. He says he wants you two

back here Wednesday morning. That gives you tomorrow to clean up things there and hopefully have a moment to relax. Go catch lobster or something."

Emma heard a seagull, not far away, "We have two bags of local apples in the refrigerator."

"That's a lot of apples to eat," Sam said.

She smiled. "Enough for applesauce and a pie for the church's bean-hole supper this weekend."

"Got it," Sam said. "Have fun.'"

Franny Maroney dropped off another casserole at the rectory. She didn't look particularly shaken by the day's events, but Colin wasn't surprised. Finian invited her to stay, but she wanted to get home to a baseball game. She was in her Red Sox shirt.

After she left, Colin set the casserole—something to do with chicken—in the oven to warm up. "Franny's seen a lot in her day, but she also doesn't mind a little excitement once in a while, provided no one gets seriously hurt."

"Luckily no one did, today, at least," Finian said.

"Close call at Hurley's, and with Jeremy."

Jeremy was in no shape to join them for dinner, but Colin brought him whiskey. He managed to sit up and take the glass. "I'm glad you don't need a sippy cup," Colin said.

"What's a sippy cup? Never mind. It's scary you know these things. Life in Rock Point. Did someone tell Georgina about today? Her father didn't commit suicide after their visit. He'd figured it out—the death caps, the sketch, Nick. By the time I found him in the park, he was too sick to get it all out."

"But in hindsight, you can see what he was trying to tell you."

"Yeah." Jeremy stared at his whiskey. "If he'd just told me early on Nick had visited him on Sunday..."

"Nick had already made sure Robin saw one of the sketches. That's why he wanted to talk to someone about poisons and myths."

"I don't know how or when—"

"Friday," Colin said. "He dropped Georgina off at her father's place."

"You've spoken with her?"

Colin shook his head. "Nick's talking, and he wrote everything down."

A smile spread across Jeremy's face and reached his gray eyes. "That's excellent news."

"Talk to me about Valerie Masterson," Colin said, sitting across from Jeremy with his own glass of whiskey. He'd barely taken a sip yet.

Jeremy cupped his glass with both hands. "She wasn't right in the head due to her brain tumor. Robin covered for her theft. He knew the nerve agent wasn't viable, and he wanted to protect her in her last days—and Georgina. He wanted her to have positive memories of her mother. I'm prohibited from telling Georgina everything, but she has good instincts and I'm sure will fill in the blanks."

"Were you complicit in the cover-up?"

"'Cover-up' is strong, Colin. I didn't say or do anything illegal or against protocols. I didn't pursue what I suspected might be true. I wasn't a senior intelligence officer at the time."

"You let Robin have time with his dying wife and kept him working in the program." Colin held his glass up but didn't drink any of the whiskey. "Tell me the truth, Jeremy. How sure were you Nick didn't have a real nerve agent?"

He shrugged. "Mostly sure."

"Ninety-nine percent?"

"Is one ever ninety-nine percent sure of anything?"

"Estimate."

"More than fifty-fifty."

"What, sixty-forty? Hell, Jeremy, you're reassuring."

"It's not our job to be reassuring, is it?"

Colin didn't answer.

"As Nick was swinging that knife and perfume bottle, it did occur to me I wasn't a hundred-percent certain if he might have put together some sort of crude nerve agent." Jeremy waved a hand, dismissive. "One wonders these things at the point of a knife, and I was right."

"Chanel."

The smallest of smiles this time.

"How close did Nick get with the knife before I showed up and saved your ass?"

"Too close, and I could have handled him."

Colin didn't argue because it was probably the truth.

"Robin was a good man," Jeremy said. "I never would have had an affair with Valerie Masterson. Her marriage was in trouble, but I like to believe she and Robin would have worked it out if she'd lived."

"You're a romantic at heart. Who knew?"

"Every now and then I need a bit of hope to penetrate my cynicism. Robin tried to be a good husband and father, but he was clueless. I stayed in touch with him and kept an eye out for Georgina. Valerie asked me to. She knew what Robin was like. She had cogent moments toward the end, and that was one of them."

Colin got heavily to his feet. "Go home as soon as you can travel, Jeremy. Take a long walk on some picturesque English country lane, and then get back to work."

"I'm not good for anything else at this point. Watch yourself, Colin. Don't make that mistake. Don't think you aren't expendable. Train people to take your place. Let them do it."

"You've saved a lot of lives in your day."

"It's the misses that haunt me. The people I couldn't save."

"You saved me."

"I'm still waiting for a thank-you note from Yank."

Colin grinned. His friend would be fine. "Wear headphones when you walk. Listen to Harry Potter. I hear the narrator's top-notch. It'll keep you from thinking too much."

"Voice of experience?"

"I kayak and listen to the oceans and the birds."

"Mainer."

And Colin knew then. His role with the FBI was changing not in some unspecified future but soon—now.

He took his whiskey into the dining room. He smiled at Emma and touched her cheek. "Let's see what Franny's cooked up for us tonight."

Georgina rallied and left the hospital that evening. She could have spent the night, but she didn't want to be alone if she didn't have to be. She reminded herself she was young, strong and determined, but she knew she needed to be with people who cared about her— people who'd helped her.

Oliver and Henrietta picked her up and drove her to the rectory. Colin Donovan, Emma Sharpe and Finian Bracken were having after-dinner whiskey in the kitchen. She couldn't face whiskey yet.

They chatted about everything and nothing—the upcoming bean-hole supper, the damage at the restaurant that caught fire, Irish whiskey versus Scotch—and she relaxed in their company. "Are you going to continue with your botanical drawings?" Emma asked her.

Georgina smiled past tears. "I think so. My father would like that. There's nothing creepy about what I draw."

"No, there isn't," Colin said.

Georgina appreciated his certainty. "Nick should have used his skills and imagination for fun graphic novels or screenplays. I draw mostly because I have time to kill when I'm not cooking, and I want to learn to identify wild edibles. I don't mingle much. I suppose I'm my father's daughter, after all."

She finally went in to see Jeremy Pearson. She was glad they were past his alias. Had she ever truly believed it? She didn't want to wake him, but he sat up, reached for her hand. "I'm sorry I didn't figure out that bastard sooner, Georgina."

"I'm sorry I didn't, either. Dad wouldn't want us to beat ourselves up over it. You were with him at the end. You heard his last words." She paused, studying this man—seeing now how hardened he was, seeing the scars for what they were. "Art consultant, huh? But you were Dad's friend not just a spook keeping an eye on him."

"We asked a lot of him, Georgina."

"He appreciated that, I think. He loved his work, and

it helps me that it made a difference. It helps a lot. He chose the painting?"

"He saw you light up when you were at the gallery, and he wanted that for you."

"He'd never have bought it on his own. He'd have thought about it and figured his good intentions ought to count for something. But I'm glad he thought about it. I'm glad he saw my reaction to Aoife O'Byrne's work."

"She's a wonderful person and a talented artist."

"Then I should keep the painting?"

"That's your call."

"Did he know your real name?"

"Yes," Jeremy said.

"I was surprised it's Jeremy. I expected—I don't know. Something rougher." But her moment of humor faded. "Did Dad have sleepless nights about the choices he'd made?"

"I think so, Georgina, but I also think he lived a good life. He made sacrifices, but he had you."

"And you were his friend?"

"Yes. I was his friend. He loved you very much."

"I do know that."

"There's much he couldn't tell you about his work, nor can I."

"He's an unsung hero in that regard, I guess. I only knew him as a crap father, and my mother…" Georgina bit down on her lower lip. "He was at her side when she died. I guess that's something."

"You two had foraging in common."

"That's true. I'll think of him whenever I grill chanterelles. Are you haunted by some of what you saw, what could happen? By the pressures?"

Jeremy grinned. "Not me. I'm not wired that way."

But she could see in his eyes that wasn't entirely true.

"We'll get you to London, Georgina. What you do after that…know that I'm here for you."

"You don't have any children, do you?"

He shook his head. "I'm married, though, to a great woman."

"She'd have been upset if Nick had succeeded. He liked that my father suffered. He did what he could to throw suspicion on me and make me doubt myself. I was in his sights, too. He wanted me to suffer the way he'd suffered." She couldn't stop the rush of words. "I had no idea he hated me. He was fun-loving and smart. He never let what was brewing inside him show, not to me. He held it in until he killed my father and tried to you, and me."

"Guy's a bastard."

Georgina smiled. "Well, that sums it up, doesn't it?"

"Mushroom poisoning is miserable. Get some rest. You're young you'll bounce back."

"Henrietta and Oliver collected my things off the yacht. They're moving into the same room and giving me the other guest room. They're engaged. Did you know that?"

Jeremy grimaced. "Just my bloody luck."

Hurley's opened unofficially for breakfast in the morning, and just about everyone in Rock Point turned out. The smell of the fire was a reminder of how close the place had come to oblivion, but the limited menu included doughnuts. Colin figured that was a good sign. He and Emma joined Henrietta, Oliver and Kevin at a table by the windows overlooking the harbor.

Emma touched his hand. "Colin."

He saw, too, and excused himself, joining his Irish priest friend, alone on the dock where they'd first met a year ago this past June.

"I want to sell the cottage," Finian said.

Colin realized he'd interrupted him midthought, but he knew what he meant. "Keep it in the family?"

Finian turned to him. "My Maine family, I hope."

With a jolt he didn't expect, Colin pictured Emma there on their honeymoon, sitting by the fire on rainy nights, walking along a sunny lane, clapping her hands at a rainbow above the bay, as if it were the first Irish rainbow she'd ever seen. Now Andy and Julianne were there. Even Yank had stayed there. Were Mike and Naomi next? Kevin and Beth? And there was Lucas Sharpe, too, and old Wendell. It'd be an easy place to rent.

Finian stared at the harbor, lobster boats bobbing in the quiet water. "This is a beautiful spot, Colin."

"That doesn't mean you're called to be here any longer, Fin. We're your friends. That's not going to change, whether you're here or in Ireland, whether you're a priest or raising sheep in Declan's Cross, back in the whiskey business."

"Henrietta and Oliver have announced their engagement. They didn't make that up. It took Oliver a while to believe he deserved happiness."

"You deserve happiness, too. Franny Maroney agrees if that helps. She cornered me at breakfast."

"I like my quiet life here."

Colin read into his words. "You don't think it'd be a quiet life with a world-famous artist."

"I said nothing of the sort, Colin. I'm a priest."

"Your family's in Ireland. You have good friends there. They never let go of you."

"I have a call, Colin. I made vows."

"What's your heart's desire, Fin?"

He turned, smiled. "Right now, I'd like a full American breakfast."

"Good. It doesn't include mushrooms."

25

The Cotswolds, England

Oliver brought the last of the dahlia tubers into the yellow stone dovecote on his farm and laid them on a worktable in his former stone-working studio. He'd carved the small room out of a corner of the historic dovecote, which his grandmother had transformed into a garden shed decades ago. Originally, pigeons were raised here, but they'd fallen out of favor as a dinner delicacy. Only a handful of dovecotes remained, dotting the rolling Cotswolds countryside.

When he left the dovecote, wiping dirt from the tubers off his hands, Oliver was surprised to find Henrietta digging dahlias out of an antique flowerpot she'd discovered in June. "I want to dry these tubers, too," she said without looking up.

"I'll add them to the table."

"I have ideas for spring." She got to her feet, adjusted

her long orange-red skirt, kicked a bit of mud off her Wellingtons. "The farm needs to be mine as well as yours or it won't work. I don't want to feel as if I can't move a vase or rip out a rosebush without you or Martin having a fit."

"Martin might fight you about a vase, but I wouldn't care. And neither of us knows a thing about roses."

She pointed a trowel at him. "Tell Martin if I move a vase, it's for good reason."

"You tell him. I'll back you up, but you don't need to go through me to speak with him."

"I adore him, of course."

"Of course."

She lowered her trowel. "I want to include you. I want us to do this together. I've never been one for objects, but I love this place." She narrowed those beautiful eyes on him. "You must speak up if you want something to stay as it is."

None of her comments were contradictory in her mind. Oliver understood this, because, he thought, he understood her, and he loved her.

She stabbed her trowel into the flowerpot dirt. "There's more. I'm excited about doing more with the farm, and figure out Aunt Posey's house—my house, I know. I want to give garden design a go for real. Jeremy knows where to find me." Her blue-green eyes settled on Oliver. "Where to find us."

"Assuming he returns to work himself."

"I doubt he'll be raising chickens anytime soon. You've made your amends, Oliver. Now, it's time for sheep and flowerpots, and Alfred and—"

"And us." He eased his arms around her, kissed her on the forehead. "You, me, our children."

"Oliver..." He heard her voice catch, and she backed out of his arms, eyed him as if he might be plotting to steal a painting. "Wait. What did you say?"

"Children." He smiled. "Really, Henrietta, someone has to listen to Freddy's opera records and read your biography of him."

She laughed then, grabbing her trowel. "Let's finish these dahlias."

Jeremy Pearson went with Georgina to her father's favorite woodland in the Cotswolds, and they scattered his ashes together, saying a proper goodbye. A goodbye he'd have wanted. Five days after their ordeal in Maine, they both needed more time to recuperate, but they would get there.

"No more yachts for me," she said as they walked through fallen leaves, as she had with her father—if not often, she thought, enough.

Now that Jeremy was fully recovered from his ordeal—and didn't have to pretend to be someone else—Georgina saw how strong and rugged her father's friend was. "What will you do?" he asked.

"I'll find work. The episode with the mushrooms wasn't my doing. Richie Hillier said he'd vouch for me as a chef, and I have previous happy clients. The Fannings aren't too happy with me. Somehow, I'm the one who brought a deranged killer on board—never mind he worked for them before I was hired."

"He's not that deranged," Jeremy muttered.

"We watched *The Avengers* together. I'm not going

to let him spoil my love of world-building stories. Tolkien, *Game of Thrones*, comics."

"You wouldn't mind a superhero of your own, would you?"

She smiled at him. "I don't need one. I have you. My guardian angel."

"Your friend, Georgina."

"Can I meet your wife sometime?"

"She'd love that. So would I. Colin asked if you were the daughter I never had. Maybe you are."

"Do I remind you of my mother?'

"You remind me of both of them, your mother and your father, but you're yourself. Would you like to see the York farm?"

"I would, indeed."

He gave her directions and met her at the picturesque, sprawling farm the following day. Oliver and Henrietta and a wire fox terrier greeted them at the entrance to a romantic yellow stone house. They gave her the tour of the gardens, the dovecote, the barn and fields. It was warm enough to serve lunch on a stone terrace off the back of the house. Henrietta explained they had word of a job at a restaurant in Stow-on-the-Wold that specialized in locally sourced produce, including wild edibles. "We'll put in a word, if you'd like," she said.

Georgina glanced at Jeremy and saw the hope in his rugged face. She smiled at their hosts—her new friends. "I would be most grateful. Thank you."

And later on, after a walk to the village, they offered chanterelles as an appetizer at dinner. "If you want them," Oliver said.

"I'd love them," Georgina said.

* * *

Emma and Colin caught a warm Saturday in Maine and went out on Rock Point harbor in separate kayaks. He could feel the cold off the water. It wasn't summer anymore, but the sky was clear, the colorful autumn leaves slowly giving way to November. He'd been kayaking out here late last summer when he'd learned about the nun murdered at a local convent. Could he ever have conjured up Emma? This life with her?

He'd been exhausted, fighting burnout. Now it was a year later, and he knew he'd done his bit as an undercover agent.

They paddled back to the docks and had chowder at Hurley's, little hint left of the fire. If Nick Lothian had wanted to, he could have injured a lot of people that day. But he hadn't wanted to. He'd been focused on Jeremy Pearson and Georgina Masterson, and getting out of Maine and on his way to what he'd wanted to do as a student—sell chemical weapons on the black market. Pie in the sky back then, pie in the sky two weeks ago.

Colin threw the kayaks into the back of his truck. Emma popped in the paddles and vests. Back at the house, she got the wild blueberries her father had picked for her out of the freezer. "I was going to save them for Thanksgiving, but tonight's the last bean-hole supper at St. Patrick's. They're expecting a crowd."

"There's nothing quite like a Maine wild-blueberry pie. People will love it."

But they had apples, too. More Cortlands, perfect for sauce as well as pies. While Emma put together the blueberry pie, Colin tackled the apples, got them sim-

mering on the stove, the house filling up with the smell
of their cooking and the cool breeze floating through
the open windows.

"I'll be doing counterintel work out of Boston," he
said as he gave the bubbling apples a stir. "I'll be training new undercover agents, too. There'll be some travel,
but not like the past five years. Yank says he might need
us both in London from time to time. He didn't explain,
but I like the idea."

"We could visit Granddad in Ireland."

"And the Brackens," Colin said. "However many of
them are there."

She set the timer on her pie and turned to him. "We
could lead quieter lives."

"We could."

"One day," she said.

He took her in his arms. "I'm not addicted to the job.
I'm not going to be Jeremy Pearson in fifteen years. I'm
going to be here with you, making pies and applesauce,
watching our kids grow and loving every minute of our
lives together."

When they returned to work Monday morning, Matt
Yankowski was at his desk, back at work full-time.
He called everyone into the conference room. Emma
remembered her first time in the offices overlooking
Boston Harbor, a dreary March day with HIT just get-
ting off the ground. She hadn't known Colin then, but
Yank had.

Sam Padgett joined them, griping about New England weather. Dark and good-looking, he grinned at
her as they went into the conference room. "The Fan-

nings are clean but they definitely have some interesting friends," he said as they took seats at the table.

Their buttoned-down boss greeted his small hand-picked team. "Let's get started. We have work to do."

26

After the last of the bean-hole suppers, the southern Maine coast, including Rock Point, went quiet before the holidays, and Finian Bracken took the opportunity to fly to Ireland for a few days. He arrived in Dublin at dawn, but jet lag didn't bother him a bit. He had breakfast at the airport and drove into the city. He visited the Book of Kells, and churches he knew from his seminary days. He was a priest—he wore his clerical garb—but he remembered himself as a lad, coming to Dublin the first time. He'd been sixteen, on his own. What had been his heart's desire then? He smiled, remembered walking in St. Stephen's Green, blushing when a pretty girl had asked him for directions to Grafton Street. He'd been thrilled he'd known the answer.

He walked to Wendell Sharpe's town house near Merrion Square, in the heart of Georgian Dublin. Lucas was still in town, the two of them deep into Sharpe Fine Art Recovery business—and grieving, Finian thought. They'd said their goodbyes to their son and father, and now they were mapping out their lives without him.

They had dinner at Wendell's favorite pub, where Colin had proposed to Emma a year ago. "Heading to Bracken Distillers tomorrow?" Wendell asked.

"Declan's Cross at first light," Finian said.

The old man smiled. "Thought that might be the case with both O'Byrne sisters there."

"We enjoyed our stay," Lucas said, ever more diplomatic than his grandfather. "We look forward to being back. I hear Emma and Colin are buying your cottage in Kerry."

"They've already signed up for a whiskey school at the distillery to celebrate their first wedding anniversary."

"They'll be fine," Wendell said. "They've got those crazy jobs, and Rock Point and Heron's Cove."

Lucas seemed confused, but Finian knew what Wendell was saying.

"Not that I'm telling you what you should or will do," the world-renowned art detective said.

"Perish the thought, Granddad," Lucas muttered.

Wendell ignored him. "But if you move home to Ireland, you have a family and friends to welcome you, whatever your calling is by then." He raised his pint. "To new adventures."

When Finian walked back to his hotel, he wasn't so sure spending the evening with the two Sharpes had been one of his finest ideas, as much as he enjoyed their company. Wendell had a knack for seeing through people, never mind it'd taken him ten years to track down Oliver York.

You're a conflicted man, Fin Bracken.

And he couldn't be, not in this religious life he'd chosen.

He arrived in Declan's Cross on a gray, misting afternoon, and he parked at Kitty O'Byrne's hotel but didn't go inside. He walked up to Lamb's Head, past Sean's farmhouse to Aoife's cottage.

When she opened the door, he could smell the peat of the fire in her stove, and feel the heat of it as he looked at her shining blue eyes. "Finian," she said. "Father Bracken."

"Will you walk with me?" he asked her.

"I'll grab my jacket."

She met him on the lane and smiled at him. "We'll take our time."

He saw that she understood, and he felt some of the knots inside him start to untangle. They set out side by side in the gray, walking toward the ruin at the tip of the headland. Aoife chatted about gardening and sheep and the hotel—her new life in Declan's Cross. Finian told her about his friends in Maine. Andy and Julianne's wedding. Hurley's. Kayaking. Apple season. Nothing about murder, poisons, fires and the dangerous work some of his friends did.

He and Aoife didn't mention art or the priesthood, or the future—or the past.

When they reached the ruins, they walked up the hill to the Celtic crosses with their view of the sea. "I've loved this spot since I was a girl," Aoife said. The wind whipped her dark hair into her face as she turned to him. "I hope it brings you the same peace and clarity it's brought me time and time again."

"You only painted it that one time, in the unsigned landscape that was stolen with the cross and the two Jack Butler Yeats paintings and wasn't returned."

She sighed out at the gray sky and sea. "Somehow I knew it was for him."

Finian realized she didn't mean Oliver York, the wealth Brit, the mythologist, the martial arts expert, the gentleman farmer, the wily art thief now in love with his childhood playmate. She meant the eight-year-old boy who'd watched his parents murdered in front of him.

"Stay here awhile," Aoife said. "I'll have tea and soup hot when you get back."

She left him there. He watched her almost skip down the hill to the lane. She knew every tuft of grass out here, all the spots that could trip her up. In a moment, she disappeared past the gravestones of the old church ruin, through the greenery that covered a stone wall.

Finian touched his fingers to a bell carved into one of the crosses. Saint Declan's bell, which, according to legend, had led him through a raging storm at sea to this part of Ireland.

Finian decided he wouldn't think too much about what was next for him, beyond tea, soup and a hot fire. For now, he was home.

* * * * *

Author Note

Rival's Break is the ninth book and the tenth title (including a novella) in the Sharpe & Donovan series, and it was as much fun to write as the first, *Saint's Gate*. Since then, I've received countless comments from readers who love diving into this world of Emma Sharpe, Colin Donovan and their family and friends. I'm humbled and grateful.

In researching *Rival's Break*, I consulted my niece, Sarah Josti, who graciously shared her medical expertise with me. My friend John Moriarty in southwest Ireland once again pointed me in the right direction on a number of questions, from whiskey to mushrooms. I once almost took a mushroom foraging class in Ireland, but it was a rainy November day and I sat by the fire instead and read! I appreciate the online sources I consulted on wild mushrooms, including the North

American Mycological Society and the Journal of Wild Mushrooming. Any mistakes and liberties are mine.

New to Sharpe & Donovan? You can find more information on my website, CarlaNeggers.com, and sign up for my newsletter. Finian Bracken appears in every story, including the prequel novella, *Rock Point*, and our elusive art thief is first referred to in *Declan's Cross*, the third book in the series. We meet Henrietta Balfour in *Thief's Mark*. The series settings of Boston, Maine (including Mike Donovan's Bold Coast), Ireland, London and the Cotswolds are ones I love to visit personally... and quietly. I'll leave the villains to fiction!

Many thanks, and happy reading,
Carla

CarlaNeggers.com